13 Gifts

Don't miss any of these spellbinding stories from Wendy Mass!

The Willow Falls series:

11 Birthdays
Finally
13 Gifts
The Last Present
Graceful

Twice Upon a Time:

Rapunzel: The One with All the Hair
Sleeping Beauty: The One Who Took the Really Long Nap
Beauty and the Beast: The Only One Who Didn't Run Away

13 *Gifts*

BY WENDY MASS

SCHOLASTIC INC.

FOR MY DAUGHTER, CHLOE, WHO HAS GIVEN ME MORE GIFTS IN HER FIRST FIVE YEARS THAN I EVER IMAGINED

This book was originally published in hardcover by Scholastic Press in 2011.

ISBN 978-0-545-31004-8

10 9 8 7 6 5 4 3 2 17 18 19 20

Printed in the U.S.A. 40
First printing 2016

The text type was set in ITC Esprit Book.
Book design by Elizabeth B. Parisi

Chapter One

Like all big mistakes, mine started with a goat.

But if I'm being totally honest, I wouldn't be riding my bike to school at dusk, with nefarious deeds ahead, if that telegram hadn't arrived last month. The goat came a little later.

The telegram came all the way from Madagascar, where maybe they don't have access to phones or computers or other modern ways of communicating. Mom's been preparing for months for our summer trip to the large island off the coast of Africa. Dad and I get to tag along while she studies the mating habits of the bamboo lemur. It might not sound like it, but this will be more fun than last summer, when we watched her catalog the scat of various woodland creatures in the forests of Ecuador.

Scat = Poop.

Mom had never gotten a telegram directly from Madagascar before, though, so I figured this must be really important. Her face went totally white when she read it. The guy who delivered it just stood in the open doorway. I think he was waiting for a tip. He didn't get one.

Mom crumpled up the telegram before I could read it, but she told Dad and me that she'd just been made head researcher of the lemur project. I'm not sure why this news freaked her out so much. It was just a matter of time until she got this responsibility.

Since the telegram arrived, Mom's been really distracted. She's even stopped asking if I've finished my homework or made any new friends (usually her two favorite topics). Whenever I try to strike up a conversation, she mumbles something and wanders out of the room. This morning I found her keys in the freezer next to the ice cream sandwiches.

Her normal approach to mothering has always been to smother and overprotect. While I was still in my crib she taught me that talking to strangers would cause my tongue to turn green. (I believed this until I was eight.) I've never been allowed to sleep over at anyone's house, and my cell phone has a GPS tracker in it that links up to her computer. Mom promised me she'd only activate the tracker if I went missing, but when I stopped to buy gum after school last month, she texted me to get a quart of milk. Coincidence? I think not.

So if I happened to have a lapse in judgment by agreeing, during a moment of temporary insanity, to steal the middle school principal's beloved goat for Shelby Malone and her DFs (devoted followers) based on the promise that I'd then be allowed to sit with them at lunch for the last two weeks of seventh grade, who could blame me? I have been set adrift by my own mother.

Tonight I'm actually going to do what Mom's been pushing me to do for years — something social with a group of my peers. Scary and illegal, but social. As much as she likes to keep tabs on my every move, she's always bugging me to make friends and do things. She's complicated like that.

I've found that standing on the sidelines works very well to keep all the middle school drama from touching me. The problem is, that sometimes trying to stay *out* of trouble actually gets you *into* trouble. Choosing not to participate in any group projects or activities isn't a popular option with my teachers. Every time I get in trouble, Mom seems so disappointed in me. She must never have done anything wrong in her entire life. She doesn't ever punish me, though. The look on her face is enough.

Well, tonight's activity probably isn't exactly what Mom has in mind, but the plan is already under way. There's no turning back now. I pedal hard, and my bike brings me ever closer to the middle school parking lot and the unsuspecting goat. I had hoped to blend in to the background during my mission (or as much as possible since I'm about a foot taller than most seventh-grade girls, thanks to my Jolly Green Giant of a father). Mom may currently be distracted with her job, but not everything slips by her. The only way I'm allowed to go riding at dusk is with bright yellow reflectors practically all over my body, a whistle around my neck, and a container of pepper spray dangling from my wrist. All this in a town where the biggest crime during the two years we've lived here was when little Richie Simon stole a hot pepper from Mr. Jones's garden. Richie claimed it had gotten stuck on the bottom of his shoe when he went to retrieve his lost baseball, but if that were true, he likely wouldn't have eaten it. Poor kid threw up so many times, and in so many colors, that even grouchy old Mr. Jones couldn't bring himself to press charges.

Actually, the biggest crime in our town's history just might be the one I'm about to commit. But I have to focus on being careful, and not let fear creep in. In the movies it's always the scared ones who do something dumb like drop their wallet with their driver's license in it. And I had a big pimple the day our student ID photos were taken, so no way is that going to be displayed on the front page of the town paper. When I reach the middle school, I hide my bike in the bushes and pray that it remains safe. It's my favorite possession.

Earlier today, Shelby had stuck a ruler in the doorjamb of the gym door so it wouldn't lock. I would never have thought of that. Not that I've considered breaking into school buildings before. Breaking *out*, yes, but not in.

I enter without a hitch and sprint through the empty gym, which feels bigger than ever. The only person I need to watch out for is the night custodian, who, according to Shelby, spends most of his time in the cafeteria, listening to music and mopping the same spot on the floor over and over. We chose this entrance because it's the farthest from the caf.

Once in the hall, I stay close to the lockers as though they offer some small bit of protection. I've gone to so many schools by this point (six at last count) that they all blend together. Same VOTE FOR ME! posters slapped up on the walls, same mud-brown lockers with papers sticking out of them at odd angles, same unmistakable smell of gym clothes, old tuna sandwiches, and cleaning solution. This could be in Anywhere, USA.

The doorknob to Principal Murphy's office turns easily. He must be pretty trusting not to have locked it. I slip inside without so much as a creak. I can literally *see* my heart thumping under my T-shirt, and I bet I could wring a cupful of water from my palms. Other than the events of the last five minutes (and one harrowing occasion in preschool when I snuck into the supply closet for more animal crackers and got locked in), I have very little experience going where I'm not supposed to go. Shelby and her DFs are stationed at posts outside the school, ready to text me if we have any unexpected visitors. I pull out my phone. No texts. That's a good sign.

The closed blinds allow only slivers of light to filter in from the parking lot, but I don't want to risk discovery by opening them or switching on the desk lamp. It helps that I've spent enough time inside these four walls to know the layout of the office even in the near darkness. That, and the fact that, at three feet tall, the goat is hard to miss.

I don't doubt my decision to steal him until I'm standing only inches away from his long, furry face. I never noticed before how one deep brown eye is almost an inch higher than the other. When combined with his slightly upturned lips, he looks sweet and goofy and a little bit confused.

I reach for him, then hesitate. Yes, it's strange that the principal keeps a goat in his office, but who am I to judge where one's affections lie? Personally, I hail from the school of thought that says the fewer things you care about, the less you'll get hurt. But that doesn't mean I should fault someone else for bringing a huge goat to work and taking him to every school activity like a trusted sidekick.

The clock is ticking and this goat isn't going to steal himself. Shelby and the DFs are probably wondering what's taking me so long. I make my decision. To make my mom happy, I will steal the goat. And I will sit with Shelby and the DFs for the next two weeks and pretend to both understand and care about everything they say. Then I'll put it all behind me and immerse myself in the courtship rituals of small, furry tree dwellers halfway around the world.

I'm not sure in what order, but as I stretch my arms around the goat's flank, light suddenly floods the room. The words "Unhand that goat!" fly at me from the doorway. My "getaway car" (Shelby's older brother's pickup truck) peels out of the parking lot with Shelby and the DFs piled in the back, and Principal Murphy gets a face full of pepper spray due to my oversensitive startle reflex.

When my parents arrive to pick me up, I try my best not to cry. Principal Murphy is doing enough of that for the both of us. Hopefully his eyes will stop watering soon and he'll regain full use of his sight. At least that's what the small print on the container says should happen in about two to three hours.

"Your daughter will be suspended for the last two weeks of the school year and will be expected to take her final exams at home," he announces to my parents.

They nod from their chairs, looking down at the large desk, rather than up at Principal Murphy. I can't blame them. Between the watering and the twitching, it's pretty gruesome.

"I will be willing to shave a week off her punishment if she gives up the names of her accomplices."

I shake my head. I may not be a joiner, but I do know that you don't rat out your partners in crime.

Principal Murphy's face darkens. But oddly, Mom's expression changes from anger and disappointment to something that almost looks like . . . relief? Happiness? Yes, there's a definite gleam in her eye. Does the fact that I had been invited to participate in an activity — *any* activity — with other kids make her so happy she is willing to overlook the fact that I just got kicked out of school?

No such gleam in Dad's unblinking eyes, though. It takes a lot for my usually laid-back father to get mad, but I can tell by the firm set of his jaw that I won't escape some sort of punishment this time.

Imagine all the trouble I'd have gotten into if it had been a *real* goat.

Chapter Two

I wake the next morning to the sound of a babbling brook. Most kids' alarm clocks beep, buzz, or play Top 40. Mine babbles, gurgles, rains, thunders, or whooshes, depending on what setting it's on. Mom feels it's important to wake up to the calming sounds of nature, as the animal kingdom and our own ancestors have done for millions of years. But honestly, the sound of water cascading over rocks is doing little to calm me now. Instead, it mocks me with its *la-di-da, just relax and enjoy the wonders of nature, isn't life grand?* attitude. I switch the setting to thunderstorm. There. Now it matches my mood.

All the kids who *didn't* get caught trying to steal a life-sized stuffed goat (and then temporarily blinding the principal) will be getting up for school right now as if it's an ordinary day. I stare at the ceiling and wonder what everyone will say about me. Even though I normally fly well under the radar, it's very rare that someone gets suspended for two whole weeks. People are gonna notice.

If this were a normal day, I'd be just about to miss the bus. Frankly, I would have expected my parents to come in here by now. I switch off the storm and sit up. In the quiet I can hear two things — the snip-snip of the gardening shears below my window, and the clack of my dad's fingers flying across his keyboard down the hall. He's in full deadline mode on his latest "zombie eats alien" book that I'm not allowed to read until I'm older.

Outside my window, the chomping sound of the shears is getting louder and more intense. Our house is all on one level, so when I peek through the blinds, I'm only about five feet above the small vegetable garden. Carrots and peapods and fistfuls of parsley fly into Mom's white wicker basket as she yanks and snips, yanks and snips. The bush to her left is full of butterflies, but she doesn't even glance at them. She's moving at least five times faster than usual. Things may be even worse than I feared. I let the blinds fall.

The only beam of light through the dark cloud of impending doom currently hanging over my head is Jake Harrison, who beams at me from his poster next to my window. I lean over and kiss his cheek. This little morning ritual always makes me feel better. He smiles back at me with those perfect white teeth and that gleam in his eye that says, *I may be a huge movie star, but I'm just a regular guy, too.* He's the only boy I could ever imagine kissing in real life, which, of course, means that I'll never, ever, kiss *anyone*, since I'd just as soon get the chance to kiss the real Jake Harrison as grow another head.

To calm my nerves, I take out my stationery. My fourth-grade teacher believed that letter writing was a dying art and matched us each up with a pen pal who lives across the country. My penpal, Julie, is the only person I tell what's going on in my life. She's not even going to *believe* this last incident. When I get it all out on paper, I address the envelope and stick the stamp on upside down, which has become a tradition whenever I write her. Then I reach into the closet and pull out the flowered hatbox that used to belong to Mom's mother, Grandma Emilia. I wedge the top free and drop the envelope inside. It lands on top of the sixty-six other letters I've written Julie in the past four years and never sent.

The frantic gardening finally stops. Even though it means having to leave the relative safety of my bedroom, I really need to use the bathroom. I wait another minute, and then open the door slowly, hoping the coast is clear. It isn't. Both parents are standing a few feet away from my door, whispering. They stop when they see me.

"We need to talk," Mom says, rubbing her chin with a gloved hand. I'm about to tell her she's just smeared dirt across half her face, but Dad has already licked a finger and is using it to wipe off the smudge. It takes a lot of effort on my part not to roll my eyes at this gesture. Honestly, he's like an eighth grader with a crush on the head cheerleader. In his eyes, I'm pretty sure Mom can do no wrong.

"Let's go out back," Mom says. Dad and I are both in our pajamas and slippers, but she doesn't seem to notice or care as she leads our little group down the hall and out the back door. The wooden picnic table under the birch tree has become our official family-meeting spot, and we head straight for it.

Once seated, Mom wastes no time with small talk about the lovely early June weather. "Trust and honesty are essential to a healthy relationship," she begins, laying her hands palm-up on the table, "and to a happy family. You have let us down, Tara, and broken our trust. There are consequences for that. Serious consequences."

My eyes widen at the harshness of her words. Each one makes my stomach clench tighter. She's never talked to me like this before. She's been hard on me sometimes, but I always felt that deep down, she was on my side. Dad squirms on the bench next to her, but remains silent.

"You're at a turning point in your life right now, Tara, and it's up to your father and me to make sure you don't go down a dangerous path."

Okay, so it's sinking in that she is most definitely *not* happy with me for trying to impress the popular kids. I must have misread that gleam in her eye last night. She confirms it when she says, "I'd like to think I raised a daughter who wouldn't do something foolish just because the other kids were doing it."

Now I can't help rolling my eyes. Doesn't she know me better than that? When have I ever followed the crowd with anything? When has anyone even asked me to? How can I explain the real reason I did it was to please *her*? I look to Dad for help, but he has chosen this moment to start pounding a nail sticking out of the table with his huge foot.

"So what are you saying?" I ask her. "I'm grounded for the next two weeks until we leave for Madagascar? I'm already suspended. Isn't that enough?"

She shakes her head. "I know this is going to sound harsh, but your father and I have decided that you won't be coming with us for the summer. Instead, you'll be going to Aunt Bethany and Uncle Roger's house in Willow Falls. You haven't seen your cousin Emily in a few years, and we think the time away from kids who were obviously a bad influence will do you a world of good."

My jaw falls open. Literally, I cannot close it. A bee could fly directly toward me and I wouldn't be able to stop it from landing on my tongue. Mom's spent the last twelve years and eleven months trying to protect me from unseen harm, and okay, maybe even spoiling me a little (probably because she feels guilty for making us move every time she takes a new teaching or researching job). Now she's sending me out on my own while she's on the other side of the world? I doubt she can track my phone from the jungle.

Dad clears his throat and faces Mom. "I know we agreed on this, Molly, but maybe a shorter visit with your sister's family would be enough? A week or two perhaps? We wouldn't want to complicate their summer plans. . . ."

With Dad's words, hope swoops in. Mom shoos it right back out. "I've already spoken to Bethany, and she's very excited about it. She's even going to keep Emily home from camp so she and Tara can spend time together. If the lemurs behave, we may not be gone the entire summer."

Still utterly astonished, I try to pull my thoughts together. No bamboo lemurs? Stuck for the summer with my little cousin who had to be rushed to the hospital for eating half a glue stick the last time they visited us? I force my mouth to work properly. "But, Mom, you hate Willow Falls. Now you want to banish me there for two whole months with people I barely even know? While you guys are thousands of miles away?"

To her credit, she has the decency to look down at the table. Her legs begin to twitch, one after the other, a habit she has when she's anxious. "You shouldn't say *hate.* That's a terrible word. And Willow Falls was a wonderful place to grow up, wasn't it, James?"

My father nods. "Indeed it was."

"Then why don't we ever go back? I know your parents aren't there anymore, but why haven't we ever visited Aunt Bethany?"

"It's complicated," Mom says, still staring down at the table. "People get busy with their lives. But now you'll have a chance to get to know your cousin. Emily is apparently a very levelheaded and stable girl, and I think she'll be a positive influence on you."

I shake my head in amazement. "She's seven and eats paste! And I'm levelheaded enough."

"She's not seven anymore," my mother corrects me. "She's eleven now and quite gifted academically. I assure you she no longer eats paste. And do you call breaking into your principal's office the act of a stable person?"

I raise my voice. "How can I have any stability when you uproot us every time the wind changes direction?"

She presses her lips together into a firm line. We stare at each other in angry silence. Dad pounds another nail. He must have a lot of faith in the lining of his slipper. Either that or he's recently gotten a tetanus shot.

When she speaks, she does it so softly I have to lean over the table to hear her. "What if I promise that if you go willingly, if you really try to get along with everyone and keep an open mind, then we won't move again?"

I shrug. "I don't believe you."

"I'm serious," she says, more firmly this time.

Dad stops pounding and raises his brows. "Are you sure you want to promise that, Molly?"

Mom folds her hands firmly in front of her and nods.

Dad turns to me. "That's a pretty good offer. What do you think?"

Honestly, I don't know what to think. It's not like where we live now is so amazing or anything. Just another suburb in a string of suburbs. My parents never move us anywhere interesting. But the thought of not having to pack up again, of not being the new kid everyone stares at, well, that's too good to pass up. "Fine, I'll do it. But I get to take my bike and my Jake Harrison poster, and if Emily eats any more art supplies you'll have to fly back and pick me up."

"Deal," Mom says, sticking out her hand.

"And we'll never move again? At least until I graduate? And I mean high school, not just middle school."

"Yup."

I take her hand and shake it.

"Start packing," she says cheerfully. "We head to Willow Falls Saturday."

Jaw falls again. "As in *tomorrow*?" I manage to squeak out. "Boy, you're not losing any time getting rid of me. What about my homework? And finals?"

"We're not trying to get rid of you, Tara. The research team I'll be heading up has already started. I had intended to meet up with them once you got out of school. Now there's no reason to wait. We'll drop you off and fly out tomorrow evening from there."

I mutter something under my breath that, under normal circumstances, would probably get me grounded for a week.

She throws me a warning glance and climbs off the bench. "We have to go to school later so you can clean out your locker. Your teachers will be dropping off your assignments in the main office." With that, she motions for Dad to follow her, which of course, he does because he knows that arguing with Mom when she's made up her mind is useless. As they stroll back to the house, Dad turns and gives me a *you can do it* thumbs-up.

Maybe a summer away from my parents won't be such a bad thing.

I rest my cheek on the table and close my eyes. Sadly, the tight ball in my stomach is a familiar feeling. I get it each time my parents announce we're going to move again. At least when we move, it's still the three of us. A loud *kreeee, kreeee* sound right next to my ear rudely interrupts my downward spiral into self-pity.

I open my eyes and lift my head off the table. I'm not alone in the garden anymore. A huge bird (a hawk? a buzzard?) is perched less than a foot from my face. Normally I would jump up and scream when faced with a giant bird with a sharp, curved beak, sitting close enough to peck my eyes out, but I'm frozen. I'm not a superstitious person by nature (and I'm turning thirteen on Friday the thirteenth, so that's really saying something), but I'm pretty sure its sudden appearance is supposed to mean something. Good luck? Bad luck? Six more weeks of winter? No wait, that's the groundhog.

The hawk tilts its head at me like it's trying to decide something. I'm being judged by a bird! Finally it ruffles its shiny brown feathers, apparently having come to some kind of decision. With a final *kreeee* followed by a *garuuunk*, it springs off the table and takes to the air. It gives a lazy flap of its enormous wings, then circles overhead in a slow glide. It's still close enough for me to clearly see its yellow feet and pointy talons. With a sudden burst of energy, it flaps quickly and takes off. A second later I feel something wet and slimy slide down the back of my head.

That can't be good.

Chapter Three

I pull my still-damp hair into a ponytail and climb into bed, exhausted. The only good thing about today is that it's over. While the lowest point of the day was definitely Mom's announcement of my banishment to Willow Falls, further humiliations and annoyances included — but were not limited to — the following:

1. It took three showers over the span of twelve hours to get the sticky hawk poop out of my thick hair.

2. First I had to endure whispers of that's her and goat and principal and pepper spray and suspended as I walked the hall of shame to the principal's office with Dad. Then Shelby Malone (now my archnemesis) passed us in the hallway and said, "Wow, Sara, your father sure is tall." And then DAD SMILED AT HER (even though she'd just called his only daughter by the wrong name) and said, "Thank you, young lady!"

3. Principal Murphy announced that since my mother informed him I will be leaving tomorrow to attend a camp for troubled teens, he doesn't want to keep me from "doing the important work ahead of me there." So he's waiving my homework assignments and will have my teachers send my final exams to the camp for one of the counselors to administer. If the words CAMP FOR TROUBLED TEENS hadn't come out of his mouth exactly as a stream of green pus oozed from his left eye, I would have focused on them more. As it was, it took a few seconds for the words to register and for my brain to start coming up with reasons why I'm totally NOT a troubled teen, whatever that means: I don't compare myself to airbrushed supermodels. I don't obsess over boys (only Jake Harrison, and who doesn't love him?). I don't hate my parents (well, maybe a little right now) or smoke behind the gym like those kids who think they look really cool but actually look ridiculous. Okay, so maybe I wear black a lot, but it's not because I'm depressed or rebelling against society or anything; it's just that I have an awful sense of style, and black matches black really well.

4. It took my father most of the car ride home to convince me that Mom let Principal

Murphy believe I was going to that camp because otherwise I wouldn't be allowed to leave town before exams were over.

5. On the positive side, the principal clearly got at least <u>some</u> of his sight back because he flinched as soon as he saw me.

6. I got home to find Mom had taken the liberty of packing my suitcase for me, and I had to repack it with the right stuff. I then refused to take a last trip to the ice cream parlor with her for our favorite, bubblegum ice cream. We always pull out the gumballs and make them into a smiley face on our napkins, and I didn't feel like smiling. Even via gumball.

"Are you still awake?" Mom asks, sticking her head in and unknowingly adding to my list of annoying things that are happening to me today.

I grunt.

"I'll take that as a yes. Can you come into my room for a minute?"

I don't even bother to ask why. None of Mom's answers to anything lately have made any sense.

"Your aunt loves jewelry," she says when I shuffle in. "I thought it would be nice if you picked out a few pieces for her."

The bottom drawer of her dresser is already open. Even though she's told Dad repeatedly not to buy her any more jewelry since she never wears any of it, he still gives her a small cardboard box for almost every occasion. Rings for her birthday, bracelets on Christmas, earrings on Valentine's Day. Once he even gave her a necklace for Arbor Day. She made him take that one back.

I cross my arms. "How would I know what Aunt Bethany would like? I've only met her a few times."

Mom doesn't answer, just stares into the drawer. Then she storms out of the room and snaps, "Just do your best."

I think Mom's moodier than me, and I'm the one who's almost a teenager. I take her place in front of the drawer and try to figure out the best plan of attack. The boxes are organized by size, so I figure I might as well start at the smallest: rings. Rings of all colors and sizes and shapes. I make a small pile of ones I've never seen her wear, then start on the next size up: watches and bracelets. Halfway through, I open a red pouch that doesn't seem to have a box to go with it. I open the pouch and shake the contents into my palm. Two identical bracelets drop out. They're simpler than the rest of Mom's stuff — each one is basically just a piece of brown leather with two red beads in the center. A gold clasp hooks the ends together. I don't usually wear jewelry either, but I really like these. Maybe she'd let me have one, especially since she has two and I've never seen her wear them. I slip the bracelets back into the pouch and set it aside.

Mom comes back as I'm putting away the last necklace box.

"How'd you do?" she asks, coming over to examine the large pile. "Looks like you found quite a lot."

I'm about to ask if I can have one of the beaded bracelets, but then I do something I wouldn't have done before my parents' decision to send me away. While Mom's focused on the choices for Aunt Bethany, I stuff the small pouch into my pocket. I'm sure if she saw me, she'd tell me something about how stealing the bracelets is my small way of asserting some power over her since I'm feeling powerless right now. It's a lecture I can do without, so I'm glad she doesn't notice.

"I'm sure Bethany will love these," she says, dropping the jewelry into a small plastic bag and handing it to me. "I'm sorry I was snippy before. It's not your fault that you don't know your own aunt. It's mine. How about I tuck you in and tell you a little about Bethany and Willow Falls?"

I hesitate. She hasn't tucked me into bed all month. Still, I let her follow me back to my room. As I climb in bed I ask her to have Dad put the bike rack on the car so we don't forget in the morning.

"No problem," she says. But even in the dark, I can tell her eyes have flicked away from mine. I have a sinking feeling that my bike's staying right here.

• • • • • • • • • • •

I was right! I'm not taking my bike with me! I know this because it's now five in the morning (!) and we're on our way to the train station (!!) so my parents can put me on a nine-hour train ride BY MYSELF (!!!), where apparently I'll be expected to make small talk about the weather with the stranger sitting next to me (!!!!).

Me = Never Talks to Strangers.

"But I just don't understand," I whine, rubbing the last bit of sleep from my eyes. "Why aren't we driving? Why can't you come with me?"

Mom turns around in the passenger seat. "Honey, we explained it all to you last night after we got the phone call."

"I think I'd remember something like that, Mom."

"Well, you did seem a bit sleepy. The airline called to say our connecting flight to Madagascar was rerouted through a different airport. We wouldn't have time to get you to Willow Falls and then get there on time. But don't worry; you'll be perfectly fine on the train. They are very used to handling unaccompanied minors."

While I try to process being an "unaccompanied minor," Dad launches into an off-key rendition of *"I've been working on the railroad, all the livelong day,"* which doesn't help me focus. "Are you sure this isn't a trick and I'm really being shipped off to that troubled teens camp?"

"Promise," Mom says. Dad just keeps singing. I put my hands over my ears and slide down in the seat.

I must have fallen asleep, because the next thing I know, we're pulling into the station. Dad hops out to get my bags from the trunk, with Mom only two steps behind. The first rays of sun land on the side of the brick building. I watch as the light cuts through the branches of the only tree, briefly transforming the dew-covered leaves into shards of green glass, then back to regular leaves. I am mesmerized by this.

Dad sticks his head in my window. "Coming?"

I shake my head.

He laughs. "Come on. We have a little going-away present for you." He holds up a small blue backpack that I recognize as the freebie he got last month for opening a new checking account. He had grumbled about not getting a toaster, as though banks just normally give out small kitchen appliances. He dangles the backpack from his wrist and lets it sway back and forth.

I climb out of the car. "Fine. But you better show me quickly. Don't I have a train to catch?"

"We still have time," Mom assures me. Like I'd actually care if I missed it.

Dad flips open the top of the backpack and reaches in. First he holds up three granola bars and a peanut butter and jelly sandwich. So far I'm not impressed. Then he pulls out a small Velcro wallet. "There's two hundred dollars in here. This should hold you over for the summer till we get home. Try not to spend it all in one place."

My eyes widen. *Two hundred dollars?* That's more money than I've ever had in my life! I could buy an iPod with that!

Mom steps forward. "You're not thinking of blowing it all on an iPod or anything like that, are you?"

I swear that woman can read my mind.

"This should help with the temptation." She reaches into the backpack and pulls out her own iPod, with its dainty little ear-buds wrapped around it.

I squeal (which I normally *never* do) and grab for it.

"It's just on loan," Mom warns as I cup it lovingly in my hands. "I added some music and a few of your favorite TV shows. I don't want you using it around the house when you get there, though. You don't need another excuse to be antisocial."

"Whatever you say." I'd agree to pretty much anything in order to get those earbuds in my ears.

At the ticket window, the woman taking our information says, "Funny. Got a *Sara* Brennan due to leave here on the same train in a few weeks. She a relative?"

My mom shakes her head, but Dad laughs and punches me playfully on the arm. He's the only one who thought Shelby calling me Sara was funny. Now, apparently, there really IS a Sara Brennan. I bet she's been planning her trip for months, not hours.

The woman covers a yawn with her hand, stamps the ticket, then tears off the side. She hands it to me, then points down a narrow hallway. "Station manager. Second door on the right."

"Excuse me?" I ask.

"For your interview. All unaccompanied minors gotta have one."

Dad leads me away from the counter. "It'll only take a minute. They told us you'd need one when we booked it."

Mom walks ahead and has already knocked on the door by the time we arrive. I hang back, but Dad propels me forward in that gentle but forceful way of his. The man behind the desk is small, with red-framed glasses and a smile.

He points to the two folding chairs in front of his desk. "Please sit."

Mom and I sit down and Dad stands behind me, his hands resting protectively on the back of my chair.

"You are Tara Brennan, age twelve?" he asks, typing into his computer. He looks up at me.

I nod.

He smiles. "You'll be thirteen soon I see, on July thirteenth. Wait, is that a . . ."

I sigh. "Yes, it's a Friday."

"Well! Hope you're not superstitious."

I shake my head.

"Only believe what you can see with your eyes, am I right?" He winks.

I nod.

"I assume you are traveling of your own free will, Miss Brennan?"

I glance at Mom. Her eyes shoot me a warning. I turn back to the man. "Yes."

He looks back and forth between Mom and me. "Are you certain?"

"Yes," I repeat. "Sorry, I've just never traveled alone before."

"Just a standard question. Nothing to worry about," he says. "Our conductors are quite used to unaccompanied minors traveling the rails. You'll have a fine time."

"Is that it?" Mom asks, glancing at her watch.

"Just a few more quick questions I'm required to ask." He pulls out a handbook from his drawer and flips to a dog-eared page. "Any life-threatening allergies?"

I shake my head.

"Are you prone to outbursts or tantrums?"

Dad chuckles behind me. I roll my eyes. "No."

"Are you capable of using the lavatory by yourself?"

"The what?"

He leans over the desk and whispers, "That's the bathroom. Sorry, gotta ask."

Dad chuckles louder.

"Oh!" I feel my cheeks go hot. "I mean, yes!"

"And lastly, will someone be waiting to pick you up at your destination?"

I turn to look at Mom. No one went over that part with me.

"Yes," Mom replies. "Her aunt and uncle will be there. I wrote their names and telephone number on the release form. Tara has a copy in her backpack, too."

"Excellent," the station manager says. "Then we're almost all set." He reaches back into his drawer and pulls out a bright yellow rubber bracelet. "You'll need to wear this for the duration of your travel with us."

He hands it to me and waits while I pull and stretch it in an attempt to get it over my hand. "Is there a bigger size?"

He shakes his head. "Sorry, they make 'em pretty small so they don't slip off the younger kids. I can give you this instead." He reaches back into the drawer and pulls out a white sticker the size of a paperback book with the words *UNACCOMPANIED MINOR* in huge red letters. "You could wear this on your chest."

I give one more yank and the bracelet finally lands on my wrist. "Thanks, I'm good."

"Bon voyage," he says with a salute.

Dad salutes in response. Mom shakes the man's hand, and I tug at the bracelet. It really is very tight.

"Does my hand look purple to you?" I ask Dad as we follow the signs to the right track.

He takes hold of my hand and turns it side to side. "Not more than usual."

"I'm serious. What if my circulation gets cut off and my hand swells up and has to be amputated?"

Dad shrugs. "Then I'll put you in my next horror novel."

"This is the gate," Mom says, stopping short.

I look up at the sign next to the door that leads up to our track. It lists all the stations. "I don't see Willow Falls on the list, Mom. Guess we better head home."

"Not so fast. You'll be getting off in River Bend, the next town over. Willow Falls is too small for a train station."

When we arrive on the platform, the train is already there. I tighten my grip on the backpack while Mom hands the conductor my ticket. He asks to see my bracelet, so I hold up my wrist. I'm fairly certain my hand is not normally the color of grape juice.

He motions us to climb on. "Train departs in eight minutes, so be sure you're off in time."

My parents assure him they will. Inside the train it's actually pretty nice. The seats are blue and green striped, with two seats on each side of the aisle. It looks clean, too. A little cramped, but not too bad. I follow Mom down an aisle as she carefully checks out each seat. The train is mostly empty since this is the first stop on the line, so I'm not sure why she doesn't just pick one.

"How 'bout this one, Mom?" I gesture to a perfectly good seat by a window with no one on the aisle.

She shakes her head. "Keep going." So we trudge through another car until finally she stops and says, "Here."

I look at the seat. It looks exactly the same as the others.

"What's different about this one?" I ask.

She takes a deep breath. "It's in the center of the train car, so there will be less sway when the train's moving. And it's facing forward; some of the others were backward. You tend to get nauseated when traveling backward. Also, the bathroom is in the next car, so it's close enough to use without having to deal with any unpleasant odors that might emanate from it. Plus there's an escape hatch above the window in case of emergency."

"Perfect," I say, dropping my backpack onto the seat. "When my hand falls off and my arm begins to gush blood, the paramedics will be able to climb right in to save me."

"That is indeed handy," Dad says. "No pun intended." He easily tosses my suitcase on the rack across the aisle from me.

"Why'd you put it over there?" I ask.

"You can keep an eye on it better than if it were above you," Mom explains before Dad has a chance. "If you get hungry, the food car is two ahead of this one. And make sure you have your backpack with you at all times. People come and go on trains, and you can't be too careful. You have your phone, so call us if you need anything. Not sure about the reception in here, though . . ." Her eyes mist up. Dad sniffles, then coughs to hide it.

At least I know they care. "I'll be fine, really." I actually have no idea if I'll be fine, but it seems like the thing to say in this situation.

"Call us when you arrive," Mom says, "and remember, we'll only be able to call out once a week, so keep your phone handy. If there's a problem, just call that number I gave you and the Institute will send someone out to fetch us."

The speaker crackles on. "Train 751 departs in two minutes. All aboard."

"Excuse me," a soft voice says from behind my dad. He steps out of the aisle to reveal a short dark-haired woman with a deep purple scarf draped over her hair and tied under her neck. She's wearing the most makeup I've ever seen on someone outside of the movies. Green and purple eye shadow, bright pink lipstick, and what has to be four coats of mascara and ten coats of foundation. She looks very glamorous. And sort of like a whole makeup store exploded on her face.

"Got four root canals yesterday," she explains, pointing to the scarf. "Cheeks swelled up like beach balls. Not pretty."

My parents nod politely and move farther out of the way to let her pass. But she doesn't even try to squeeze by.

"I couldn't help but overhear," she says. "Your daughter is traveling alone?"

Dad nods. Mom's eyes suddenly lock on a spot over my shoulder, like there's something only she can see. There better not be ghosts on this train. Then she takes a deep breath and focuses again. "We're in a hurry," she tells the woman. "So —"

The woman holds up two tickets. "I have an extra ticket for the club car. First class. Full meal service and lovely accommodations. My daughter was supposed to travel with me but got called away on business. You know how it is with these modern women." She tries to smile, but then winces and brings her hand to her cheek. "Still waiting for those painkillers to sink in. Anyhoo, I've got an extra one if you think she'd like it." She pauses. "*Ticket*, that is, not painkiller."

"This seat will do fine," Mom snaps, a bit rudely if you ask me. I know she doesn't approve of women wearing a lot of makeup, but it's no excuse to get snippy.

"You're sure, now?" the woman asks, looking from Mom to me.

Since I've never traveled first-class anything, I say, "First class sounds pretty nice, Mom."

"This will do fine," she repeats firmly.

"All right," the woman says, turning around.

"I don't see the harm —" Dad starts to say but is cut off when the conductor steps into the car. It's a different guy from the one who let us on.

"Last call!" he shouts from the doorway. "You folks traveling with us today?"

My parents shake their heads.

"Better get a move on, then."

Mom leans over to hug me, and holds on so tight that when she stops I feel more alone than ever. She rushes down the aisle without looking back. Dad leans in and whispers, "You go take that woman up on her offer. You deserve it." I pull back in surprise. Dad almost never goes against anything Mom says. He gives me one more squeeze before hurrying after her.

They wait outside my window until the train pulls away from the platform. We wave at each other as the station gets smaller and smaller. The last thing I see is Mom leaning into Dad and him putting his arm around her. My eyes burn and I blink away tears. Being alone on the train is bad enough. Being alone on the train and crying about it is that much worse.

When I'm sure the train is out of my parents' sight, I stand up, hold on to the back of the seat across the aisle, and pull down my suitcase. I figure someone will eventually sit next to me, so if I have to make small talk with someone, it might as well be with a lady who's nice enough to offer me a first-class ticket.

It's not easy maneuvering down the aisle, but I only bump one person in the knee and he had his leg really far out into the aisle to begin with. Now that the station is far behind, the train has picked up speed. I try not to look as the scenery whizzes by. Throwing up right now would not make me very popular with my fellow passengers.

After realizing I'm going in the wrong direction and turning around, I finally find myself in front of the door marked CLUB CAR. I press the button and the door glides opens. I blink and stare, wide-eyed. I might as well be on a whole different train! The seats look twice as wide and ten times as soft as the one I was just sitting in. The walls are dark wood rather than the white plastic that I'd seen as I walked the length of the train. Silk curtains billow down from the windows, swaying in time with the motion of the train.

My arrival has caused pretty much everyone in the car to look up from their papers, books, knitting, and wine sipping. I can't help noticing the white tablecloths on the seat-back trays. A young woman in a fancier version of the conductor's outfit approaches me. She places a bottle of red wine back on the little counter at the front of the car and wipes her hands with a cloth.

"Can I help you?" she asks. "Are you lost?"

I shake my head but I'm not sure what to say. Maybe this was a mistake. I don't even know the nice lady's name. "Um, I have a ticket. Kind of."

"She's with me," a voice calls out from the back of the car. The glamorous woman in the scarf leans into the aisle and waves her extra ticket. The conductor (waitress? both?) leads me to the back, where I smile gratefully at the woman.

"Darling!" she says, throwing her arms around me. "I'm so glad to see you! I was wondering when you'd get here." As she pulls away I think she's winking at me but it's hard to tell with all the makeup.

"Um, thanks! Yeah, you, too!"

The conductor/waitress smiles. "Make yourself comfortable. Would you like anything to drink? Some soda?"

I never get soda at home. "Yes, please."

She takes my suitcase and places it in the wooden cabinet above our heads, right next to a first aid kit and extra pillows. I think for a second about Dad putting it across from me before, but it's different back here. Much safer. This is first class!

I smile politely at the man on the other side of the aisle reading his newspaper. He nods politely in return. And my parents think I'm antisocial! I plop down in the seat next to my new best friend and turn to thank her. Her only response is a gentle snore. Guess those painkillers must have kicked in. I admit I'm kind of relieved. Even though I no longer believe that talking to strangers will turn my tongue green, it's best not to take unnecessary chances.

The time speeds by much quicker than I'd have thought possible. Between the iPod, my books, the three-course lunch, and the generous helping of free snacks and soda, I hardly even notice the time passing. And those painkillers must be pretty strong because my new BFF hasn't woken up.

And the best part? Halfway through the ride, the conductor/waitress notices me tugging on my bracelet and offers to help. I hold out my arm eagerly. I guess I'm not really unaccompanied anymore anyway! She snips the bracelet right off with a pair of scissors from the first aid kit. *So* much better. I rub the thick red dent and watch my hand slowly return to its usual handlike color.

The gentle motion of the train is hard to resist, and I drift in and out of sleep. Every time the train stops at another station I jerk awake. My seatmate sleeps through it all.

I've been putting off using the bathroom but those four sodas have left me no choice. Heeding Dad's words, I grab my backpack and bring it with me. It feels unnecessary — I can't imagine a safer place — but I do it anyway.

Which is why it's so surprising when, an hour later, the train pulls into River Bend station and I disembark (after a groggy but warm good-bye from my sleepy seatmate), to find that my backpack is empty except for a soggy peanut butter and jelly sandwich, my aunt's phone numbers, and a strip of bright yellow rubber that makes me feel more like an Unaccompanied Minor than ever.

Chapter Four

To say that I'm panicking at this moment might be an understatement.

I have no money, no iPod, no phone, and the River Bend train station is not much more than a patch of land in the middle of a cornfield. The other two people who got off with me are gone. Any minute I expect hail to start falling from the sky because that would just be my luck.

The clock on the brick wall of the station says 5:15. The train arrived only fifteen minutes late. Has Aunt Bethany come and gone? Unable to think of anything else to do, I open my suitcase. I know it's impossible for the stuff from my backpack to have migrated here, but I rummage through it anyway. I have a pair of pajama bottoms in one hand and a sock in the other when I hear a wooshing sound above me, followed by *kreeee.* I crouch even lower before looking up, expecting the worst. Bats maybe, or another beady-eyed hawk.

Not a hawk. *Two* hawks. Two hawks playfully circling each other above my head. I instinctively cover my head with my hands (and the pajama bottoms and sock). Fortunately, the birds seem a lot more interested in each other than in me. A minute later, the larger one extends one clawed foot (talon? paw?) to the smaller one, who grabs on and they fly away together.

If Mom were here, she'd whip out her camera and follow them. She's fascinated when animals (or people) act differently than research dictates they should. Two birds holding hands (feet? paws?) isn't something you see every day. I actually go so far as to reach into my pocket for my cell phone to tell her about it when I realize that I no longer own such a thing. The panic returns and I turn back to the rummaging.

The next noise I hear is the clomping of heavy shoes on the pavement behind me. I shove everything back inside and look up to find a man hurrying down the platform toward me, the laces of his hiking boots flying around his ankles.

It's been a few years since I've seen Uncle Roger, but this tall, blond guy in green cargo shorts, sunglasses, and a T-shirt encouraging people to SAVE THE KOALAS definitely isn't him. This guy can't be more than twenty-two years old. As he gets closer, he holds up a cardboard sign with *TARA* printed on it in big purple letters. Purple letters outlined with glitter.

"Might you be Tara?" he asks, tilting his head and grinning.

I nod and zip up my suitcase.

"Ace!" he exclaims, folding the sign and tucking it in his back pocket.

Even though he's smiling really wide and doesn't appear to have any concealed weapons and is tall in a comforting reminds-me-of-Dad kind of way, it still feels weird being alone with a strange guy in the middle of nowhere. Not being judgmental, but any guy who uses glitter qualifies as strange.

If pushed, I'd have to admit that, strange or not, he's downright good looking. In a *doesn't*-remind-me-of-Dad kind of way. His tan skin really makes his straight white teeth stand out. The only person I've ever seen with whiter teeth is Jake Harrison and, of course, I've never really *seen* him.

"I expected you to be a wee ankle biter, but you're almost full grown! Here, let me get your port." It's hard to figure out where one word ends and another begins. I've never heard someone with his accent before. If everyone in town talks this way, I'm going to be in big trouble. He grabs my suitcase, grins at me again, and takes off toward the parking lot at the end of the platform. I have no choice but to follow since he has my last remaining belongings.

"Your aunt will get all up me for being late, but first my car was cactus so I had to borrow your uncle's car and then there was a big bingle on Elm Street. I'm lucky I got here at all!"

My aunt would *get up him*? His car is a *cactus*? Four out of every five words he says don't make sense.

He pulls a pack of gum from his pocket and holds it out to me. "Want a chewie?"

I shake my head.

"Not my bowl of rice either," he says, putting it away. "But my oldies always said to make sure to have something to offer a new cobber like yourself."

A cobber doesn't sound like a good thing to be.

The only car in the parking lot is small and red and sporty. It seems impossible that a grown man could fit in it. But he strolls right over, opens the trunk, and tosses my suitcase inside. Then he goes over to the passenger door and holds it open for me.

When I don't make a move to get in, he says, "Oh, do you need to use the dunny? Or did they have one on the train?"

I follow his eyes to the Porta-Potty on the side of the station and feel my cheeks redden. I shake my head and speak for the first time. "I'm sorry; who *are* you? My aunt and uncle were supposed to pick me up."

He slaps his hand on his forehead. "Oops! Forgot to introduce myself. My blokes always tell me I yabber so much I forget all the important stuff. The name's Ray Parsons. I'm an offsider for your rellies. Errands, upkeep around the house, assist your uncle in his lab, that sort of thing. They're good folks. Pretty decent way to make a quid while I'm in the States, actually."

"My *rellies*?"

"Bethany and Roger. Your rellies."

"You mean my *relatives*?"

He shrugs. "If you want to use a longer word to say the same thing."

I narrow my eyes at him. "How do I know you're telling the truth?"

He holds both hands palms-up. "She'll be apples, I promise ya."

"Seriously, you're saying all these words but they don't make any sense."

He laughs. "How do you know *you're* not the one who doesn't make sense?"

Before I can reason out an answer, he says, "Why don't you ring them up? You got a mobile?"

I'm pretty sure that means a cell phone. I shake my head. "It's sort of missing at the moment."

"No worries," he says, tossing me his own.

I pull out the paper with the contact information and dial their home number first. Answering machine. I hang up without leaving a message and try the number listed under Aunt Bethany's cell. As soon as the call goes through, Aunt Bethany yells, "Ray! Have you got her? Tell me you have her. Her parents have been trying her cell and can't reach her. And something about the GPS being out of range? Ray! Ray?"

"It's me, Aunt Bethany. Tara. Ray lent me his phone." I turn my back to him and lower my voice. "I just wanted to make sure he wasn't, you know, trying to kidnap me."

I hear a chuckle behind me, but I ignore it.

"Didn't he give you our note?"

"What note?" I turn back to face Ray.

"D'oh!" he exclaims, hitting himself on the forehead again. "Forgot about that, too." He pulls a folded piece of paper from his back pocket and hands it to me. I scan it quickly. Apparently Emily had a big fencing tournament that they couldn't miss so they sent him to fetch me. I hand the note back to him.

"You still there, Tara?" Aunt Bethany asks, the phone breaking up a little. "We'll be home soon after you arrive. Sorry about this."

I tell her it's fine and give the phone back to Ray. It's not like I could expect them to rearrange their schedules for me. I wouldn't even want them to.

Ray "yabbers" the whole twenty minutes it takes to get to the house. I manage to pick up a few colorful phrases. He had to "chuck a U-ee" at one point when he started going down a one-way street the wrong way, and then he told me some story about a "bloke" of his who wanted him to "chuck a sickie" last week so they could go to the movies. People apparently do a lot of *chucking* in Australia, which is where I finally figured out he's from.

Aunt Bethany's house is just as I imagined, on the outside at least. It's very big, with a freshly mowed lawn, three-car garage, and a circular driveway made out of paving stones, not blacktop like a normal driveway. The crisp smell of apples hangs in the air, although I don't see any apple trees.

"Out back's a hole for a pool," Ray says as he grabs my suitcase from the trunk.

I follow him up to the large red front door. "A hole?"

"Yup. The mister and missus can't agree on the shape of the pool, so there's been a hole for a year now."

"Wow, Ray, you just said two whole sentences that I understood!"

He grins. "That bloody well won't happen again!" As he unlocks the door he says, "The Aussie lingo comes out stronger when I first meet someone. You'll get used to me."

I'm not planning on getting used to anyone. I'm about to tell him this when I hear Mom's voice in my head telling me to be polite. So I don't say anything at all.

A large SUV squeals into the driveway and we both turn in the doorway. Emily jumps out of the backseat practically before the car stops moving. She's grown a lot since I last saw her, but compared to her I still look freakishly oversized. She's dressed in a thick silver outfit that covers every inch of her except her head and makes her look more like an astronaut than a fencer.

A large silver medallion dangles from her neck that says 5TH PLACE and her light brown hair whips around her face.

"Tara!" she yells, leaping up the two porch steps. "I'm so glad you're here!" She reaches around to give me a big hug but it's kind of awkward because she's wearing all this padding and her arms aren't very long. She squeals and says, "This is going to be so much fun!"

When Emily lets go, Aunt Bethany hands her the fencing helmet that rolled out of the car after she jumped out, and takes her place in the hug. "You're so tall! Just like your dad!" She and my mom have the same light olive skin and dark brown hair, but other than that they don't look anything alike. For one thing, Aunt Bethany is wearing a dress and heels, full makeup and nail polish, and has jewelry on every place one can wear it including her ankle. If my mom puts on a skirt it means someone died.

Uncle Roger strolls over and pumps my hand with a huge grin. I remember now how straight he stands, with his chest sort of puffed out, but not in an arrogant way. He has lost some hair and grown a mustache in the few years since I've seen him. Even though he's probably ten years older than my parents, he doesn't have any gray hair. I wonder if it's because he's rich and doesn't have to worry about a lot of things. Every time we move to a new house I spot a few more gray streaks on Dad.

Everyone asks me questions at once. "How was the train?" "Are you hungry?" "Do you want to see the town?" "Do you want to call your parents?"

I really don't want to talk to my parents, but I don't want them to worry, either. "I lost my cell phone on the train," I explain, "so maybe you can call them?" I know they won't be too mad about me losing the phone since Dad loses his every other week, but I'm not planning on telling them about losing everything else. Not until I absolutely have to.

"No problem," Uncle Roger says. "We can get you a new phone tomorrow. You got replacement insurance?"

I nod. Unable to think of anything else to say, I opt to stare at the ground. All this attention is making me miss the peace and quiet of the train, where no one bothered me. Ray picks up my suitcase, clears his throat, and says, "Tara probably wants to get settled upstairs. You know, wash the train off her."

"Of course she does!" Aunt Bethany says, whisking me inside. Ray bounds up the long, carpeted staircase with my suitcase while I stare around me in all directions. A chandelier with at least a hundred diamond-shaped crystals hangs over what looks like marble floors. I've only seen marble floors in museums before. A huge living room off to the right is filled with leather couches and fancy paintings and a coffee table with three books spread out in a fan shape. I can't see what's at the end of the long hallway that leads off from the foyer. It looks like a house from the pages of a magazine. And it smells like lemon.

"Emily will show you the way to your room and help you settle in. She's so excited you're here!"

Emily nods vigorously. "C'mon, let's go upstairs." She grabs my arm and pulls me toward the stairs. I let my hand glide over the dark wooden banister as we climb the winding staircase. If the guest bedroom is anywhere near as nice as what I've seen so far, I'm sure it will be double the size of my room at home.

I follow Emily down the hallway, the carpet so plush that I can't even hear our footsteps. She passes room after room of closed doors, then stops at the last one on the left and flings open the door. "Here it is!"

We are facing a large room that is clearly Emily's own. Her bed is unmade, and clothes, books, papers, trophies, and fencing equipment lie scattered around all surfaces, including the two twin beds. The top of her desk is piled high with thick textbooks and three-ring binders.

"Make yourself at home," Emily says, stepping neatly over what is probably a crumpled school uniform but could just as easily be last year's Halloween costume.

I don't move. "But this is *your* room."

She opens her arms wide. "*Our* room."

My heart sinks as I catch sight of my suitcase at the base of the second bed. I've never shared a room with anyone. I want to ask how there isn't a guest room in a house this big, but what comes out instead is, "Were you, um, searching for something and that's why it looks this way? Or you left your window open and a tornado passed through?"

Emily shakes her head and begins peeling off her fencing uniform. "Nope. It's always like this. All the true geniuses were slobs." She points to two posters sharing the space above her headboard. No pop stars or movie stars for her. Instead, my cousin has posters of two old men on her wall.

"That one's Einstein, right?" I ask, pointing to the one of the guy with crazy white hair sticking out in all directions.

She nods. "And trust me, he was too busy figuring out how the universe works to bother with picking up his socks."

"Or combing his hair," I mumble. "So who's the other one?"

"That's Euclid, one of the greatest mathematicians of all time."

"Um, why do you have a poster of him over your bed?"

She grins. "I'm hoping some of his genius will seep into me while I'm sleeping! I'm trying to figure out one of the Millennium Prize Problems. They've stumped the greatest mathematical minds in history, but I think I'm getting close. The winner gets a million dollars!"

"Wow." But what really surprises me is that she doesn't seem the least bit embarrassed by revealing such a geeky thing.

She leans over and pats Euclid's cheek lovingly. I take a deep breath and make my way across the room, avoiding placing my feet directly on anything breakable. I push aside a winter coat that likely hadn't been worn in the four months since winter ended and sit down on the edge of the bed.

"Hey, sorry about the whole squealing thing before," Emily says, down to white leggings and a T-shirt now. "I'm not really a squealer. It's just that I promised Mom I'd be more enthusiastic about things other than trying to prove the underlying structure of the universe through mathematical equations." Without pausing to take a breath, she says, "It's just that math is so amazing. It's like this huge puzzle, only you don't know what pieces to look for so you keep trying all these different ones and suddenly one fits!" She looks over her shoulder at her posters with obvious admiration. "Like Einstein said, 'As far as the laws of mathematics refer to reality, they are not certain; and as far as they are certain, they do not refer to reality.'"

I have only a passing acquaintance with what she just said,

but clearly I won't have to worry about my little cousin eating glue sticks anymore. "Um, you're interested in fencing, right? So it's not all about math."

She glances at the open door then leans closer. "Fencing's okay. I'm just doing it to prove I can be as well-rounded as the next kid at my school. Anyway, I wanted to thank you. Since you're here now, I don't have to go to camp this summer." She shudders. "I hate camp."

"You shouldn't say 'hate,'" I tell her, surprised — and kind of annoyed — that Mom's words come so easily.

She laughs. "You sounded just like my babysitter Rory when you said that. Okay, I *strongly dislike* being told I have to swim in a cold lake infested with all sorts of bacteria and fungi, and forge lifelong friendships with my bunkmates only to turn on them when color war starts."

It occurs to me that my cousin talks a lot. "You have a boy babysitter?"

She tosses all her fencing garb into the middle of the floor. I watch the helmet roll off and thump against the dresser. "Why would you think I have a boy babysitter?"

"Isn't Rory a boy's name?"

"Not in this case."

"Oh." And that's where the conversation peters out. My mind drifts to the meager contents of my suitcase, and how there's barely space in this bedroom for the few things I brought with me.

"I know what you're thinking," Emily says, tossing her fencing medal over a bedpost stacked high with them.

None, I notice, better than fifth place. Maybe she should stick to math.

"You're thinking I'm a little old for a babysitter," she says.

Actually, I had been thinking about how silly my Jake Harrison poster would look next to Emily's white-haired geniuses. Not that Jake isn't smart. I hear he gets straight A's from all his on-set tutors.

"I'm at that awkward age," Emily explains, even though I didn't ask. "Too young to stay home alone, too old to need someone to watch me. Anyway, Rory's more like a friend. She's in seventh grade, same as you."

I want to tell her that officially, I'm not in seventh grade anymore, having been kicked to the curb by an oversensitive principal. But I'm not sure what mom told Aunt Bethany, so I keep quiet and Emily keeps talking.

"I'm sure you'll like Rory a lot. She's funny without trying to be. And she's kind of klutzy, too. We know you'll want to socialize with your peer group while you're here, so Mom planned a party for you to meet everyone."

I don't think I've heard anyone other than my mother use the words *peer group.* Well, maybe the school social workers. But I've never heard an eleven-year-old who sounds as grown up as she does or who talks as *much* as she does. The words *party* and *for me* are enough to make me want to crawl under the blanket (if I could find it) and sleep for two months. "You really don't have to plan anything for me, I don't really like —"

Aunt Bethany walks in as I'm about to say *parties.* "All unpacked?" she asks.

A little knot forms in my stomach. It's probably homesickness, but since I've never been away from home before, I can't be totally sure. "I'm about to start," I reply, kneeling down next to my suitcase and knocking over a stack of CDs in the process.

Aunt Bethany frowns. "Emily! I told you to clean up this room before Tara arrived!"

"But, Mom, I thought I had longer and then —"

My aunt holds up her hand. "Just clean it now."

"Fine," Emily grumbles and begins tossing things from her bed to the floor.

"When Tara's unpacked, the two of you can come down for dinner." She shuts the door behind her.

"Sorry you have to clean your room because of me," I tell her, not really sorry at all because frankly, all the stuff everywhere is giving me a headache.

Emily sighs. "It's okay. I have a geometry test next week and haven't been able to find my protractor for a month." She starts yanking things off her bed and shoving them underneath, where they are likely to remain until she goes off to college. I'm about to tell her that I don't think that's what her mom meant by cleaning up, but I'm the guest here and it's none of my business.

Everything in my suitcase is jumbled from when I went through it at the train station. The bag Mom packed with her jewelry has made its way to the top of the pile. I set it aside so I can bring it down to dinner. Jake's poster is still on the bottom, folded in a way that would keep his face crease-free.

"What's this?" Emily asks, picking up the little red pouch with the bracelets I "borrowed" from Mom in it. Before I can stop her, she opens it and shakes out the contents into her hand.

"Two of the same?" she asks, lifting one up to admire it. "You bought us friendship bracelets!" She slips one right over her wrist without even needing to unclasp it. Then she hands the other one to me. I hold it between my fingers, unsure what to do next.

"Want me to help you put it on?"

When I don't answer, she plucks it from my hand and attaches it around my wrist. I've never had friendship bracelets with anyone. I hope it doesn't come with some level of responsibility that I can't possibly live up to. I have to admit, it fits perfectly. I wonder why my mom never wore it. Emily is twisting her arm side to side, admiring hers, too. How am I going to get it back from her at the end of the summer? How do I get myself into these situations?

"And what's this?" she asks.

In a flash, Emily lifts Grandma's hatbox out of my suitcase. I reach for it and grab on to the bottom part. Unfortunately, she's gripping the top so tightly that when I pull on the bottom the whole thing opens up and my letters go flying out. I scramble around to pick them up before she can get too close a look. I only brought them in the first place because it would have been like leaving my diary at home. I'm sure Julie the Pen Pal has forgotten all about me after I didn't answer her first letter. Or her tenth. That's when they stopped coming.

"Wow, what are all those? Letters from friends?"

When I don't answer, she says, "You must be really popular."

"It's not really like that." I stick the last letter back in the box and hold out my hand for the top.

She holds on to it a second longer than necessary. "My mom has some old hatboxes like this. They were Grandma Emilia's."

"This was hers, too." I wedge the top back on. "My mom said she had a whole collection."

Emily nods. "Grandma was a really famous actress, you know. At least in Willow Falls." She stares at the hatbox, almost longingly, then says, "Everyone tells me I look just like her. Does anyone tell you that?"

I look up to see if she's serious. If people thought we both looked like our grandmother, that would mean we looked like each other, too, which we totally don't. Instead of pointing that out to her, though, I shake my head. "I've never met anyone who knew her, since we've never lived here."

"Right!" she says. "Duh. I wasn't thinking. Why'd your parents move from Willow Falls anyway?"

I shrug. "I never asked and they never said."

Her eyes soften as pity pools inside them.

"My mom likes to move a lot," I explain. "I guess she just got tired of living here. But don't feel too sorry for me. I've lived in plenty of small towns in the middle of nowhere. I'm sure they're just like Willow Falls."

She shakes her head. "Not like Willow Falls. This town is . . ." She trails off, searching for the right word. Finally she finds it. "*Special.*"

"Sure, whatever you say." I stare down at the jumbled contents of my suitcase. I know it's silly to be jealous of someone because they actually like where they live, but I can't help it.

"Hey," Emily says, "I'd be bummed, too, if my parents were somewhere really cool where no kids are allowed, but we'll have fun here, I promise."

I wonder if that lie originated from my mother or from Aunt Bethany, but I'm glad to know that Emily doesn't know the real reason I'm here. "Thanks," I mutter.

She returns to throwing her piles of stuff onto other piles of stuff. After a minute of silence, she says, "I emptied out the bottom drawer of the dresser for your things. Will that be enough space?"

I nod.

"Maybe you should unpack later, though. I forgot my mom wanted us to come down for dinner. She gets super-cranky when she's hungry."

I zip up my suitcase, not in the mood to unpack anyway. "My mom gets like that, too," I tell her, glad to be talking about something other than the "specialness" of Willow Falls.

"It's kind of weird," she says as she opens the door, "how they're sisters, but hardly ever see each other. I always figured if I had a sister we'd be best friends."

I shake my head. "I always figured if I had a sister we'd hate each other."

She grins and marches into the hall. "You shouldn't say 'hate.' "

I smile at the back of her head, and the tightness in my chest loosens just the littlest bit.

Chapter Five

Instead of heading downstairs for dinner, Emily leads me past the stairs to the opposite end of the hall. She stops in front of the last door, where big black letters tell us to KEEP OUT. Ignoring the warning, she opens the door and marches right in. I hesitate. I hadn't planned on breaking any rules within my first hour of arrival.

Emily yanks me inside and shuts the door behind us. It's dark. It's also colder than in the rest of the house. I shiver. She flips on the light and my eyes instantly widen.

Long wooden shelves cover all four walls, from floor to ceiling. As far as I can tell, the stuff on the shelves is a mixture of toys, action figures, old-fashioned candy and chocolates with labels in other languages, comic books, bobbleheads, baseballs and footballs and soccer balls with autographs scribbled on them, and cookie jars covered in a thin layer of Bubble Wrap. Other than the balls, which are in plastic containers, everything else is still in its original packaging. A long, rectangular table sits in the center of the room with a single computer, a printer, and enough packing supplies to keep a small post office afloat for a year.

Emily trails her hand along one of the spotless shelves. "Pretty wild, right?"

"What is this place?" I whisper.

She laughs. "Why are you whispering?"

"The sign on the door?" I point out, voice still low. "I figure that means we don't want to get caught."

"Dad doesn't mind if I come in here. As long as I don't touch anything."

My eyes scan a row of Star Trek toys. "I thought your dad was an inventor."

"He is. But not everything is as big a seller as the Sand-Free Beach Towel or the Odor-Absorbing Sock Monkey. So a few years ago he started buying and selling collectibles. Mostly buying." She gestures to a shelf full of neatly stacked comic books. Each one is tucked inside a plastic slipcover. "He has two or three of each of these. He doesn't like giving anything up."

An astronaut Barbie Doll with the words LIMITED EDITION sprawled across the box stares down at me from the top shelf. "Don't you ever want to play with any of this stuff?"

Emily shakes her head. "I'm too busy. Between school and fencing and trying to solve my math theorem, I don't have much time for toys anymore."

In the bright light I can see gray smudges under both her eyes. I wonder if she stays up very late reading those thick books of hers. "Um, maybe we should go down for dinner? I know my mom always gets really mad if whatever she made gets cold."

"It's not really like that here," Emily says, opening the door. "You'll see."

It seems like at least *one* of the many closed doors we pass on the way back down the hall should be a spare bedroom. It also seems like the smell of food should be in the air. But even when we reach the bottom of the stairs, the only thing I smell is lemon-scented furniture polish.

The pile of delivery menus on the kitchen table explains a lot. I see Chinese food, Japanese, Thai, Mexican, Italian, and a place for deli sandwiches. Who knew Willow Falls was so multicultural? Aunt Bethany walks in from the adjoining laundry room with a stack of towels. "I ordered pizza. It'll be here in a few minutes."

"We can wait on the porch for it, if you want," Emily offers.

Aunt Bethany hands her the money. "Don't forget the change. Last time you gave him a ten-dollar tip!"

"C'mon, let's go out the back way." Emily leads me through the laundry room and out the back door. She steps onto a large patio with a barbeque grill and table at one end, and a large vinyl shed at the other. Most of the rest of the backyard is taken up by the huge hole where the pool is supposed to be.

"My mother told me you like to ride bikes," Emily says. She makes no mention of the gaping pit of dirt, earth, and rocks with the hastily constructed plastic barrier around the edges that doesn't look imposing enough to keep even a chipmunk away.

I guess I shouldn't be surprised that Mom told them stuff about me, but I am, a little. "At home I used to ride every night after dinner." I don't tell her how hard it's going to be not riding.

I already miss feeling the wind on my cheeks, that sense of freedom, of using my muscles and feeling strong.

She opens the latch on the shed and the door swings open easily, letting out a musty smell. "You can use mine while you're here. I never use it."

My heart leaps. "Really? That'd be great!" Then my eyes land on the bike. It's pink. Like bubblegum pink. Knotted tassels hang limply from the handlebars, a white wicker basket secured between them. Stickers of Clifford the Big Red Dog cover the banana seat. One gear, no hand brakes.

"I know it looks small," Emily says, "but if you raise the seat you'll be able to use it."

My thank-you comes out a bit forced, but Emily doesn't seem to notice.

"You can go for a ride right now, if you want, while I wait for the pizza guy."

I eye the bike, which looks like something I would have ridden when I was seven. "Um, that's okay. I'll just wait with you."

"No!" she says, so forcefully that I take a step back.

She seems just as surprised herself, because she quickly adds, "I mean, it's fine, I can do it myself."

"Okay. I'll, um, go unpack."

"Okay," she says, visibly relieved that I'm not going to follow her. She shuts and latches the shed.

I watch until she disappears around the side of the house. Have I worn out my welcome already? Maybe I should have made a bigger deal over the bike. I'm tempted to climb down into the hole and hide out there until the summer is over. I peer over the edge and am sorry to see that the mixture of dirt, tree roots, and slabs of wood doesn't look very inviting.

So I push open the laundry room door, only to hear a male's voice say, "Oomph!" and a second later, the sound of glass shattering on the tiled floor. I peek in to see Ray staring down at the remains of something green.

"I'm so sorry! I didn't see you. I hope that wasn't a really expensive . . . bowl? Vase? Glass frog?"

"Bowl," he says cheerily. "No worries. It wasn't exy. Only cost a few quid. And that one was just for practice anyway."

"Practice for what?"

"I'm a glassblower," he says, thumping his chest. "'Tis a noble profession."

"A glassblower? I thought you worked here, for the St. Claires."

"I am a wearer of many hats."

I'd expected Aunt Bethany to come running when she heard the crash, but now I can hear her on the phone somewhere else in the house. "Guess we should clean this up."

"Too right!" Ray grabs a dustpan from the shelf above the huge washing machine. He carefully picks out the larger shards and sets them aside, then starts sweeping up the smaller pieces into the bin. I stand there, feeling useless. He ducks into the kitchen to dump the bin into the trash and comes back with one of those ziplock freezer bags. He instructs me to hold it open while he puts the larger pieces inside. When we're done he says, "I'll go over the floor in here one more time with the mop, make sure I didn't miss anything. You can throw that out under the sink."

I nod and head over to the sink, where I slide out the garbage can. I'm about to drop the bag in, but something about the way the glass catches the light from the window makes me feel a little dizzy. I stare down at the bag, at the jagged, beautiful shards, and am reminded of how the sun had transformed the leaves into shimmering glass outside the train station.

I don't know why, but I can't throw it out. I close the cabinet and without turning to see if Ray is watching, I take the bag and run upstairs. I hide the bag of glass inside Grandma's hatbox, then close the suitcase back up, still unable to unpack.

Suddenly I'm overwhelmed with exhaustion. The long, strange day has finally caught up with me. I start to move everything from the bed, carefully at first, but then just sweep it off with my arm. I climb on top of the pale yellow blanket and close my eyes. I'm sure Emily will come get me when dinner comes.

In the haze of half sleep, I imagine I can hear the glass tinkling inside the bag, trying to fit itself back together. But of course that's impossible. You can't unshatter a bowl any more than you can unsteal a goat.

Chapter Six

The sound of my stomach growling startles me awake. I expect to see Emily's messy room but instead I find myself in darkness. I squeeze my eyes shut and open them again. How did it get dark in the ten minutes I'd been lying down? I catch sight of my alarm clock on the night table and groan. 2:13 A.M.! I am clearly the worst houseguest ever. On the other side of the room, I can just make out Emily asleep on her back, a book open on her chest.

I tentatively lift the corner of my own blanket and am relieved to see that even though I'm now barefoot, my clothes are still on. It would have been really embarrassing if Aunt Bethany had put me in my pajamas like I was a little kid. She must have plugged in my clock, though, which means she was in my suitcase. I wonder what she saw.

I realize I have no idea where the bathroom is. My bladder tells me I can't wait till morning to find out.

Creeping across the room on my tiptoes, I do my best to step around the piles that I can just make out thanks to the full moon shining through the blinds. I make it to the door without Emily waking up.

The closed doors up and down the hall mock me. Seeing no

other option, I put my ear up to the first door I come to. I don't know what I'm expecting to hear but it's not like I can knock. After a few seconds of hearing nothing, I open the door to reveal a closet full of sheets and towels. Gentle snoring wafts into the hallway from the next room. I hurry past it, glad I hadn't tried that knob. Barging into my aunt and uncle's bedroom in the middle of the night would really not be a step in the right direction.

The room next to theirs is the one where Uncle Roger keeps his collectibles, so I turn around and start down the other side. A faint ray of light peeks out from underneath the first door. Just like a night-light in a bathroom would! I lean close to it, and, hearing only silence, eagerly push it open.

Nope. Not a bathroom. Judging from the blueprints, charts, magazine articles, and newspaper clippings fluttering on the long white walls, along with the most random assortment of stuff I've ever seen, I'm pretty sure I've just stumbled onto Uncle Roger's lab. Every surface is covered with machinery of some kind, from tiny screws to what looks like an airplane engine but probably isn't because who has an airplane engine in their house? Huge rolls of cloth in every color line the left side of the room. One corner is full of beakers and test tubes and jars marked DO NOT DRINK. Lamps and vacuum cleaners and tires and tubes, bundles of wire and row upon row of metal filing cabinets fill the rest of the space. It's as unorganized as the Collectibles Room is tidy.

I trace the light source to a tall lamp next to the desk. Or what I'm assuming is a desk since I can't see the surface of it. Emily must feel very at home in this room.

Should I turn off the light? I probably should. Waste of electricity and all that. I take a few steps toward it, careful not to trip over the stack of magazines in the way.

"Going on walkabout?" an amused voice asks from behind me. "And I thought they only did that Down Under."

My body tries to take a step backward and whirl around at the same time. As a result, I get tangled in my own legs and fall right over the magazines, which splay out in all directions.

"Sorry, didn't mean to startle you," Ray says, bending down to help me. "Just came to check when I heard noises up here."

"Why are you always sneaking up on me?" I grumble. "Because here in America, it's considered *impolite*."

"Oh, it's impolite Down Under, too. It's just fun."

"I was trying to find the bathroom."

"In here?"

I sigh. "Can you just show me where it is?"

We walk out into the hall. "Last door on the left," he whispers.

I lower my voice, too. "Then what are all these other doors?"

"They all open into the lab. Your rellies knocked the walls down to make it one big room."

I should have realized that. "Hooroo," Ray says and leaves me at the bathroom door with a wave. I figure that either means "good night" or is Australian for "Don't wander into your uncle's lab again or I'll be forced to tell him." Or maybe it's his imitation of an owl. If he weren't so cute, I would have lost patience with him three conversations ago.

By the time I get back to the bedroom, Emily's blankets have become a tent. The only sound is the rustle of pages turning.

I'm about to tell her she doesn't have to hide under there on my account; the glow of the flashlight wouldn't bother me. Then I hear "But if the square root of the integer is nine . . ." and I decide to tiptoe past her bed instead. I wouldn't want to disrupt a genius at work.

Only when I've climbed back into my bed does it occur to me to wonder why Ray would be here in the middle of the night.

. . . .

The next time I wake up, it's to the sound of my alarm playing "light rain."

"Rats," Emily mutters sleepily. "It's raining."

I reach over and shut it off. "It's just my clock, see?" I lift the blind to show her the sun outside, but she has already rolled over and doesn't respond when I call her name.

Even though it's only seven o'clock, I'm wide awake. Except for my brief journey in the middle of the night, I've been sleeping for twelve hours. I may be hungrier than I've ever been. I slip on my shoes and sneak past Emily again. The other doors are still closed and no one's in the kitchen when I get there. I'm halfway through my third bowl of Rice Krispies when Ray strolls in eating a roll and carrying a newspaper.

"G'day!" he says with his mouth full. "Not to be a knocker, but you must really like that outfit."

I look down. I'm still in the black pants and black T-shirt I wore on the train. Instead of commenting on that sorry fact, I ask, "Do you, like, *live* here?"

"In the guest room down the hall," he says, then shoves the rest of the roll in his mouth.

The guest room that should be *mine*, I can't help thinking.

He sits down across from me and opens the paper. I quickly finish my cereal and bring the bowl to the sink.

"See you later," I say, turning to go back upstairs.

"Getting ready for your party?"

I stop in my tracks. I'd forgotten all about that! The cereal in my belly congeals into a solid lump. "Do you think I can ask them to cancel it? I'm really not a party person."

"Nope. Your aunt loves to throw parties."

"I, um, I think I need fresh air." I hurry outside and over to the shed. I need to be riding. It always helps me sort things out. Tools of all shapes and sizes hang from metal hooks that run the length of one wall. I find a wrench and raise the bike seat as high as it will go. A few swishes with an old rag and the spider-webs are gone. The tires are completely flat, but a bike pump solves that. I check under the seat to make sure no spiders are lurking, then walk the bike past the giant hole and around to the front yard.

The tires are a lot thicker than I'm used to and it's hard to build up any real speed on the flat streets. But the air on my cheeks feels good, and I can move around easier without all the usual reflective gear.

After a few minutes, I can relax enough to put the looming party out of my head and take a look around. The houses are all pretty large, larger than the ones at home, but none as large as Emily's. Not too many people are outside yet, only two dog walkers and a little kid on his bike. The kid and I nod at each other as we approach on opposite sides of the street. He glances at my bike and then up at me and then down at my bike again. I pretend not to notice and keep riding.

After a few more times around the block I figure I better get back in case anyone's looking for me. As soon as I enter the backyard, I hear a very strange sound. Not chanting, not singing, but a combination of the two. The voice is male. I don't know what language it is, but it's definitely not Australian. And the voice isn't deep enough to be Uncle Roger. The only thing is, I don't see anyone.

I walk the bike as silently as possible through the still-damp grass. The voice gets louder and louder. I look around for a hidden tree house, but see only leaves and sky. There's only one other option. But who would willingly hang around the bottom of a pool pit? Maybe the boy fell in and it's up to me to rescue him. I don't have much practice in the rescuing department. I glance up at the house. The upstairs rooms are still dark. Guess it's up to me. When I reach the edge of the hole, I kneel down and peek over, afraid of what I might find.

A boy around my age with short, spiky brown hair and wire-rimmed glasses is sitting cross-legged on one of the wooden boards. His eyes are closed, and he's swaying slightly as he chants/sings. Sometimes the words are really hard and guttural, and sometimes they're soft. It's not unpleasant, just . . . different. Almost like it's from another time and definitely another place. As far as I can tell from this distance, the boy doesn't look wounded in any way. I think I'm off the hook on the rescue.

I start to back up before he spots me, but of course my sneaker catches on a rock and sends a bunch of dirt and pebbles skittering down the side. The singing stops abruptly.

"Is someone up there?" he calls out.

Would it be really bad to just leave? Probably. So I step into view. "Sorry. I didn't mean to bother you."

He scrambles to his feet. "No, I'm sorry. I hope I didn't wake you up."

I shake my head. My experience talking to boys my own age is pretty much zip. That goes double for boys chanting in a foreign language from a really big hole in the ground.

"You must be Emily's cousin," he says.

I nod.

"I thought she told me you weren't coming for a few weeks."

I want to tell him he misunderstood her, but then I'd have to explain how I only pepper-sprayed the principal a few days ago, and I have no desire to share my life story with a strange boy. I look around for a ladder or rope, but don't see any. Changing the subject I ask, "Did you, um, fall into the hole?"

He shakes his head. "Good acoustics down here. Nice echo effect off the dirt walls. And more privacy than at my house. I live across the street. Your aunt lets me practice over here."

"Practice for what?"

"For my bar mitzvah. It's in a month. I'll, you know, become a man. According to tradition."

That explains the foreign language. There are a few Jewish

kids in my grade, but I hadn't been invited to any of their bar mitzvahs. "Well, I should, uh, let you get back to it."

"Wait," he says. "You don't have to go. I mean, if you don't want to."

Considering this has been the longest conversation I'd probably ever had with a soon-to-be-thirteen-year-old boy outside of science lab, I figure I shouldn't push it. I shake my head and say, "I've got to take a shower." Then I cringe. Did I really just tell him I needed to shower? Head down, I scamper away before I can further embarrass myself.

Uncle Roger has taken Ray's place at the table, the newspaper half-obscuring his face. "Eggs?" Aunt Bethany asks me, holding out a skillet. Oil sizzles and pops all around the pan. I can't help noticing she's wearing makeup even though it's early on a Sunday morning. Maybe she sleeps with it on. I thought only women on soap operas did that.

I shake my head. "I'm sorry about last night. I didn't mean to fall asleep."

"Not at all," she says. "You'd had a long day. We saved you some pizza; it's in the fridge."

"Thanks." I'm waiting for her to ask where I'd gone, but she doesn't say anything. I clear my throat and say, "Um, I was just out riding my bike, I mean, Emily's bike. I should have left a note or something."

She cracks an egg over the pan. The oil sizzles louder. "Ray told us," she says, tilting the pan so the egg spreads evenly. "We want you to feel comfortable here, so feel free to do whatever you'd normally do at home."

I'd rather not admit that at home my mother makes me tell her every time I step out of her sight. And I have no desire to wear body armor while biking in a strange town.

She glances at my outfit. "Perhaps you'd like to shower and change before the barbeque?"

I redden. "I was just about to."

"Towels are in the hall closet," she says, then lifts the pan off the stove. With a flick of her wrist, the fried egg jumps out of the pan, flips in the air, and lands in the center of the pan. She beams in satisfaction.

"Cool," I say.

She waves her hand. "Don't be too impressed. Eggs are the only things I know how to make that don't taste like burnt bricks."

The head behind the newspaper nods in agreement.

I'm halfway out of the kitchen when Aunt Bethany calls out to me, "Wait a sec." She leaves the pan on the stove and picks up my arm, the one with my mom's bracelet. "This looks familiar."

I can't think of what to say without admitting it was my mother's, so I blurt out, "I have a whole bag of jewelry for you from Mom. It's upstairs."

She lowers my arm and smiles. "I saw the bag last night. I figured it was either your mom's or you're an international jewel thief posing as my niece. Speaking of your mother, you should call her now, before the plane takes off."

She's probably right. But I really, really don't want to talk to my parents. Mom can always tell when I'm hiding something. Even over the phone. She's truly gifted that way. I'm still not ready to tell them I lost everything they gave me.

"Darling?" Uncle Roger asks, calmly resting the paper on the table. "The eggs?"

We both turn to look at the stove. Black smoke pours from the pan. Aunt Bethany groans and runs over. I take the opportunity to run the other way.

I find Emily sitting up in her bed highlighting a section of her math book. This must have been the one she was reading under the covers.

She grins and points out the window. "It's sunny now! I was afraid your party was going to get rained out."

Too bad my alarm clock doesn't have the magical ability to make *real* rain. "You guys don't have to throw a party for me, seriously."

"It'll be fun," she insists. "You'll get to meet my friends, and I invited Rory and some of her friends, too."

I can't figure her out. Yesterday she didn't want to hang out with me, now today she wants me to meet her friends.

"Great," I say without any actual enthusiasm. She turns back to her book, and I grab clothes and shampoo from my suitcase. My Jake Harrison poster is still folded exactly like I had it, so that's good. The hatbox looks undisturbed, too, which means Aunt Bethany didn't find my letters and the bag of broken glass. I'm not sure which would be harder to explain. I wedge the suitcase under my bed between a stuffed lizard and a plastic pumpkin filled with Halloween candy wrappers.

Halloween = Eight Months Ago.

The bathroom window looks out onto the backyard, where Bar Mitzvah Boy is still chanting. He never told me his name. I guess I didn't tell him mine, either. The echo from the hole makes his voice sound deeper and richer than it did in person. More confident, too. I stand and listen for a few minutes until I begin to feel like I'm eavesdropping on a private moment, which is silly of course since he's singing outside for anyone to hear.

The air vent under the window pumps the odor of bacon into the room, and it smells like home. Not *my* home, because Mom almost never cooks bacon, but someone else's home that I'm not a part of. I turn on the shower, eager to drown out the strangeness of everything. The sound of the pounding water does drown out the boy's voice, but the steam only heightens the bacon smell.

I probably should have called my parents before their flight left. Even though Aunt Bethany told them I arrived safely, they're probably worried that they haven't heard from me directly. Although if they were so worried about me, they wouldn't have sent me here. Now they'll just have to wait till they get their weekly phone access.

By the time I'm done showering and dressing and drying my hair, the chanting has stopped. In its place is the hustle and bustle of party preparation. I peek out the bathroom window. Balloons have been tied around the trunks of various trees, adding color to the yard. Aunt Bethany, in a pink flowery dress, directs Uncle Roger to place a tray of burgers on the patio table.

I back away from the window and return to the bedroom. Emily has moved to her desk and is scribbling an equation in her notebook. Once again I'm afraid to disturb her. She erases, scribbles again, chews on her pencil, then sees me at the door. "Hi, cuz," she says, closing her books.

"Don't stop whatever you're doing because of me."

She makes a face. "Mom only lets me work on my math theorem for an hour a day. Time's up."

I wonder if Aunt Bethany knows that Emily works in the middle of the night, too. "Hey, I just saw your dad carrying out plates of food. I thought your mom only made eggs."

"She does," Emily replies, plucking a skirt and top from various parts of the floor. "All the food is catered from a restaurant in town."

"But I saw that big grill outside?"

"That's only for decoration. Dad took out all the moveable parts a long time ago. I'll have to show you his lab later. You should see what he's able to make out of a rubber band and a bar of soap."

I don't tell her I already had a middle-of-the-night peek. I leave her to dress and go back across the hall to watch the action outside the bathroom window. The backyard is filling up quickly with partygoers of all ages, crowding onto the patio. I watch as a boy with black curls and a pretty blond girl walk in together. Seeing the top of their contrasting heads isn't what catches my eye, though. It's the fact that they're wearing what look like chalkboards around their necks. Sure enough, a few seconds later the girl yanks hers a bit to the side, picks up the end of a long string attached to the top, and begins writing. I can't see the chalk from here, but I can see the white words beginning to appear on the board.

The boy reads it, nods, and scribbles something on his own board in response. None of the other kids around them seem the least bit fazed by their behavior. I don't get it. Are they not able to talk, like, they're mute from some traumatic experience? That's so sad. I watch for a few more minutes until Emily joins me in the bathroom.

"You ready to go downstairs? I'm sure people are looking for you. You're the guest of honor after all."

I shake my head. I honestly don't think I can go down there. I don't even think if I'm dressed right for a barbeque in Willow Falls.

She leans over, pinches my cheeks (hard), and fluffs my hair. I stare at her. "What was that for?"

"My mom does that when I'm about to do something social. 'Gotta have pink in your cheeks!'" Emily's imitation of her mom is spot on. Then in her normal voice she says, "Um, do you have anything more, I don't know, *colorful* to wear?"

For the second time this morning, I look down at my outfit. Black shorts, brown T-shirt, brown and tan striped sneakers. I shake my head. "This is pretty much as colorful as I get. I probably shouldn't go down there. You know, dressed like this. And your clothes would be too small so don't even offer."

She sighs dramatically. "You're *going*. Remember, I got out of camp because I promised to help you acclimate. Now let's go down there and acclimate!"

"I don't know what that means," I say, trying to stall.

She rolls her eyes. "It means mingle. Adjust to the new environment."

I sigh and grudgingly follow her downstairs. I stumble a little as we near the back door and the noise filters in from the party. A little voice in my heads whispers, "Just smile and nod and it'll be over before you know it." It takes a second to realize that little voice is actually Emily whispering in my ear.

So I put on a smile and start nodding as we step out onto the patio.

"Maybe skip the nodding," Emily whispers. "You look like a bobblehead."

I stop the nodding.

Emily immediately heads over to two girls, dragging me along by the elbow. "These are my friends, Emily C and Emily B."

The Emilys say hello in unison. I wonder if they practice that or if it comes naturally if you have the same name as someone. I've never met another Tara before, so I wouldn't know.

"So let me guess," I ask my cousin, "you're Emily S?"

Emily shakes her head. "No, silly. I'm Emily A."

"But your last name starts with an *S*."

Emily C leans over like she's telling me a secret and says, "It's about class rank, not last names."

Emily B adds, "We're not supposed to talk about class rank. Our school is all about fostering a sense of self-worth in a noncompetitive environment."

"We don't think that accurately reflects the real world, do you?" Emily A asks me.

"Um, no?" It must have been the right answer because all the Emilys nod in approval. B and C excuse themselves and head off to the soda table as the boy and girl I saw earlier wearing the blackboards come over. Up close I see that the girl has a lot of freckles and her blond hair is a little puffy. She keeps trying to smooth it down with her hand. I expect them to start writing on their boards, but to my surprise, the girl turns to me and says, "Hi! I'm Amanda!"

Okay, so maybe only the boy can't talk and this Amanda girl is such a good friend that she uses a board to talk to him. I stare at her open, smiling face. Emily elbows me. "Tara," I say. "My name is Tara."

"And this is Leo," Emily says, stepping aside so the black-haired boy can join the circle.

I give him a little wave. Should I say hello? I'd feel weird talking to him when he can only write. But maybe the wave was rude? While I'm trying to figure it out, he says, "Hi, Tara. Welcome to Willow Falls."

I take a step back, looking from one to the other in surprise. I don't get it. They can *both* talk. A woman with hair the exact yellow shade of Amanda's calls to them from the other side of the patio. She's kneeling in front of a little boy with four hot dogs sticking out of his mouth.

"Coming, Mom," Amanda replies. Then to me she says, "That's our friend Rory's little brother, Sawyer. We're supposed to be watching him until she gets here."

The two of them hurry off and I turn to Emily. "Um . . . what's with the blackboards?"

"Oh, right! That must seem weird to someone who isn't used to them."

"Just a little."

"It's pretty simple, really. They can't talk to each other. I mean, not out loud."

"Why? Are they in a fight or something?"

Emily shakes her head. "Not this time, but Rory told me that when they were all in fifth grade Amanda and Leo were in a huge fight and didn't even go *near* each other for a whole *year*. Then something happened that they won't tell anyone, some big secret, and they've been best friends again ever since. Then last summer they started using the blackboards to talk to each other. Or they text. But that's rude to do in a group."

I watch the little boy, Sawyer, spit his half-chewed hot dogs into Leo's hands. Leo makes a face, but I can tell he isn't really grossed out. "How long are they going to stop talking for?"

She shrugs. "Who knows? Those two are weird." The other Emilys return and my Emily tells them (with way too much enthusiasm) that she thinks she found "an inconsistency in the XY coordinates" in the math homework. This is my cue to exit.

I wander over to the pool pit and look down, half expecting to find Bar Mitzvah Boy. Instead, I see a stuffed green bunny lying at the bottom, one ear flopped over its face. A minute later the owner of the bunny announces himself with a howl and a wail. *WHEREISMYBUNNY?!* reverberates through the backyard as the boy who tried to eat too many hot dogs bursts into tears.

I want to tell him the bunny is in the hole, but there are so many people and they would all be looking at me. I do manage to sort of point into the hole, but no one really notices. Bar Mitzvah Boy appears from the side of the house, heading right toward me. He reaches the edge and looks over. "He's here! I'll get him!"

"The Hamburglar to the rescue!" a girl standing next to him declares. I hadn't noticed her at first, but she must have been running alongside Bar Mitzvah Boy the whole time. It's like she blended into the background or something. She's wearing a brown and white sundress with brown sandals, which is sort of the perfect outfit for a summer barbeque and makes me feel even more underdressed. Drat my utter lack of fashion sense.

Then she turns and looks straight at me. Our eyes connect for only a second, but it's enough to give me a strange sort of jolt. I've never seen eyes like that before. I don't think it's the color, which is your basic green. But as soon as she looked at me, I got this weird déjà vu feeling. Like I've met her before, while knowing absolutely that I haven't. How could I not have noticed her right away?

The little boy runs over to her and wraps his arms around her waist. She laughs and says, "Don't worry, Sawyer. David Goldberg's going to rescue your bunny." I realize the girl must be Rory, Emily's babysitter and sister of the little boy.

Bar Mitzvah Boy = The Hamburglar = David Goldberg?

David thumps his chest and says, "I shall return." He crosses to the other side of the pool and starts climbing down. The rocks sticking out of the side make almost as good a ladder as a real one. Except that the rungs of a real ladder don't fall off with no warning. David slides down about a foot, joined by falling pebbles and dirt on either side of him. The crowd that has now gathered lets out a collective gasp.

"I'm fine," he calls as he regains his footing. He straightens his glasses and continues the rescue. Soon he's on his way back up, stuffed bunny clamped between his teeth.

"You could have just tossed it up to us," Rory says, pulling the bunny's ear from David's mouth.

He shrugs and dusts the dirt off his knees. "Wouldn't be as dramatic."

Rory holds the bunny up by the opposite ear, kind of distastefully. She shakes off the dirt before lowering it into Sawyer's waiting hands. She gives one last shudder as he hugs it.

She must really not like dirt.

I'm starting to feel a little weird standing here like I'm a part of their conversation. Then David says, "Rory has a thing against bunnies." It takes a few seconds to realize he's talking to me. I guess it wasn't the dirt, after all.

Rory stomps her foot. "The bunny tried to kill me, David. He would have gone after my whole family next. Or he might have followed me here one time while I was babysitting Emily. And then after he destroyed *her* whole family, he would go across the street for yours!"

He rolls his eyes. "So you keep saying."

I have this fear that if I don't talk to Rory soon, she'll walk away. And even though I don't know why it matters to me one way or another, I only know I don't want her to go. So I ask, "Your brother's stuffed animal tried to kill you?"

David chuckles. "It was a pet bunny," Rory explains. "I only had him for a few weeks. It's very frustrating because no one believes me about the evil that lurked within him." She glares at David as she says that last part.

"That must have been scary," I say, because I want to be on her side.

"See?" Rory says. "Even a stranger believes me."

"She's not a stranger," David says. "Her name's Tara, and she's Emily's cousin."

Rory beams at me. "You're the guest of honor, then!"

I feel my cheeks get warm, first because David knew my name, and second because I've rarely been a guest before, to say nothing of the guest of honor. "I guess I am," I admit. "And David's the Hamburglar?"

He nods. "When my mom and I moved here in third grade, my only friend for a while was this kid Connor. My last name's Goldberg, so he started calling me Burger, then Hamburger, then the Hamburglar. It just stuck."

Amanda and Leo appear from out of the crowd, blackboards swinging on their chests. "Rory," Amanda says, "I thought you said your brother only eats pizza and soft pretzels."

"He added hot dogs last month."

"We learned that the hard way," Leo says, wiping his hands on his jeans.

Amanda turns to David. "Nice rescue, Bee Boy."

David thumps his chest again, then bows deeply.

Bar Mitzvah Boy = The Hamburglar = David Goldberg = Bee Boy?

Noticing my confused expression, Amanda explains, "It's from a thing that happened in fifth grade."

"Did he get stung by a bee or something?"

Amanda and Leo laugh. "No," Amanda says, "he looked like one."

I glance at David, who, in his blue shorts and white button-down shirt does not in any way resemble a bee. Emily was right; these two are a little odd.

"I didn't look like a bee," David insists.

"Yeah, you did," Amanda says. "You were wearing black and yellow, and you flew out of the classroom door like, well, a bee toward a flower!"

David shakes his head. "I still don't understand how you just happened to show up that day with a spare drawing of the periodic table in your pocket. I would have failed for sure, otherwise."

"Doesn't everyone carry a spare periodic table in their pocket?" Amanda asks innocently. "Hey, remember how you almost killed Leo when you banged the door open?"

David looks confused. "I don't remember Leo being there."

Leo scribbles something on his board and tilts it toward Amanda. She slaps herself on the side of the head. "Oh, you're right, Bee Boy! I was thinking of something else."

Leo loops the chalk back over his blackboard and turns to me. "Tara, after the party, do you want us to show you around town?"

In my whole life, a boy has never asked me to go anywhere with him. I take a closer look at him. Leo's definitely cute, with blue eyes, a dimple, and that dark black curly hair. He and Amanda stand very close to each other, but not in a way that makes other people feel left out. Even though he's obviously not asking me on a date, I honestly have no idea how to respond.

"It'll be fun," Amanda insists. "We'll show you all our favorite places. And I bet we can get a ride out to Apple Grove after."

Apple Grove doesn't sound all that exciting. But I've lived in enough small towns to know that you take your fun where you can get it. The four of them are waiting for an answer. Mom would be thrilled. I'm here less than twenty-four hours and already four kids my age want to hang out with me. With no breaking and entering involved. I look from one to the other. They all seem so . . . nice. A little strange (okay, a *lot* strange), but nice.

But I just can't do it. "I . . . I lost my cell phone on the train," I tell them, staring at a random spot over Leo's left shoulder. "Or it was stolen or something, I'm not really sure. But my uncle's going to take me to replace it this afternoon."

Rory grabs hold of my arm. Normally my first instinct would be to pull away. I'm not used to being touched by anyone who isn't related to me. But I fight the urge because it's Rory and there's something different about her.

"That's not a problem," she says eagerly. "We could take you there. The phone store's right downtown. They moved from the mall last summer. Robert's still the manager, though."

This girl sure knows a lot about the phone store.

As though reading my mind, she says, "I spend a lot of time there."

I take that to mean Rory has a crush on the store manager.

"So, Tara," David says. "How come you decided to spend the summer in the thrill-a-minute town of Willow Falls?"

I stiffen as they all turn toward me expectantly. I mumble something about my mom's job until Aunt Bethany saves me by showing up with a plate of hot dogs. I could tell them the "no kids allowed" story, but I really don't want to lie. I just don't want to tell the truth, either. I make sure to chew my hot dog slowly and thoroughly, so hopefully by the time we're done eating they'll have forgotten that the question is still hanging in the air, with no good answer to satisfy it.

Chapter Seven

We only pass through one traffic light on the way into downtown Willow Falls. I've lived in some small towns, but this one is the smallest and quaintest of them all. Old-fashioned streetlights line Main Street, and the *bump bump bump* of Uncle Roger's tires tells me we're driving on cobblestones. I spot a small library, a diner, music store, bookstore, toy store, a few clothing stores, and a movie theatre. Each one has a brightly colored awning hanging over the door, so they all kind of match. Uncle Roger's is the only little red sports car on the road, though. I'm surprised I haven't heard any complaints from the passengers in the backseat. That might be because they're squished in so tightly the air is being sucked from their lungs.

"Here we are," Uncle Roger says, pulling up next to the curb.

"Thanks for driving us," I tell him.

"My pleasure. You sure you don't need me to help deal with the insurance?"

From the cramped backseat Rory squeaks, "I've got this one, Mr. St. Claire."

I hop out and push my seat forward so the others can exit. Rory untangles her arms and legs and climbs out first, followed by Amanda, Leo, and David, who makes a loud *umph* sound as he pushes himself out.

"Okay. Call me if you need to be picked up."

I watch as he pulls away and then I follow the others into the phone store. All the people working in the store turn to look. Their faces light up.

"Rory!" One of the women actually claps.

A guy wearing a blue suit and a manager's badge hurries out from behind the counter. "Two months now, right? A personal best for Rory Swenson!" He clutches a small red notebook in one hand and a pen in the other. He must be at least in his thirties. Late thirties, even. Why would Rory have a crush on this guy?

Rory puts her hands on her hips. "What makes you think I'm here because I lost my phone?"

The manager's smile fades. "Aren't you?"

She sighs. "Yes."

"Rory!" Amanda says, laughing. "Are you serious?"

Rory nods and slumps her shoulders. "I know, I'm pathetic." But then she straightens up and points to me. "But I'm not *only* here for me. This is my new friend, Tara. She lost hers, too."

I give a little wave.

The manager beams. "Any friend of my best customer is a friend of mine. Want to see the book?"

Quick as a flash, he spreads open the small notebook and flips to an early page. He drops his finger onto it and says, "Here she is! Under fifteen minutes to lose her first phone. It's still a companywide record! Then a few weeks later she brought in a waterlogged one, then a month after that was my personal favorite — her phone was run over by a bulldozer."

Rory blushes. "They were about to plow down all the apple trees Amanda and Leo planted. And that cute little birdbath. It's been up there since Willow Falls was founded."

Amanda puts her arm around Rory's shoulder. "Throwing your cell phone at that huge bulldozer was very brave."

"Hey," Rory says, jutting out her chin, "it worked, didn't it?"

"That, and the grant from the city," David says.

Rory kicks him in the shin.

Ten minutes later, Leo and Amanda have had a full conversation through their blackboards, David has played with every electronic gadget on display, and Rory and I have filled out the paperwork to get our new phones. The manager goes into the back for a minute, then comes back with our replacements. Mine looks exactly like my old one, which still looked brand-new since I almost never used it.

Rory takes one look at mine and her eyes grow wide. "Wow! That's a beauty. You're so lucky."

I don't want to let her know that I never use it, since that would make it obvious that I don't have any friends. Maybe she's already guessed that, though, since I haven't said more than a few words to any of them. Still, all I tell her is that my mom is really overprotective and paranoid, so she insisted on the best possible phone.

"My parents are like that, too," she says. "Overprotective, I mean. Or at least they used to be. They're much better now. But I can still only get this lame one. It doesn't even have a real keyboard for texting! Can you believe that?"

I shake my head in solidarity. Truly, though, I've only sent a handful of texts in my entire life, and most were to my parents telling them when I'd be home after school.

While she and I sign the little red notebook (which the employees enjoy just a bit too much, if you ask me), Amanda takes my new phone and programs all of their numbers into it. I've never had anyone's number stored in my phone except my parents'. I'm honestly not sure why they're being so nice to me. Maybe it's for Emily's sake, so she won't be stuck with me all the time.

"See you in a few days, Rory!" the manager calls after us as we head out.

"No, he won't," David says as we head away from the store.

Rory sighs. "Yeah, he probably will."

"Let's take Tara to the community center," Amanda suggests, pointing across the street at a large white building. "There's always something fun going on there."

Rory shakes her head. "My mom's taking an aerobics class. It would be too embarrassing."

So we start walking. We pass the music store, where Leo and Amanda wave at two guys setting up a display in the window. I do a double take when I realize they are identical twins. "That's Larry and Lawrence," Amanda says. "They let me practice my drums downstairs whenever my sister claims she can't possibly do her homework with all the racket."

"I never knew any girls who played the drums," I say and then wish I could take it back. Seriously, I should not be allowed to talk to other humans.

"She's really great," Leo says. "You should hear her play."

"Aw, shucks," Amanda says, elbowing him playfully.

Okay, now I'm positive they're a couple. I look ahead at David and Rory, who have stopped in front of another display window, this time at the Willow Falls Historical Society. They're pointing at something in the window and laughing. It's clear that they're good friends, but I don't get the same vibe as I do from Amanda and Leo.

"Why don't we go in here?" Rory suggests when we catch up. "What better way to learn about Willow Falls than to see a two-hundred-year-old stuffed raccoon in a rocking chair?"

I look inside the big glass window. It's pretty much what I would expect from a historical society. Cramped and dark, with a big wooden desk, some old-fashioned musical instruments, a few couches and chairs, and shelves of books and knickknacks.

"It's really dusty in there," Leo says, backing away from the window. "My allergies would act up."

"And I heard it's haunted," Amanda adds, waving us forward. "Just keep walking and don't look back."

"Wow, some people really don't like history," David mutters as we follow them past the window.

"Seriously," Rory agrees.

Halfway down the next block, I catch sight of a little side street that the others walk right past. It's not even wide enough for a car to go down. I guess it's more of an alley than a street, but I spot a tiny watch shop, and a few other stores whose signs I can't read from this angle. "What's down here?" I ask. The others stop and walk back to me.

"My grandfather took me to that one when I was a little kid," David says, pointing to the watch store. He wrinkles his nose. "I remember it smelled like cigars and feet."

Rory peers into the alley. "I've always just walked past this," she murmurs. "Let's see what else is down there." Amanda and Leo exchange a quick glance, but they follow along.

Like Main Street, the alley road is made of cobblestone. But in this case, many of the stones are misshapen and cracked, and we have to watch our steps carefully so as not to trip. Both the watch store and the barbershop across from it are closed on Sundays. A shoe repair store, also closed, reveals itself past the barbershop.

"What's this place?" Rory asks, stopping in front of the last store on the right. A thick layer of dust and grime covers the big window, but the letters at the top of the glass are still legible and a sign on the door declares they are open weekdays only. "'Angelina's Sweet Repeats and Collectibles,'" she reads aloud. As soon as the words are out of her mouth she backs away, nearly tripping on the edge of an upturned stone. "We should go back."

"Why?" David asks. "Let's see what's inside." Before Rory can protest, he uses his sleeve to wipe a large circle of dirt from the window and peers in. "Empty," he declares with a shrug.

Only it *isn't* empty. The area he cleared off is enough to expose shelves and tables full of various small objects — books, toys, comics, clocks, sporting goods, dishes, clothes, shoes, and even more that I can't make out in the gloom of the darkened shop. "More like the *opposite* of empty," I reply, turning away from the window to smile at him. David's kind of funny, which makes it easy to be around him. And I don't usually find anyone easy to be around.

He smiles back, a little uncertainly, though. "Only if you call cobwebs and an overturned trash can the opposite of empty."

My smile wobbles. I'm not sure how I'm supposed to respond now. How long do we each pretend to see something else? Darn my lack of social skills! A quick motion next to me catches my eye, and I turn in time to see Leo grab Amanda's arm. Face pale, Leo opens his mouth to speak. But before he can utter a word, Amanda clamps her hand over it and shakes her head. Leo's eyes widen. Clearly, he realized he had just been about to speak to her. I can't imagine what the big deal is. They can just stop and start their strange game any time. He lets go of her arm and she pulls her hand away from his mouth. They look at the rest of us, then back at each other.

Leo picks up his board. *HER not HIM?* he writes, his hand shaking with each letter. He tries to shield the board from the rest of us, but since I'm right next to Amanda, I can see it. Then she writes back, *OFF BY A DAY?* then erases it with her forearm. She turns to Rory and, in a voice that she probably hopes sounds casual, asks, "Hey, Rory, so what do *you* see in the window?"

"I . . . I'm not sure," Rory says, backing away another few feet. "Tables? And some shelves and stuff?"

"Very funny, Rory," David says. "Is this because I don't believe your bunny was intent on world domination?"

Rory looks pleadingly at Amanda, and then at me, then back at Amanda. At this close range I can see Amanda has gone as pale as Leo. So pale that her freckles are almost gone. I must have missed something somewhere. Are we joking around, or aren't we? Why does Rory look so scared, and Amanda and Leo so freaked out? What does "Her not Him" mean? Her who? And Him who? And doesn't David know he's dragging out the joke by insisting the store is empty? I think I'd like to go home now. I'll settle for Emily's room.

To my relief, Rory says, "Can we just go?" She spreads her arms wide and herds us down the street like she's wrangling cattle. Amanda and Leo both take one last glance at the store window before allowing themselves to be ushered along.

Right before we reach the corner of Main Street, Amanda puts her hand on my arm. As before with Rory, my first instinct is to shake it off. Her grip is pretty tight, though, so it's just as well that another part of me doesn't.

"Are you okay?" she asks, her eyes wide with concern.

I'm not used to someone I just met looking so deeply into my eyes. I squirm a little and glance down at the cobblestones. "I . . . I think maybe I should call my uncle to pick me up."

"I think you're supposed to come with us to Apple Grove. I mean, I think you'd really like it."

When I don't answer, she adds, "Rory's dad is probably already on his way to bring us." Playing the drums must make her hands superstrong. If she doesn't let go soon, I'm going to have five bruises in the shapes of fingers.

Rory catches up to us, and Amanda drops her hold on my arm.

"Let's just go to Apple Grove now, okay?" Rory asks. Her brows are still a bit furrowed, but she looks less freaked out than before. "You're coming, right, Tara?"

"Um, I guess I am."

"Good!" Rory says, linking her arm with mine.

Rory = Hard to Say No To.

While we wait outside the Willow Falls Diner for Rory's father, Amanda and Leo huddle together, scribbling furiously on their boards, erasing, and rewriting over and over.

"Um, have they always done stuff like that?" I ask Rory and David in a low voice.

"I don't know," David whispers, watching them out of the corner of his eye. "Rory was friends with them first, and then when she started babysitting for Emily across the street, we just all started hanging out and became really good friends. They've done some strange stuff since I've known them, but this whole blackboard thing has gone on since last summer."

"I'm sure they have their reasons," Rory says. Her eyes dart anxiously down the street toward the alley.

David shrugs. "I just wish they would tell us what it is."

"Maybe they *can't* tell us," Rory says.

It's one thing not to tell a stranger like me, but what could keep them from telling their closest friends?

As though they could hear my thoughts, Leo and Amanda abruptly stop writing and turn to look at me. I quickly bend down to tie my sneaker. Only my sneakers are slip-ons, so I pretend I have an itch on my ankle instead.

Thankfully Rory's dad pulls up to the curb before I scratch my skin raw. As she leads us to the car she says, "I should warn you, my dad's a little, well, *different*."

"My dad's pretty different, too," I tell her. "He writes about zombies for a living and is, like, seven feet tall."

David whispers, "But does he have a green stripe in his hair?"

"Last year it was blue," Amanda adds from behind.

I can see the stripe as soon as Rory opens the passenger door. It's hard to miss since the rest of his hair is blond. It's a normal-sized car (unlike Uncle Roger's), but it's still a tight fit in the back. I hope I remembered deodorant this morning! As we pull away, Rory gestures to the backseat and says, "Dad, this is Tara St. Claire. We met her at the barbeque today."

Rory's dad looks in the rearview mirror. I give a little wave. It's all I can do considering my arms are pretty much pinned at my sides. Then I say, "It's actually Tara Brennan, not St. Claire. My mom and Emily's mom are sisters."

The car jerks to a halt and we all bounce forward, then back.

"Dad?" Rory says worriedly.

He twists around in his seat to face me. "Your mother and Bethany St. Claire are sisters? Your mother's Molly?"

"Uh-huh."

He peers closer at my face. "And your last name is Brennan?"

I nod.

He breaks into a huge grin. "You're Jim Brennan's daughter!"

I nod again, a bit more hesitantly this time. Maybe he's a fan of my dad's books? Dad doesn't have that many fans, but some of them can be pretty hard-core.

"Jimmy Brennan's daughter!" Rory's dad exclaims, shaking his head. "I don't believe it. Jim and Molly!" He stares at me, continuing to shake his head in amazement. I find myself staring at the green stripe. I wonder if it fades away or if he's stuck with it until it grows out.

"Um, Dad?" Rory says, tugging on his sleeve. "We're sort of in the middle of the road here."

"Oops, sorry," her dad says, turning forward in his seat. He pulls back into the flow of traffic, still shaking his head in wonderment.

"How do you know Tara's parents?" Rory asks him.

"We all grew up together," he says, grinning. "Molly and Jim were an item before the rest of us even *thought* about dating. From eighth grade on, they were inseparable. Then after high school they moved away and never came back. We all figured they'd get married, and now here you are. Living proof!" He glances in the rearview mirror at me, and shakes his head again. "Molly and Jim's kid. Wow. Wait till I tell your mom! And, Leo, your dad was a few years ahead of us in school, but he'll remember them, too!"

It continues like that all the way out of town, past some cornfields, past the Willow Falls Shopping Mall, and onto a dirt road with a small white sign that reads WELCOME TO THE NEW APPLE GROVE. We pull over next to the sign and climb out.

"I'll be back to pick you guys up in about half an hour," Rory's dad says, leaning out of the car window. He beams at me. "You're tall, just like Jimmy. Good ol' Jimmy Brennan! Hey, are your parents in town, too?"

I shake my head. "They're in Madagascar for the summer." I leave out the part about how they banished me to Willow Falls before they left.

He laughs. "Madagascar? What are they doing there?"

I feel my cheeks start to burn. "My mom is leading a research team to, um, study the mating habits of the bamboo lemur."

He laughs again. "You're making that up!"

I shake my head. "Nope. That's what she does."

He thumps the steering wheel in delight. "Good ol' Molly! Be sure to tell them Doug Swenson says hello, okay?"

"Okay."

He pulls away and Rory says, "I mentioned the weirdness of Dad, didn't I?"

"You did," I reply as we walk away from the road.

I don't know what I'd expected of a place called Apple Grove, but I'm pretty sure apples figured into it somewhere. As far as I can tell, though, Apple Grove is just a clump of about twenty-five tiny trees in the middle of a clearing behind a shopping mall. None of the trees are higher than my waist, and most are considerably shorter. Some need sticks to hold them up, others are surrounded by wire mesh, still more peek out from under mounds of fertilizer. A few unplanted ones have canvas bags wrapped around the bottom, for extra protection, I guess.

A small fountain completely covered in crusted-over bird droppings sits a few feet in front of the trees, like an old queen presiding over her subjects. Was this the birdbath Rory sacrificed her phone to save? I'd have to go on record as saying it probably wasn't worth it.

Amanda inhales deeply. "Ah, smell those apples!"

I would say she's crazy, that these trees are completely bare, except that the smell of apples really *does* fill the air. Apples and apple pies and apple tortes and apple turnovers. "Where's that smell coming from?" I ask, turning around in a circle.

"Not you, too!" David groans.

Rory and Amanda share a quick look. Amanda writes something to Leo, who nods eagerly.

"You smell it, too, Tara?" Rory asks.

"The apples?" I ask. "Doesn't everyone?"

David shakes his head. "Only girls can smell it, apparently."

I look over at Leo, who reddens slightly and immediately starts pulling at the collar of his T-shirt like it's suddenly gotten too tight. I just *know* he can smell it, too. Why would he let David believe he can't? What would be the point of that? Maybe they just don't want David to feel left out. For kids who only became friends not that long ago, they really protect each other. For the second time since I've been to this town, I get a pang of jealousy. I don't like it. I've made it a habit not to long for things. It makes not getting them a lot easier to handle.

"Come on," Amanda says, running over to the first row of trees. "Come see what we've done. Apple Grove used to be a really important part of Willow Falls. Over a hundred years ago, the families who lived here exported apples all over the state."

Leo makes these wide sweeping motions with his arms. "Can't you just picture it? The townspeople used to string lights up in the apple trees and hold weddings and school dances, and boats would sail back and forth on the river. It used to be such an amazing place." He lets his arms fall to his sides. "But the river dried up, the people who lived here passed away . . ." He pauses for a moment, than continues. "The houses eventually came down, and years later the mall went up, destroying the few trees that were still producing fruit. Amanda and I got permission to plant new apple trees in this small clearing." He glances around. "Guess it doesn't look like much."

"It'll take a few more years until the trees grow fruit," Amanda says, gently touching one of the thin branches. "And some might never. But the ground remembers how to grow apples, so we have hope."

Leo grins at me. "If you promise not to laugh, we'll show you how we help them grow."

"Forget it, Leo, no way," David says, crossing his arms.

"Why not? You do it all the time."

"Yeah, but that's with you guys. Tara's going to think I'm a total dork."

"She probably already does," Rory jokes. "So you might as well go ahead."

He shakes his head and presses his lips together.

"Come on," Leo says. "You're going to have to do it next month in front of a hundred people. You can't get shy now."

He sighs. "Fine. But you know it doesn't really help the trees grow."

"Sure it does," Amanda says. She touches a tiny leaf on a spindly branch. "I'm sure this little guy wasn't here last week."

David rolls his eyes. "All right. Assume the position."

The other three immediately sit down on the grass, and to my surprise, keep going until they are fully lying down. "Come on, Tara," Rory says, patting the ground next to her.

I hesitate. I don't normally get too freaked out by bugs, but when I was seven we lived someplace where you couldn't go on the grass because of fire ants. Fire ants hurt. I don't think I've lain in the grass in six years. I guess it must be safe in Willow Falls or they definitely wouldn't be doing this. So I lie down next to Rory and try not to think of what might be crawling in my hair.

It's late afternoon by now, so the sun is off to the side and not shining right in our eyes. The sky is completely blue and cloudless, and the smell of apples is stronger down here for some reason. After a few seconds, the heat of the earth rises up beneath me. It feels nice, and I relax into it. And then suddenly I feel like I'm moving. My fingers instinctively grab on to the blades of grass to either side of me. I know we're not supposed to feel the spinning of the earth on its axis, but I swear I do. I have this flash of fear that if I let go, I'd go hurtling into outer space. I shut my eyes tight and try to catch my breath, which seems to be coming faster and faster.

Panting Like a Dog Around Kids You Just Met = Really Embarrassing.

Chapter Eight

"Are you okay?" David asks.

I open one eye to see him standing above me, looking down in concern.

I open my other eye, experiment with turning my head from side to side, then take a deep breath. I think I'm back to normal. "Sorry, go ahead and do the . . . whatever it is you're doing."

"You're sure?" he asks.

"I'm sure," I say quickly, anxious to have the focus be off me.

"All right." David steps back until he's next to the fountain. He clears his throat. "This is called 'Shalom Rav,'" he says, then starts singing.

It's a Hebrew song, that much I can figure out. But it has a much softer melody that the chanting I heard in the pool hole. His voice is really smooth and the song is actually really, really beautiful. Lying there, feeling the warmth from the earth below me and the warmth from the sun above me, and the warmth from David's song in the air, I feel something I've never felt before. A sort of connectedness to everything. It still feels like the earth is spinning beneath me, but it's not unpleasant now.

Then the song is interrupted by a different kind of singing. *Kreeee, kreeee, kreeee.* I lift my head and there they are, perched on the edge of the broken fountain, legs entwined with each other. I push myself up onto my elbows and stare at them while David keeps singing. I've never seen a hawk in my entire life, and now they're everywhere, and apparently they're all friendly — well, with each other anyway. Unless . . . I'm no expert on hawks, but I would swear these are the same ones I saw at the train station. Could one of those hawks actually have been the one who visited me in my backyard at home? I immediately dismiss the thought. It's hundreds of miles from here. Unless it hitched a ride on the train, it would be impossible.

David finishes his song, and the others sit up and clap. I clap, too. He was really, really good. I could only tell he was nervous occasionally.

"Aw, it was nothing," David says, waving away the applause. "Anything to help the trees."

The hawks rustle their feathers, almost like they're clapping, too.

"Look," Amanda says, pointing at the birds. "It's not only nature you can charm. It's also the animal kingdom. Max and Flo love your singing, too."

I look around in surprise. "You guys know those birds?"

They all nod. "They've been in Willow Falls for decades," Leo says. "My parents remember them from when they were teenagers. Some kids named them Max and Flo. The names just stuck."

"I think it's very romantic," Rory says wistfully. "They're like lovebirds. Except, you know, they're hawks. You never see one without the other."

Well, that decides it. It was bad enough having one bird facing me down in my backyard, I'd have noticed if there were two.

While the others are tending to a tree that has started falling over, I gravitate to the fountain and watch the hawks for a minute. The smaller one is using its beak to clean the feathers on the larger, who then rustles them contentedly. Some unseen signal must have passed through them, because they both lift off with a mutual *garunk*. But as they fly overhead, something about the bright yellow feet on the larger one seems awfully familiar.

"Look out!" David yells. I look down from the sky in time to see him running right at me. He places his hands on both of my shoulders and shoves. I stumble back, unable to catch my balance before falling onto my butt. I watch in horror as a stream of bird droppings hits David squarely on top of his head.

David falls dramatically to his knees. "Hamburglar down," he calls out weakly. "Hamburglar down."

"Wow!" Rory says, suddenly appearing at my side. "He took a bullet for you! Well, a bullet of bird poop!"

I scramble to my feet, ignoring the ache in my butt from the hard ground. I stare at David, unsure of what to say, or even think. No one has ever done anything like *that* for me before.

"I'm pretty sure this means you're indebted to him for life," Leo says.

Some bird poop slides from David's hair onto his glasses. He takes them off and wipes them on the bottom of his shirt.

"I . . . I don't know what to say," I manage to squeak out. "You didn't have to do that."

"Don't worry," he says, putting his glasses back on and blinking. "Purely selfish on my part. A bird pooping on your head is supposed to be good luck. So since you're the reason it happened, that means *you* must be good luck. That's why you came to Willow Falls this summer, right?" He grins. "To bring me luck for my bar mitzvah."

My stomach twists. I'm absolutely positive my parents weren't thinking of David when they sent me here. I point to the side of his glasses. "Um, there's still a little . . ."

He quickly wipes them off again. "No one happens to have a tissue in their pocket, do they?" He's still holding on to his button-down shirt, and I bet he's wondering if he should just take it off and use it to wipe his hair. But if he felt comfortable doing that he would have done it already.

"Hang on," Rory says, "I've got something." She unwraps a thick strip of canvas from the bottom of one of the unplanted trees, then repacks the dirt firmly around it. I never would have thought of that.

"This is why we keep her around," Amanda tells me, smiling proudly at Rory. "She's resourceful."

David lowers his head, and Rory does as good a job as she can to clean him up with the rag. Good thing his hair is so short. Prior experience has taught me it's much worse with long hair. And if it weren't for David, I'd be finding that out all over again.

"I'm pretty sure I'm not good luck for anyone," I assure him when Rory finishes. "I mean, I'll be turning thirteen on Friday the thirteenth, so that's a whole lotta thirteens. I'm not superstitious, but it can't be *good* luck."

He shakes his head. Some of his hair is matted together and it doesn't move. I try not to stare.

"If you weren't good luck, why would *your* thirteenth birthday and *my* bar mitzvah be the same weekend?"

Amanda and Leo raise their eyebrows at that, then turn and huddle together with their boards. I try to ignore their frantic scratching and reply, "Um, a coincidence?"

Rory makes this strange sound that's a cross between a chuckle and a snort. Then she says, "There *are* no coincidences in Willow Falls."

I look at her in surprise. "What do you mean?"

"Leo told me that when we first started becoming friends," she replies. But instead of explaining it, she turns to the closest unplanted tree and asks, "Hey, Amanda, think this little guy is ready to be planted?"

But Amanda is too busy with Leo to answer.

"Will you come to it?" David asks, ignoring the others. "My bar mitzvah, I mean?" He stands up and brushes the dirt off his knees. "Unless you have other plans. Like, maybe your aunt is planning a birthday party?"

I grimace at the thought that they'd throw another party for me, and shake my head.

"So it's settled, then. You'll be my good luck charm. I've been practicing for a year and a half, and I'm still not very good. As you can see, I could use all the luck I can get." He points to his matted hair.

Without waiting for an answer, or for me to tell him I'm really not cut out to be anyone's anything, he grabs Leo and they run off to see who can push stones the farthest or some other boy-type thing that involves rocks and brute strength.

Amanda and Rory immediately spring into action.

"She's about Kylie's size," Amanda says, eyeing me up and down.

Rory nods in agreement. "Yeah, but no offense, your sister doesn't seem like the type to lend clothes."

"She's actually been a lot nicer lately. Well, when she and her boyfriend are getting along, that is. I'll ask her on a good day." Then Amanda turns back to me. "Unless you brought a nice dress with you?"

I'm a bit shell-shocked from all that just happened, so it takes me a few seconds to figure they're talking about dressing me for the bar mitzvah. I look down at my drab clothes. "Um, this is pretty much as fancy as I get."

"That's okay, I don't usually wear things like this either," Rory says, lifting the hem of her sundress. "I got it for a birthday party last year that I thought would be a really big deal." She pauses, and glances at Amanda, who gives her this nod of encouragement, which is weird. Then Rory asks, "You know how sometimes you expect something to go one way, but then things end up being totally different? That happened to me a lot last year. Seriously, a LOT. Most of the time things didn't turn out so well, but sometimes they turned out way better than I could have imagined. And maybe that's how it will be for you . . . or maybe something totally different."

Rory = Not Making Sense.

"Um, I'm not sure what you mean."

Amanda lightly touches my arm. "I think what Rory's trying to say, is that sometimes you wake up in the morning, and things are suddenly really weird. And, well, maybe you don't understand it right away, or maybe not really ever. But you just have to trust that . . . oh, I'm not explaining it very well. Maybe I should just ask . . . is Willow Falls like you expected? What about the people here? Has anyone, you know, surprised you?"

I squirm, not sure what the right answer is and not wanting to insult anyone. Any time we move to a new town, I set my expectations so low that if anyone even smiles at me in the hall it's a victory. So these people have already surprised me just by saying hello! To say nothing of an Australian personal assistant who I can't understand most of the time, a math-genius cousin with a father who has rooms full of weird stuff, a boy who chants in pool holes and whose singing makes trees grow, two best friends who use blackboards to talk to each other, or Rory, with the evil bunny and the strange way she has of both blending in and standing out. And then there's the matter of those hand-holding hawks that seem to be following me. But for all of *them* this is their normal life. How could I tell them how strange they are, even if they're asking me?

Finally I say, "Well, my parents only decided I was coming here three days ago. So I didn't have time to build up any real expectations of the town, or, you know, the people here."

A quizzical look flies between them. They don't even try to hide it this time.

"Really?" Rory asks, knitting her brow. "Just three days ago?"

"Uh-huh. It was very last-minute. My mom's job got moved up, so I have to finish the last two weeks of the school year online." Okay, so there may be a few gaps in the story, but I didn't actually *lie* about anything.

"Huh," Amanda says, giving me another head tilt. Then she mumbles something about being right back and strides off toward the boys, blackboard swinging so fast it hits her on the chin. She yanks Leo aside and writes something on her board. I can't help thinking it's about me, but what could she possibly have to say? I barely told them anything.

Rory touches me gently on the arm and turns me a bit so my back is facing the others. "So," she says breezily, "have you been to a bar mitzvah before?"

It's obvious she's changing the subject, but this time I don't mind. I shake my head.

"Me, neither," Rory says. "David's, like, the only Jewish kid in town. He's been learning everything through this online program his mom signed him up for."

"Really? You can do that?"

She nods. "And there's no temple near here, so the service and the party afterward are going to be at the community center. That reminds me, I have to look for a gift."

My eyes widen. A present! Of course presents go along with bar mitzvahs. And from what I remember hearing at school, they're pretty expensive ones. Rory must have seen my expression because she says, "Definitely don't worry about a gift, Tara. David wouldn't expect that at all."

But Mom's voice in the back of my head tells me otherwise. "I wouldn't feel right going to a party without a gift." And before I can stop myself, I add, "My parents gave me spending money for the summer, so I'll just use part of that."

Rory's dad pulls into the parking area and that effectively ends our conversation. I follow the others to the car. Maybe the stores in Willow Falls will accept magic beans instead of money. It worked in *Jack and the Beanstalk*. Or wait, maybe it didn't. Although if I actually *owned* magic beans, I'd use them to go back in time and un-pepper-spray the principal. Then I'd be off to Madagascar, where no one would expect anything from me for two whole months. (I'm pretty sure none of the lemurs would be declaring their manhood with a ceremony requiring a big gift and a fancy dress.)

"Look what I found!" Rory's dad exclaims when we reach him. He's standing outside the car, waving a large book in his hand. The words *Willow Falls High School* are emblazoned on the front in gold.

"Daaaad," Rory complains, her hands on her hips. "Not that old yearbook again! I've told you before, my friends don't want to see pictures of your high school rock band. We get it, you were cool once."

"Very funny, darling daughter," Rory's dad says, flipping the book open. "But I brought it because I thought Tara might like to see something." He holds the book out to me, open to a page near the end. I take it, and everyone crowds around to see. A large banner proclaims PROM KING AND QUEEN, with a full-page color photo underneath. A dark-haired girl in a pink dress steadies a small silver tiara on her head with one hand, and clutches a bouquet of white roses with the other. At her side is a skinny boy in a white tuxedo, all gawky arms and legs. I recognize the picture right away. Mom told me how Grandma had begged her to wear that dress to the prom, and how she'd donated it to the local Salvation Army the very next morning. Next to the picture, Dad had inscribed a message to Rory's father: *I'm sure you'll find your prom queen one day. Let's hope she's not a zombie.* Then below it he'd drawn a cartoon zombie with skin dripping off his face.

Rory's dad chuckles. "Your dad always did love his monsters."

"He writes books about them now," I tell him.

He slaps his thigh. "Man, that's great! Just great!"

"Wow," Rory says, peering over my shoulder, "you weren't kidding about your dad being really tall. Have you ever seen this picture before?"

I nod, handing the book back to her father. "My parents used to have it up on their bedroom wall." As I say it, I realize I haven't seen it in the last few houses. Was it lost in a move somewhere?

This time I climb into the car last so I'm squished up next to a window. I spend the ride back into town staring out of it, wondering how I'm ever going to come up with the money to get David a gift. I tune out the conversation in the car, which has turned to talk of final exams next week. What if they actually ask me to hang out again, only next time they want to get ice cream or go to a movie? I won't even have pocket money to pay for any of that stuff. Plus, I still have to figure out a way to replace Mom's iPod before the end of the summer.

Probably, Aunt Bethany and Uncle Roger would give me any money I needed, but I don't want to feel even more indebted to them. They're already housing and feeding me. Plus, how could I ask them to lie and not tell my parents that I lost the money? Me lying is bad enough; I can't ask others to lie for me. And, as much as I don't want to admit it to myself, my pride is at stake. It's just embarrassing that I couldn't hold on to the two most important things my parents entrusted me with.

I'm deep in thought about how I could take advantage of my height and pretend to be older in order to get a job somewhere in town, when Jake Harrison's name reaches my ears. I can't help but tune back in.

Next to me, Amanda asks, "When does the movie open again?"

I blurt out, "In six weeks!" exactly as Rory gives the same answer from the front seat.

Leo and David groan. "Looks like we have another Jake Harrison fan on our hands," David says.

Amanda grins. "I don't think Rory can be considered a fan anymore."

Rory twists around and glares at Amanda. She gestures ever so slightly toward her dad.

Amanda mouths the word *sorry*. David giggles and Rory glares at him, too, before turning back around. I look out the window again. I'm probably supposed to wonder what that was all about, but nearly thirteen years of not getting interested in other people's lives has trained me well. The only reason I'm even mildly curious this time is because it has to do with Jake. How could someone be a fan and then stop being one? Whatever the reason, Rory obviously doesn't want to discuss it in front of her father. I don't blame her. I would never want to talk about boys in front of my dad, either. Not that I could imagine an occasion where that would ever come up.

My thoughts turn to Dad's inscription in the yearbook. He was clearly just as smitten with my mom back then as he is today. The little cartoon he drew was pretty funny. He used to draw whole comic books for me when I was younger. He always made me a superhero of one kind or another — kindergartner by day, vanquisher of evil by night. His comics would probably give most little kids nightmares, but I loved them. Mom told me once that Dad thought about writing and illustrating comics for a living, but he didn't think he could make enough money at it.

I start recognizing houses and realize we're only a block away from my aunt's. If Dad hadn't given up, maybe one of *his* comics would be in Uncle Roger's Collectibles Room. Maybe an early edition of *The Day Tara the Great Destroyed the Zombie Queen and Then Ate a Grilled Cheese Sandwich* would be worth a ton of money.

I sit up straighter in my seat. *A ton of money!* For *one* comic. Hadn't Emily said her father had duplicates of some of the ones in his collection? Would he really notice if one went missing? That room looked like it hadn't been touched in years. I mean, I could write my name in the dust on some of those shelves.

As I climb out of the car, Rory calls out, "Hey, do you want to come with us to the Willow Falls Diner after school tomorrow? They have great chocolate-chip pancakes."

Well, that was fast. I hesitate, one hand still on the door handle. This day was hard enough. How long until they figure out I have nothing to offer their merry little band?

But it's Rory asking, and like I said before, Rory = Hard to Say No To.

"Okay," I reply. "Thanks." I watch from the porch as Rory's dad pulls around the circular driveway. I keep standing there long after the car has disappeared down the street. I can't make myself go inside, because once I do, I'm going to have exactly twenty-two hours to figure out how to steal a comic book and sell it without getting caught.

And that will be the worst thing I've ever done.

Chapter Nine

Emily has finally switched off her flashlight. Still, I dare not move until I'm sure she's sound asleep. My stomach growls, and I can easily imagine that it's admonishing me for what I'm about to do, rather than complaining because I had only picked at the leftover barbeque Aunt Bethany had served for dinner. She'd wanted to know all about my afternoon. Did I like Rory and her friends? Do I think I'll hang out with them again? What did I think of Willow Falls? Stuff like that. I told her everyone had been very nice, that they'd invited me for pancakes already, and how Rory's dad had been friends with my parents but hadn't known they'd gotten married.

Aunt Bethany stopped chewing her baked beans. "Well, your mother pulled away a bit from her other friends once she started going out with Jimmy."

This was news to me. It doesn't really make sense since Mom always talks about how important her friends were to her.

"You girls would never do anything like that, right?" Aunt Bethany asked, pointing her fork at both of us in turn. "Boyfriends come and go, but your girlfriends will be with you forever."

Only in my mom's case, her boyfriend never left.

Emily rolled her eyes and said that she wasn't planning on dating until she won the math prize, or left for college, whichever came first. Uncle Roger said, "Amen to that." I didn't say anything since I don't have any friends to drop in the first place.

Only maybe that's not true anymore, because if I didn't have friends, would I be staring at Emily's bed right now, waiting for her to sleep so I can proceed with my plan? Would I risk getting caught stealing again? I press my hands over my eyes. Being almost thirteen is very confusing.

Emily's breathing has become even. The time has come. The clouds block most of the moonlight, so the obstacle course that is Emily's room is more challenging tonight. I grab my phone off the night table, glad to actually have a use for it. I hold it out in front of me, allowing the glow to guide me safely around stacks of books and piles of clothes.

The light in Uncle Roger's lab is off, and I don't have to worry about Ray barging in on me again since he's out with his "mates." I tiptoe past Emily's parents' bedroom and stop in front of the door marked KEEP OUT. Heart pounding, I don't allow myself to hesitate more than a few seconds before slipping inside. I shut the door as quietly as possible and hold my breath until I'm sure no one is coming.

The room is nearly pitch black, which I quickly chalk up to the fact that there are no windows. I hadn't noticed that last time. I guess the light and heat from the sun would fade the collectibles. That must be why it's so cold in here, too. Wouldn't want the foreign chocolate to melt!

The pale light from my phone casts strange shadows, making the room appear longer, the shelves taller, than they were when

Emily brought me here. The faces of the action figures and bobbleheads that fill the shelves seem suddenly menacing. I hurry past them, averting my gaze from their accusing eyes.

The comic section consists of three huge plastic bins, each divided by hanging folders. I balance the phone on the edge of an upper shelf so I can use both hands to flip through the comics. The first bin is full of the usual superhero suspects like *The Avengers*, *Green Lantern*, *The Fantastic Four*, *The Flash*, *Superman*, *Justice League of America*, *Spider-Man*, *The Incredible Hulk*, and *Batman*. The next contains ones I've never heard of, like *Tales to Astonish* and *Journey Into Mystery*. I'm surprised to see comics like *Archie* and *Richie Rich* in the last bin, along with a few relatively recent ones like *Hellboy*, *Buffy the Vampire Slayer Season Eight*, *The Sandman*, and some manga from Japan. My father would be impressed for sure. The largest folder is nearly bursting with monthly editions of *The Uncanny X-Men* from the 1970s. I stop at a section of *Mickey Mouse* titles from the 1940s and pull a few out. Uncle Roger owns at least two of each copy. Like the others, each one is tucked inside a plastic slipcover. I don't really think of Mickey Mouse when I think of comics, though. I drop them back into the folder.

I'm about to step over to the next bin when the sound of a door opening and closing freezes me in place. My mind races to come up with excuses. The best I can think of is "I couldn't sleep and was looking for reading material." It's pretty lame, but it's better than the truth. I brace myself for the inevitable and turn to face the door.

No one is there. I'm still alone! It wasn't this door! That means either Emily woke up to use the bathroom or Uncle

Roger had a late-night flash of inspiration and is in his lab. I strain my ears, but can't hear anything that would confirm who is in another room and why. Either way, though, someone is up, and that means I'm in danger of getting caught. I reach blindly into the last bin, grab a comic, and slip it under the elastic waistband of my sweatpants. I'm halfway across the room before I remember my phone. I dash back, reach out for it, and knock it right off the shelf. Luckily, my superfast reflexes that got me in so much trouble with the pepper spray actually work in my favor tonight, and I manage to catch it right before it hits the floor.

As I step into the hall, I hear the unmistakable flush of a toilet. Emily! Had she noticed my empty bed? If so, she must have expected to find me in the bathroom. I just have to hope she didn't look over at my bed before she went out.

I race toward the bedroom, grateful to the plush carpet for masking the sound of my feet. I duck into the room and dive under my blanket just as the light in the bathroom turns off. I turn my head, close my eyes, and pretend to sleep.

Emily's bed creaks as she climbs back into it. I hold my breath. Is she going to ask where I've been? But all I hear is the rustling of pages and the click of the flashlight. There she goes, under the covers again. Honestly, I don't know how she functions on so little sleep. If I weren't on the verge of a heart attack from all this stress, I'd be impressed with her dedication. I can't think of a single instance in my life when I've tried that hard at anything, which is a depressing thought.

Ever so quietly, I slip the comic out from under my pajamas. I don't know much about collectibles, but I do know that they're worth more if they're not creased by someone sleeping on them! I slide the comic off to the side of the bed and move as far away as possible. Once my heart rate returns to normal, exhaustion overtakes me. At first I try to fight it, wanting desperately to stay awake until I can get the comic someplace safe.

A loud snore from Emily wakes me up a few hours later. The light from the moon is still pretty bright, so I can see clearly. She's sleeping on her side, with her back to me. Moving quickly, I lean over the far edge of my bed and feel underneath for my suitcase. I slide it out about a foot and get to work on the zipper. It sounds SO LOUD, but Emily keeps right on snoring. I flip open the top and see Jake's smiling face. At first it makes me feel better to have something so familiar to look at. But then I catch a glimpse of disappointment in his eyes and have to turn away.

Still hanging over the edge, I reach behind me for the comic book. Fortunately I'd managed not to destroy it in my sleep. I lift up the poster and the bag of broken glass, and carefully rest the comic on the bottom of my suitcase. I cover it back up, and push the suitcase back under the bed, where, hopefully, the stuffed lizard will guard over it.

The next time I wake up, the light is streaming through the blinds, and the clock says 8:03. I rub my eyes. Another school day has arrived and I have no school to go to. I glance over at Emily's bed. It's empty. I'm surprised I didn't hear her get up.

"Hey there," Emily's voice says, causing me to nearly jump out of my skin. I flip over to find her kneeling by the side of my bed, fully dressed in her school uniform, with my suitcase out in front of her. All I can do is stare as she pulls on the zipper.

"Sorry if I woke you," she says. "I can't find one of my schoolbooks, and I just wanted to make sure it wasn't mixed up with yours. Is it okay if I check in here?"

My brain simply cannot process what's happening. I want to say, *Wait, stop, don't*, but all that comes out is a crazed gurgle. She must have interpreted that as a yes, because she flips open the top. When I see that, I fly off the bed and am at her side in a flash.

"Hey, you like Jake Harrison?" she asks, apparently not noticing my Olympics-worthy leap.

We both stare down at my poster, me trying not to faint from fear, her grinning. "I like him, too," she says. "Why don't you put it on the wall?"

She reaches down for the poster, but I'm too fast. I quickly shut the lid, just barely missing her fingertips. "I'll do it while you're at school. Your book's not there, sorry."

She sighs. "That's okay. It just means I'll be Emily B today. When you forget your books, you lose points."

"You'll always just be Emily to me," I joke, hoping to distract her as I push the suitcase under the bed with my toe. Had she really gone in there to look for her book or did she suspect something? Her expression seems sincere, but I don't know her well enough to know how good a liar she might be.

She glances over at the clock, then begins rushing around the room shoving various objects into her book bag. My legs are too wobbly to stand much longer, so I sit on the edge of the bed and watch.

Aunt Bethany walks in, fully dressed and made up already. "Hi, girls. Tara, did you sleep okay?"

"Yes, great," I reply, perhaps a little too quickly. "I mean, the bed's really comfortable." I inwardly groan. What a stupid thing to say.

"Good. I know it's hard to adjust to a new place. Emily, Dad's downstairs waiting to take you. I'm just going to talk to Tara for a few minutes."

Emily dashes out of the room calling out her good-byes. I place my hands on my lap, telling myself not to worry; Aunt Bethany doesn't know anything about the comic. How could she? Unless . . . could there have been security cameras in that room? What if they'd watched the whole thing from their bed-side table?

"This came for you this morning," Aunt Bethany says, handing me a folded piece of paper. "It's an e-mail from one of your teachers."

I never thought I'd feel so relieved to see a homework assignment. "Thanks." I don't open the paper yet because I can see she has more for me.

"I wanted to give you this, so you can come and go as you please." She places a silver key in my hand. It's attached to one of those stretchy bands so I can wear it on my wrist. I push it on there now, right next to the red rope bracelet. I see Aunt Bethany looking at the friendship bracelet with that same puzzled look as when she first saw it. Then she shrugs and gets up. "Well, you have our phone numbers if you need to reach us. You have the run of the house, and if you go out, just leave a note. Do you want me to drive you to the diner to meet Rory and her friends later?"

I shake my head. "I figured I'd ride Emily's bike, if that's okay."

"You know the way already?"

I nod. "With all the new towns I've lived in, I've had a lot of practice learning my way around new places."

Aunt Bethany's face softens. "Moving all the time must be hard. Molly never used to have this need to always be on the go. I don't know where it came from. Is it your dad?"

I shake my head. "It's always Mom's decision. Out of nowhere, she'll decide we have to pack up and move. But I'm pretty sure we're going to stay where we are for a while now."

"Good!" she says, leaning over to pat my arm. "I hope you're right." She leaves me in the room, shaking her head as she goes, mumbling about how it's a shame not to give a child roots. I sit there until I hear her car pull out of the driveway. Then I spring into action. I wash up, get dressed, and grab the little backpack Dad gave me. I take a minute to look at the comic before sliding it inside the backpack. *The Fantastic Four.* I know a little about that one. I think the lady can turn invisible and the one guy is, like, made out of rocks or something. And one guy stretches? I'm tempted to read it, but I don't want to risk smudging the pages or anything. The cover states that this is issue #12, and that it was printed in 1961. That sure sounds old enough to be worth $200.

I head down to the laundry room, where everyone leaves their shoes. As soon as I step into the kitchen, I'm greeted by Ray, in green plaid pajamas, holding up a plate of what looks like ground-up . . . *something.* "Ready for brekkie?" he asks.

I'd totally forgotten about him! I shake my head. "Not hungry."

"Go on," he says, thrusting it out toward me. "Give it a burl. I bet you'll like it."

I shake my head again.

He shrugs. "Suit yourself."

I hurry into the laundry room and he follows me, stirring his concoction. "Where are you off to so early?"

I slip into my sneakers and open the door. "Just riding my bike into town. I want to get there when the stores open."

He laughs. "You don't have to rush. Throngs of shoppers won't be descending on Willow Falls any time soon."

I wish I'd just told him I was going out for exercise. Now he's going to expect me to come back with something. "You're probably right. See you later." I close the door behind me.

He opens it and calls out, "Stuff downtown can be exy. Before you buy anything, tell 'em Ray sent ya. Ask for the mate's rate."

"Sure thing," I reply, "whatever that means." I fling open the shed doors. Nope, the bike didn't get any bigger. I have to pump the tires again and shake a beetle out of the helmet, but soon enough I'm heading into town. It feels strange being the only kid between six and eighteen years old out on a school day. I wonder if people think I'm cutting school. Or maybe they think I stole a little girl's bike and am making my (slow) getaway!

I don't stop peddling until I reach the corner of Main Street and the alley. Ray was right. I certainly won't have to compete with many other shoppers. I spot some seniors going into the community center, and two moms pushing strollers into the library. Other than that, though, downtown is pretty empty.

There are no sidewalks in the alley, and I can't ride on the broken cobblestones. No other choice but to push the bike. The watch-repair store is closed, as are all the others I pass. When I reach the last one on the right, I lean my bike against the wall and peer into the circle David had wiped off. Angelina's Sweet Repeats and Collectibles is as full of stuff — and devoid of people — as it was yesterday. I check the times on the door. The sign only says OPEN WEEKDAYS, but doesn't give any specific hours. Well, I have nowhere else to go, so I reach around for my backpack and settle down next to the door to wait.

I drum my fingers on my legs. I wish I had something to read. Something other than *The Fantastic Four*, sealed up tight in its protective bag. According to the cover, they meet the Hulk in this one. I guess he didn't become *incredible* until later.

Not much to look at in this alley. None of the colorful awnings of Main Street, no flags waving from flagpoles, no life of any kind really, not even a breeze. And David was right — it does sort of smell like feet.

Hunger is starting to creep in, and I wonder if I should have accepted Ray's offer of brekkie. Still, refusing to eat anything I don't recognize has served me well up to this point. I pull the backpack onto my lap and unzip the outside pocket. Success! One of the granola bars Mom packed me for the train is still mostly intact. I inhale it, then look up and down the alley for a garbage can. Nope, none of those, either. I shove the wrapper back inside my bag, where my hand lands on a piece of folded paper. My homework! I'd forgotten I stashed it there. At least it will be something to read.

I expect to see a list of questions on some boring topic or another, but instead, Mrs. Schafer, my English teacher, has written me a letter.

Tara,

Principal Murphy filled us in on what happened last week (although some of the details are a bit unclear). Obviously you are going through a difficult time right now, and the other teachers and I don't want anything to derail your progress at the camp. Our experiences are what shape our lives, and as the great philosopher Socrates once said, "An unexamined life is not worth living." Therefore, we have agreed that if you write an essay at the end of your program, reflecting upon what you have learned from your experiences, we will accept that in place of individual final exams. You will not be graded on your words, only the effort made to complete the assignment. The choice is yours, of course. Please e-mail me back and let me know what you decide.

All our best to you in your time of struggle,

Mrs. Schafer

I grip the paper tight and reread it through twice more. *Progress at the camp. My time of struggle.* My teachers are picturing me at this camp for troubled teens, probably alone in my bunk, crying because no one understands me. I'm not sure life in Willow Falls is quite that bleak. Okay, so maybe right this very minute, I'm sitting alone in a deserted alley trying to sell a stolen comic book so I'll have even the slightest chance of fitting in with the kids in this town, but I don't think that's really the same thing.

If I tell Mrs. Schafer the truth — that my mom made up the whole camp thing so she could leave earlier on her trip — well, Mom would look really bad. So basically, I'd be a much better daughter by taking the offer.

"How long have you been sitting there?" a woman's voice booms from behind me.

I jump to my feet. My backpack goes flying from my lap, and the letter drifts to the ground beside it. A short, old woman with white hair fills the open doorway. Her raised eyes and pressed lips manage to convey both annoyance and amusement at the same time.

"Um, a while I guess."

"Did you think to knock?" she asks. "Or try the doorknob?"

I shake my head. "The store looked closed." I swoop down to grab my backpack, and stuff the letter in my pocket.

She sighs and mutters something about needing to get better lighting. "So what are you looking for? Some vintage blue jeans? I have a mood ring from the eighties that turns green when you're happy and black when you're mad. All the teenage girls love 'em."

I shake my head and am about to tell her about the comic, when I'm momentarily distracted by a large brown birthmark on her cheek. It looks like a chicken. Or no, more like a duck. And it kind of wiggles when she talks.

"No? Well, come on in, then," she says, propping the door open. "Take your time and look around; I've got plenty of everything."

I glance at my bike on the sidewalk. I guess it should be okay to leave it. No one has walked by in all the time I've been here. I follow the woman inside. The store reminds me of Uncle Roger's room, except a lot less organized. But where his room has a layer of dust on everything, I can't see even a speck in here. I barely have time to think about how odd that is because the shelves are so full of hats, toys, dishes, old clothes, costumes and scout uniforms, books, art, *everything*, that it's hard to maneuver through the aisles without bumping into things.

"You break it, you bought it," the woman warns as she walks up to the front counter.

I steady a foot-tall ceramic figurine of a ballet dancer that I definitely don't want to have to buy, and clear my throat. "Actually, I'm hoping you'd buy something from me."

She gestures to the shelves. "Sorry, but I'm focusing on more selling these days, less buying. Gotta clear out some inventory."

My shoulders sag. "Oh."

She pulls a large calculator out from under the counter and starts going through a stack of receipts. Is that it? Am I supposed to leave? If she doesn't buy it, I can't imagine anyplace else in town that would.

After a minute of standing there awkwardly, I pull out the comic book and rest it on the glass counter. "Um, do you know where else I can go? I really need to sell this."

With an exasperated sigh, she turns away from the calculator and picks up the comic. "*Fantastic Four* #12, eh?" Her eyes flicker to my face. "Let me take a closer look." She grabs a pair of rubber gloves from a box next to the register and puts them on. I figure this is a good sign. Then she carefully pulls the comic out of the clear cover and holds it up to her face, tilting it slightly to catch the overhead light.

"No sign of rust on the staples, corners not blunted, ink is bright, good reflectivity." She ticks these qualities off matter-of-factly, then lays the book back on the counter and lifts up the front cover. She gently rubs her fingers across a few of the pages, nodding with satisfaction. "Supple paper, no brittle edges, minor signs of wear at the spine."

She closes the book and pats the cover. "Near mint condition," she declares as she slides it back into the covering.

I lean forward eagerly.

"But I can't buy it from you."

My face falls. "Why not?"

"Because I'd have to sell everything in the store to come up with enough money."

I frown. "All I really need is two hundred dollars. Will you take it for that?"

She scoffs. "First of all, I can't give you two hundred dollars for a comic that's worth fifty times that. I have my reputation to uphold as proprietor of this fine establishment."

Ugh. If it weren't for Emily's bladder, I would have had time to choose more wisely.

"And second," she says, crossing her arms in front of her

ample chest, "I'm fairly certain Roger St. Claire isn't ready to sell it."

My mouth suddenly goes dry. "How . . . how do you know it's his?"

The duck wiggles as she says, "Simple. I sold it to him."

Chapter Ten

Horrified, I reach out for the comic book. But Angelina is faster. She snatches it off the counter and takes a step back. Holding it over her head, she asks, "So what are we going to do about this?"

I take a few seconds to size up the situation. She's not much taller than a kid. My arms are long, and the distance between me and the other side of the counter is short. I could easily lean over the counter and grab the comic and run out of the store. But besides not having the nerve to do that in a million years, where would it get me? She obviously knows my uncle.

I sigh in defeat. "Are you going to tell on me?"

She narrows her eyes. "The theft of such a valuable item is a serious crime. If I had bought it from you, I would have been an accessory to that crime. Don't you think there should be consequences to all this? As an adult of, shall we say, advanced years, isn't it my duty to teach you a valuable life lesson?"

Perhaps I should have thought this whole thing through a little more. Why hadn't it occurred to me that as such a big collector, Uncle Roger would obviously have a relationship with the woman who ran the town's only collectibles shop? I haven't been very successful at talking my way out of things in recent days, but I have to try. I take a deep breath and try to look as repentant as possible. "I already know stealing is wrong, and I promise I'll never do it again. Please, don't tell my uncle. He's been so nice to me, welcoming me into his home when my parents are gone and everything. I'd feel really bad if he found out."

She lowers the comic until it's hanging by her side. "Your parents are gone? Where are they?"

"My parents . . ." I pause, taking note of the concern in her voice. Maybe she's starting to feel sorry for me. "They left me on my own for the summer while they're on the other side of the world."

Her face softens. Encouraged by this, I keep going. "And I don't have any money, and I didn't want Uncle Roger to have to pay for everything for me, and I have to get this boy, David, a bar mitzvah gift, and honestly, there are two or three copies of each comic and I didn't think he'd miss this one." Everything I said this time was true, although not the whole story.

"What did you say your name was?" she asks, placing the comic on the counter between us. I still don't dare take it.

"Tara Brennan."

She tilts her head at me, in that same way Rory and Amanda did yesterday, like she's trying to figure me out. I do my best to keep eye contact, to show that she can trust me. I notice that while she is clearly very old, there's something different about her eyes. Like they belong in someone else's face. Which, of course, is a totally crazy thing to think about someone's eyes, but right now they're looking straight into me and it's making me even more nervous.

Finally she gives a quick nod and says, "Well, Tara. Let's make a deal, shall we? You're asking me not to tell your uncle you were about to sell off one of the most valuable comic books in his collection, correct?"

I nod, a bit worried about where this is heading.

"In exchange for my silence, are you willing to work for me?"

"Work — like here in the store?" I look around. It wouldn't be so terrible to come in here for an afternoon or two. Maybe organize the merchandise a little better. Or take inventory or something.

But she shakes her head. "Not in the store. I've had my eye on a few items around town. Nothing valuable, some trinkets. Bric-a-brac really. It would be your job to obtain these items for me."

"You want me to get you bricks? Like, from the side of a *building*?"

"Not bricks. *Bric-a-brac.* The kind of things you see here in the store. A little of this, a little of that. I'll give you the list."

"Okay." That's not so bad. So I'll do a few errands for her. It will give me a chance to get to know the layout of the town better.

"And to prove I'm not the world's meanest boss, I'm going to give you the two hundred dollars you were looking for, in exchange for doing this job for me."

My eyes open wide in surprise. I'm going to get the money after all, just for picking up some stuff! And I can return the comic to the Collectibles Room, without anyone in the family even knowing it was gone. I'm so relieved I could squeal. Although, like Emily, I'm not a fan of squealing girls.

"I wouldn't spend that money too quickly if I were you," Angelina warns. "Not everyone is going to hand over their belongings just because you ask. You might need to pay for them."

I knew it was too good to be true. "You mean the stuff hasn't been paid for yet?"

She shakes her head.

I get a sinking feeling. "Do these people even know you *want* their things?"

She shakes her head again. "Nope. That's where you come in. You get to convince them to hand over the goods."

"How am I supposed to do that?"

She shrugs. "You'll have to offer them money, or charm them with your winning personality. Stealing the goods, I feel the need to point out, is *not* an option."

She bends down and rummages under the counter. All I can see is the top of her shoulders. I assume she's digging around for the money to give me, but when she resurfaces, she plunks an old-fashioned tape recorder on the counter instead. "I don't trust making lists on paper," she says, sliding the tape recorder closer to me. "Paper burns, it drifts away. These babies will last forever."

Honestly, the thing must be forty years old. Inside the scratched window lies a single cassette tape. Whatever words had been written on the label faded into blue smudges long ago. "What do I do with *this*?"

She rolls her eyes. "You take it home and listen to it. The list of objects is on there. I'd start tracking them down right away if I were you. It might take you some time to find them."

My jaw drops. "You mean you're not going to tell me who has them?"

"Don't know myself. They're here in town somewhere." She waves her arms around as if that's helpful in any way.

I grip the edges of the counter. "But what if I can't find everything?"

She leans over the counter and puts her hand on mine. It is surprisingly comforting. "If you can't get everything on that list, you will simply return the money. Oh, and either you'll tell your uncle about the comic or I will."

I yank my hand away. Obviously I'll have spent all the money by that time. Where would I get another two hundred to pay her back? I couldn't. And of course I don't want Uncle Roger to know about the comic. Which means I have no choice but to find everything on that list.

Quick as a flash, she presses a combination of buttons on her cash register and the drawer shoots open. She counts out ten twenty-dollar bills and hands them to me. I zip them up into my bag, then check the zipper twice. There's no way I'm losing ANY money this time.

"Um, I don't mean to sound ungrateful," I say, forcing myself to make direct eye contact, "but maybe there's something I can do here instead? I'm really good at organizing things. Or I could sweep or dust. I mean, no one knows me in Willow Falls, so wouldn't it just be easier if *you* asked them for these items, instead?"

"Believe it or not," she says, "some people have been known to lock their doors when they see me coming."

"Why? Because you're always asking for their stuff?"

"Sure, we'll go with that explanation. And now that you mention it, you'd be best off not telling them it's for me."

"But people must sell you stuff all the time, the shelves are full of —"

"No need to come back until you have everything on the list," she says, cutting me off. "I'll see you here in a month, let's say July thirteenth."

"But that's my thirteenth birthday," I blurt out, although saying it makes me sound like I'm about two years old. And it's not like I have other plans that day.

She peers closer at me. "You know what happens when you turn thirteen, don't you?"

"You become a teenager?"

She scoffs. "Much more than that. At thirteen your soul becomes settled in your body. You become the core of the person you will be for the rest of your life. And thanks to me, you'll have paid off your debt to society by completing this job. You can enter your teen years free and clear."

I've had pretty much enough of this. "Honestly, isn't 'debt to society' a bit much? Selling the comic book would only have affected one person. If he even noticed."

"You truly believe that?" she asks.

I nod, more confidently than I feel.

She shakes her head. "Our actions have long-lasting consequences, of which we often have no knowledge. They ripple far out into the universe."

"I know that." After all, me being sent to Willow Falls is proof of how well I know that. "But trust me, I'm a sit-this-one-out kind of girl. I don't get involved for that exact reason. I don't want to ripple anyone's universe."

She puts her hand on mine again and, again, I relax a tiny bit. "Well, you're off the sidelines now, kid. Welcome to the game."

Then she steps into her office and closes the door behind her.

I rock back on my heels. This is *sooooo* not how I thought my morning would go. My brain is swirling. Souls solidifying? Me, in the game? How can I be in the game when I don't know any of the rules?

After five minutes of her not returning, I see no other choice but to accept her terms. I slide the comic into my backpack and reach for the tape recorder. I can barely lift it! It must weigh thirty pounds! How did Angelina make it look so effortless? She must be stronger than she looks. I lug the old machine out of the store, clutching it to my chest with both arms. There's gotta be a dozen better ways to make a list of something.

By the time I get back to the house, I'm exhausted from the effort of balancing the tape recorder on top of Emily's wicker basket, which I'll now have to replace due to it being totally squashed. I'd had to keep a hand on the machine at all times, which meant leaning over the handlebars and riding at a really awkward angle.

Thankfully no one else is home or else it would have been hard to explain the sudden appearance of a giant tape recorder from the days before people walked on the moon. I can tell that

Aunt Bethany has come and gone again, because there are shopping bags piled up on the stairs.

The first thing I see when I get up to the bedroom is a large red and white shopping bag on my bed. I rest the tape recorder on the desk and peek inside the bag. Clothes. A lot of very colorful clothes that are way too big for Emily. I dump out the bag until it looks like a rainbow exploded on my bed. Had Emily told her mom about my lack of wardrobe? Or maybe Aunt Bethany saw it for herself when she put me to bed that first night. It was really nice of her to do this, but everything's so . . . bright.

Leaving the clothes where they are, I return to the task at hand — returning the comic. Even though I didn't see any cars, I still put my ear up to the door of the Collectibles Room. Satisfied that all I hear is the hum of the central air-conditioning, I turn the knob and push. But the door doesn't budge.

It's locked! How could it be locked? I feel the panic rise up in me. Uncle Roger would have had to lock it sometime between midnight last night and now. Why would he do that? Did he know someone had been there? Did he know it was me?

I feel way too obvious standing here in the hall. Someone could come home at any minute and see me holding it. I need to hide the comic somewhere really good. It can't be in my suitcase, since both Emily and Aunt Bethany seem to have no hesitations about going in there. I stare down the hall. The lab! All those piles of magazines that couldn't have been looked at in five years. If I slipped it in between them, it would blend right in.

So I listen at the lab door, then push it open. Everything looks just as it did that first night when I stumbled into the room by mistake. I head right for the magazines and slip the comic inside an issue of *Inventors Digest* from seven years ago. I stack a few more issues on top of it, then stand back. Looks good. And if Uncle Roger *did* happen to come across it, maybe he'd think he left it there himself by mistake. Until I can get that other door open, this will have to be a good enough option.

Now, on to the tape recorder. I sit at Emily's desk and examine it from all sides. I press the little button that's supposed to release the tape cover, but nothing happens. I try to wrench it open to get at the tape underneath, but it won't let me lift it enough to get my fingers in there. It would help if there were a button that actually said PLAY so I could tell if the tape still worked. I rub my finger over the large black buttons and can feel the symbols carved into them that must have been white once. I choose the one with the triangle on it and press it down. Nothing but a click as it releases back up. I try the one with the circle. Then the one with the arrows pointing right. Then pointing left. Finally, the square. Why would Angelina have given me a broken tape recorder?

"You should check the batteries," Uncle Roger suggests from the doorway. I jump up so quickly that my knee bangs against the underside of the desk. The pain shoots through my leg, but I'm too busy trying to block his view of the tape recorder to pay it much attention. Darn that plush carpet that I had been so thankful for when it was ME sneaking around!

"Sorry to startle you. Just got home and wanted to see if you'd had lunch." He steps over to the desk and peers around me. "Is that one of my old tape recorders?"

"Um, I . . ." How can I lie to him after everything that happened today? But how can I tell him the truth? So I compromise and say, "Actually, I got it in town today."

He lights up. "You like old machines, too, eh? Wait'll you see all the junk I've got. C'mon, I'll show you."

So I follow him back to the lab, where I have to pretend I've never been before. "Wow, you sure have a lot of stuff."

He nods, grinning like a little kid. "You never know when you'll need a little knob or a tiny piece of wire, or when two totally different objects will inspire a brand-new invention. That's how the Sand-Free Beach Towel came to be." To my horror, he goes over to the piles of magazines and says, "You're welcome to look through any of these for inspiration of your own. Some of them go back from before Emily was born." He is literally standing six inches away from where I hid the comic. The universe is seriously playing games with me.

He chuckles and nudges one of the piles with his foot. "I should probably clean this room more often. Emily gets her messy habits from me, I'm afraid."

I force myself to laugh along when really I just want to sink into the floor. I need to get him away from the magazines. "Hey, would you happen to have some extra batteries I could try in the tape recorder?"

"You mean you don't want to take it apart?" He looks disappointed.

"Actually, I'd rather just get it to play."

He sighs and points to a set of plastic bins in the back corner. "Batteries of all sizes and shapes. Help yourself to whatever you need."

"Thanks." I grab handfuls of all different types and shove them in my pockets.

"Hey, have you seen the Collectibles Room?" he asks, practically giddy at the chance to show it off. "Your aunt organized it, so it's nice and orderly."

Once again, I'm stumped for an answer — do I say I've been there, or that I haven't? Fortunately, once again, he doesn't wait for one. "C'mon," he says, "you'll love it."

I hesitate before following him. Does he know about my trip last night? Is this a setup? I trudge along behind him promising myself that if I survive this, I will be a much better person in the future. We reach the door, and to my surprise, he turns the knob rather than reaching for a key.

He tries the knob again, pulling and pushing at it. "That's strange," he says. "I never lock this door. I don't even have a key." He tries it again. "Hmm. The only way to lock it is from the inside. Someone must have turned the latch and then shut the door behind them."

I wonder if they have tornadoes in Willow Falls. I wouldn't mind if one swept me up right about now. There's no doubt in my mind that I'm the "someone." I must have done it in my hurry to beat Emily back to the bedroom.

"That's okay," I say, slowly backing away. "I can see it another time." I leave him muttering about which tool would be the best to open it.

I close the bedroom door and make a decision. I'm going to do this impossible job for Angelina as quickly as possible, so I can pay off my debt to society, as she so dramatically put it. Then the money will legitimately be mine, and I can have a (semi) normal summer in this (semi) normal little town.

It takes five minutes to wrestle off the cover of the battery compartment since I refuse to go ask Uncle Roger for a screwdriver. I pull out four corroded C batteries, and replace them with new ones. This time when I press the button with the triangle, the tape moves around the little plastic circles with an accompanying whirring and crackling sound. I lean closer, but that's all I hear. No list, no anything.

I pace back and forth in front of the desk. To calm myself down, I start folding the clothes from Aunt Bethany. Some kids throw stuff when they're frustrated; I fold things. I'm about to start on the shorts when I hear a baby crying. I step over to the window, but the house is too far from the neighbors for the sound to travel all the way here. I cross to the door. No, it's not coming from outside in the hall.

Now, along with the crying, a woman has started to sing a lullaby. Her voice is very pure and sweet. It finally dawns on me that the sounds are coming out of the tape recorder! The woman gets through the first few lines of "Hush, Little Baby, Don't You Cry" when the tape clicks and a man's voice comes through. "All right, let's try that again," he says. A woman — a different one from the singer — replies, "Do you really think this will work?" The man says, "As long as we don't tell her he's coming. She'll be too nervous." Then another click and the singing returns, without the baby crying. Then the tape cuts to a group of people laughing. Then Angelina's voice comes on and she starts reciting a list of random objects. Finally! My guess is that whoever sold the tape recorder to Angelina's store a zillion years ago left the tape in it. Angelina — and a lot of other people before her — taped right over it.

After a few tries, I figure out how to rewind the tape so I can write down the list from the beginning.

One wicker basket with handles in the shape of hearts

One gray wool blanket with two-inch red stripes around the border

One brass candlestick in the shape of a fish

One large white shawl with the initials ER on the left corner

One knife with a black handle inside a red sheath

A 2-ounce purple glass bottle with a silver stopper

One long strand of pearls with a gold clasp

One leather-bound copy of the Bible, black, Book of Genesis repeated twice

One wooden key with the words Made in Willow Falls 1974 carved in the shank

One black steamer trunk with gold latch

One violin, silver plating on back reads
Sam, 1902

One bottle of apple wine, 1925, brewed by
Ellerby-Fitzpatrick Brewers

One wooden cane, handle shaped like a
duck's beak

The list finally ends, and soon after, so does the tape. I play it twice more to make sure I've gotten everything down correctly. Then I climb into my bed, throw the covers over my head, and pray for a miracle.

Chapter Eleven

I'm about twenty minutes early to the diner to meet Rory and Leo. Rory already texted me that Amanda has band practice and David's mom dragged him to the tailor to get his bar mitzvah suit fitted. I'm kind of glad it's a smaller group.

While I wait, I ogle the desserts in the glass case by the counter. Having (much) more freedom than at home is all well and good, but I need to actually remember to do things like eat and drink now and then. The chocolate cakes and pies in the case look so good that I'm afraid my mouth is going to water.

"Can I help you?" a waitress asks, appearing at my side. Her name tag reads HI, MY NAME IS ANNIE. ASK ME ABOUT THE CHOCOLATE-CHIP PANCAKES. "Everything here is homemade, you know."

"No, thanks, I'm —"

She waits for me to finish, but I've suddenly lost the ability to speak. All I can do is point frantically behind her at the umbrella stand, where, since it's not raining, there are no umbrellas. There is, however, a wooden cane with the head of a duck on top.

She looks where I'm pointing and turns back to me. "Are you all right, hon? You're getting kinda pale."

"That . . . that cane. Did you see who came in with it?"

She laughs. "Honey, I wasn't even born yet when that cane showed up. My dad owns the diner, and he's convinced one day the owner will come back to claim it."

I lick my suddenly dry lips. "Do you think there's any chance he'd let me have it? I, um, know someone who's looking for it."

Her eyes widen. "You do?"

I nod, hoping she won't ask for details.

"Let me go ask. He's in the kitchen." She slips behind the counter, and when she pushes through the swinging doors, a blast of warm air fills the little waiting area. I can see the corner of the griddle where pancakes and fried eggs sizzle in straight lines.

I take this opportunity to inspect the cane up close. It's gotta be the one from the list. How many wooden, duck-headed canes could there be? This one is definitely old, with most of the paint chipping off the wood. I can tell the duck's bill used to be white, and there's still a smudge of green on each eye.

The doors swing back open behind me and the waitress comes out, followed by a white-haired man with a sweaty forehead and twinkling eyes. He wipes his hands on his apron and sticks one hand out toward me. I shake it, not sure what else to do.

"I'm Joe Milazo. You're the young lady asking about the cane?"

I nod.

"That thing showed up one day thirty-five years ago. Been waiting for the right person to come for it, I expect. Whatcha want it for?"

My brain freezes. I only got the list a few hours ago. I've been too busy feeling sorry for myself from the comfort of my bed to come up with a plan of action. I scan through the options. I can't use Angelina's name since she told me that would likely backfire on me. I can't steal it when the person's not looking because my days of stealing things are seriously over. Which leaves making up some kind of story.

Making Up Stories = Lying = Not a Good Thing to Do When Trying to Pay Off Debt to Society.

But what choice do I have? I figure I'll start as close to the truth as possible. "I . . . I know this lady who collects old canes and, um, things with ducks. I know she'd love this one."

"Canes and ducks, eh?" he asks.

I nod. "Yup."

"This guy's been like a part of the family." He pats the top of the duck's head. "Sure would be hard to let it go."

"I can pay you," I offer. Maybe I should have led with that one. I have the money from Angelina stuffed deep into my sock. I no longer trust wallets. They disappear too easily.

"Well now, that wouldn't be right seeing as it wasn't mine in the first place." He turns to his daughter. "Annie, what do you think would be a fair trade?"

"Hmm . . ." She taps her long nails on the dessert counter. "I know! We're short a dishwasher today."

Mr. Milazo grins at me. "Whatya say? Ready to roll up your sleeves and dive in?"

Great, just great. Rory and Leo are going to walk in here any minute and find me up to my elbows in suds and grease? But if I let the very first thing from the list slip through my fingers,

I'm never going to finish. I glance over at the cane and sigh. "Okay, I'll do it."

Annie laughs. "We wouldn't really make you wash dishes."

"Just testing your commitment," her dad says with a wink.

"Oh," I reply weakly. "Good one."

Annie's cell phone rings. She reaches into her pocket and answers it, holding up a finger for us to wait. Her dad shakes his head and nudges me. "Kids these days with their cell phones, right?"

I chuckle politely in response, glancing anxiously at the door.

Annie slips her phone back into her pocket and says to her father, "That was Shelly. She apparently told the leader of her Sunshine Kid troupe that she sold fifty boxes of cookies instead of five. We now have forty-five extra boxes of cookies in our garage. Either we sell them by six P.M. tomorrow or pay for them ourselves."

Mr. Milazo claps me on the back. "I think we found you a job!"

Annie beams. "How'd you like to be a Sunshine Kid?"

"A what?" I ask, hoping I misheard.

"They're like Girl Scouts," she explains. "Except their uniforms are yellow and orange instead of green and brown. And they let boys in. Oh, and their cookies aren't as good. And they sing."

"So you want me to dress up in a uniform and sell bad cookies? And *sing*?"

"I didn't say they were bad. Especially if you put ketchup on them."

Ketchup?

Annie's dad walks over to the umbrella stand and pulls out the cane. Without a word, he presents it to me very solemnly, like he's handing me a really important gift. It's heavier than it looked in the stand. Very solid, and obviously well made since it's held up all these years. Strange to think that someone wouldn't have come back for it once they realized it was missing.

"Fine, I'll sell the cookies," I mutter. "But I'm *not* singing."

"Wonderful!" Mr. Milazo booms.

"What's wonderful?" Leo asks, walking through the door with Rory. "Is today buy-one-get-one-free pancake day?"

"No such luck, my boy," Mr. Milazo says, thumping Leo on the back like they're old friends. "This young lady here is going to be an honorary Sunshine Kid! She's going to sell forty-five boxes of cookies by tomorrow afternoon!"

"Is that right?" Leo asks, raising an eyebrow.

I give a little wave with the hand not currently leaning on the cane for support.

Rory puts her hands on her hips. "Tara's new in town. What have you two done to her?"

Mr. Milazo touches his hand to his chest. "Who, me?"

"Is that smoke?" Rory asked, sniffing the air.

"Hey," Leo says, "if you're out here, who's making the pancakes?"

Mr. Milazo's eyes widen. He turns and runs back through the swinging doors without a word. Smoke billows out behind him.

"Seat yourselves," Annie instructs us, running after her dad.

Rory leads us past the counter, where a group of women are eating ice cream and laughing. I glance hungrily at their bowls as we pass, and notice one lady picking out her gumballs and arranging them on her napkin. For the first time since I've been in town, it sinks in that my mother grew up here. And Dad, too! They probably came to this very diner, maybe even sat at that very counter. It makes me feel both closer to them, and farther away.

We settle into the last booth. "Sooo . . ." Leo begins, glancing at the cane next to me on the seat. "Anything you'd like to share with us about your day?"

I look from one to the other. "Um, not really. It's been a pretty ordinary day. You know how it is in sleepy little Willow Falls."

"We do," Rory says, not taking her eyes from my face. "That's why we know it wasn't an ordinary day."

I squirm, the cushion squeaking underneath me. It's impossible to turn away from Rory's intense gaze. "Well, I guess I do have to sell forty-five boxes of cookies by tomorrow."

"And why is that, exactly?" Rory asks.

"It's kind of a long story."

"We've got time," Leo says. "You're gonna have to spill it sooner or later, unless you want to sell forty-five boxes of really tasteless cookies all by yourself."

"They're not that bad with ketchup," I mutter. He's right of course. I can't sell the cookies by myself. Unless *I* buy them all! I do a quick calculation. Rats. I'd use up most of the money from Angelina right there.

I sink deeper into the bench cushion. I might as well be back at school right now, trying to talk my way out of having to work with others on some project. The last time I agreed to be a part of a group, I wound up getting suspended. "I don't have a good track record of playing nice with others," I explain. "Ask any of my teachers."

"At least tell us what's up with the cane," Rory says. "My little brother, Sawyer, quacks at it every time we come in here. I've never seen Mr. Milazo take it out of the umbrella stand before. Why would he just give it to you?"

I shrug. "I guess my charm and winning personality won him over."

Leo laughs. "No offense, but I'm pretty sure there's more to it than that."

The waitress approaches the table and places one large chocolate-chip pancake in front of each of us. I hadn't even seen anyone order. I think I could eat all three by myself. Leo digs into his pancake, but Rory doesn't touch hers. She's still waiting for an answer from me.

I sigh, glancing longingly at my plate. "If I let you help me sell the cookies, will you stop asking me about the cane?"

"For now," Rory agrees, cutting into her pancake. "But there's not much time if we're going to sell forty-five boxes by tomorrow. I'll pick up the cookies from Annie. I've babysat for her kids before; she lives right around the corner from here."

"Then what?" Leo asks. "Her kids will have covered their neighborhood already."

"True," Rory says. "Why don't we start at the community center? That's our best chance of having a bunch of people in one place at a time. We'll need to get uniforms, though. No one's going to buy cookies from Sunshine Kids dressed in school clothes."

"Amanda was a Sunshine Kid in third grade," Leo says, "but I'm sure her uniform wouldn't fit anyone."

"I know where to get them," I say quietly.

Rory grins. "Great!" she says, as though it's perfectly normal that I would know such a thing after being in town only a few days. "Then let's get going." She pushes Leo across the bench until he has one leg in the aisle.

"Wait, what about our pancakes?" he asks, grabbing on to his plate like it's a life preserver.

Rory looks down at our mostly untouched pancakes and Leo's half-eaten one, then grabs the pile of napkins from the center of the table.

"Good thing you hadn't put syrup on it yet," I tell Leo as he stares dejectedly at the wrapped-up pancake in his hand. "That'd be really messy."

"Go get the uniforms," Rory instructs us. "I'll take the cane, pay the bill, and get the cookies, and we'll meet at the community center in half an hour."

Thirty seconds later, Leo and I find ourselves out on the street, clutching our pancakes. The butter grease is seeping through the napkins. I turn to him. "Is she always this . . . this . . ."

"Bossy? Determined? Good at helping out others whether or not they ask? Yes."

I hope letting Rory take the cane with her wasn't a huge mistake. I've only known her a day, and she does have a history of losing things. I can't wait a second longer to eat, though, so I unwrap my pancake and eat it like a taco. Leo quickly digs into his, too.

"These are really good," I say, not even caring that I have chocolate all over my hands and pancake crumbs on my chin.

"You never forget your first Willow Falls chocolate-chip pancake." He shoves the rest of his into his mouth and licks each finger in turn. I guess I should feel good that he feels comfortable enough around me to do that, but it's kinda gross. After wiping his mouth with the greasy napkin, he says, "So where are we going to get the uniforms?"

I swallow the bite I'd been chewing. "You know that store we found at the end of the alley yesterday?"

He nods cautiously. "What about it?"

"I saw some in there when . . ." I trail off. I don't want to let him know I was in there today. "I saw them when I looked in the window. There's a whole rack of scouting uniforms."

He turns both ways, like he wants to make sure we're alone. "Okay, but let's hurry."

I can tell he's eyeing my pancake as we cross the street, so I tear the remaining piece in half and give it to him. We're about to turn down the alley, when the door of the dress shop opens and a woman comes out, followed by a boy with a black suit slung over his shoulder. It's David!

"Hi!" he says when he sees us. He glances at the food in our hands. "Did they run out of tables at the diner?"

I hurriedly wipe my face with the back of my hand as Leo replies, "Something like that."

"You must be Bethany's niece," David's mother says, checking her phone with one hand and fishing around in her pocketbook with the other. "Tara, right?"

I nod. She's much older than my mom, but very pretty, with the curliest hair I've ever seen. She finds her keys and pulls them out. "David says you're going to be his good luck charm."

"Mom!" David says, shifting the suit so I can't see his face.

"Oops, sorry," she says, patting him good-naturedly on the head. "Was I not supposed to say that?"

He groans.

"Here," she says, lifting the clothes away from him. "Why don't I take this home, and you can play with — I mean *hang out* with — your friends?"

"Thanks, Mrs. Goldberg," Leo says.

She presses a button on her keys and the trunk of a car parked in front of the store lifts up. She hefts the suit inside and slams it shut. "I hope you enjoy your time in Willow Falls, Tara. There's more to it than meets the eye."

"I've noticed that," I reply.

She pulls away and David says, "I didn't tell her about you, she overheard me talking to my friend Connor."

"You talked to Connor about Tara?" Leo asks.

David reddens again, or should I say, reddens *more.*

"He came over last night to play video games," David says, "and I was telling him about being nervous for the bar —"

"It's okay," Leo says. "I'm just bustin' ya."

"I could say something right now about boys who write poems," David says, "but I won't."

Leo crosses his arms. "What's wrong with a boy writing poems?"

They start playfully shoving each other. I don't have much experience with teenage boys, but I do know this could go on for a while. "I hate to break this up," I say, stepping between them. "But we're in kind of a hurry."

David gives Leo a final shove, then steps back. "Where are you guys headed? Hey, wasn't Rory supposed to be with you?"

I don't even know where to start with the story. Leo says, "How about I fill David in on things while you go pick up the uniforms?"

"Are you sure?" I ask. "Don't you want to try them on for size?"

"I trust you," Leo says, glancing at his watch. "You better go. We'll meet you at the community center, okay?"

Leo leads David away, and I can tell he's purposefully turning him so he doesn't see where I'm going. I turn down the alley and wonder if it's because David acted all weird about the store, claiming it was empty.

The door to Angelina's store is open, but she's nowhere in sight. I head over to the uniforms and start going through them.

"Don't tell me you found everything on my list already?" she asks, popping out from behind the next rack of clothes.

Seeing her makes me want to ask about a hundred questions, but something in the way she's narrowing her eyes at me makes me think that wouldn't be a good idea. "Well, I did find one of them," I tell her, "but I need some Sunshine Kids uniforms in order to get it."

She raises one brow. "In *your* size?"

"Give or take a few inches."

She looks me up and down. "Hmm, I may have a few in extra-large." She reaches over to the rack and pulls off a yellow T-shirt with a big orange sun embroidered on the front. A pair of orange shorts with yellow suns running down the legs is attached to the hanger underneath. "Almost forgot." She pulls aside the shorts to reveal a yellow hat made out of felt.

I groan. "Great, it comes with a hat."

"Luckily for you, that's just for the boys. You get a skirt!"

"I'd rather have the hat," I mutter.

"How many do you want?"

"Two of each." I don't want to leave out David now that he's here. Although once he sees these, he'll probably be begging to be left out.

Angelina tosses me the one she's holding, then pulls three more from the rack and piles them on my arms. I'm trying to think of how to tell her that the list of items she requested is going to be impossible to find. I got lucky with the cane, I'm sure. Maybe if I had a year, rather than a month, I'd have a fighting chance.

"That'll be twenty-five dollars," she says, holding out her hand.

My jaw falls open. "You're *charging* me?"

"Wouldn't be in business very long if I gave things away for free."

I look down at the pile of orange and yellow clothes, faded in various places from years of wear. "Can't I borrow them for a day or two? I'll wash them after."

"Fine," she says. "But after this you're on your own. That's why I gave you the money."

I want to argue that I'll need that money for whatever comes ahead, but I know where that argument will get me. "Thank you," I say instead. I turn to go, then ask, "Any chance you want to buy a box of cookies?"

She only looks at me, unblinking. I hurry out of the store before she changes her mind about the uniforms.

. . . .

The main room of the community center is larger than it looks from the outside. It's filled with couches and card tables, a big stage along the far wall with curtains that have seen better days, a few vending machines, and some open cabinets with board games and books piled inside. A big bulletin board filled with notices and announcements hangs on the wall by the door. There's a flight of stairs to my left, and a long hallway leads to more rooms on the other side. I can hear little kids playing down the hall, dance music, and a man calling out bingo numbers. Most of the couches and chairs are filled with white-haired people chatting and playing cards.

Leo and David pop up from one of the couches and wave me over. "This is Bucky Whitehead," David says when I arrive. "He's the oldest person in Willow Falls."

"Second oldest," the old man says, folding a newspaper in his lap.

David looks surprised. "Who's the first, then?"

"So those are the uniforms, eh?" Leo says, obviously trying to change the subject. "They look a little small."

But Bucky answers anyway. "Angelina D'Angelo, of course."

"Who?" David asks.

"The woman who runs the shop in town," I tell him Although, honestly, she doesn't look nearly as old as this guy. Leo kicks me in the shin. Why doesn't he want me to talk about the shop?

"Angelina owns a shop now?" Bucky asks, shaking his head. "That old girl gets around."

I'm about to tell him that the shop looks like it's been there forever, but Leo's foot is poised only inches from my shin, ready to strike again. So instead I say, "It's nice to meet you," and try to free a hand to shake his. Instead, I wind up dropping half the uniforms on the guy's feet. "Sorry!" I bend down to grab them, but David and Leo beat me to it.

David holds up one of them as far away from him as possible.

"It won't bite," I tell him.

"It might. This thing doesn't look like it's been washed in ten years."

"At least you don't have to wear a skirt."

His response is drowned out by the screeching of metal wheels on the hardwood floor. Rory shows up, dragging a red wagon behind her piled high with cookie boxes. "I borrowed this from the daycare room. Pretty spiffy, right?"

"Oh, yeah," Leo says. "With that wagon and these uniforms, we're going to be the most popular kids in school."

Rory drops the wagon handle in horror. It clangs on the floor. "You don't think anyone will see us, do you?"

David puts his hand on her shoulder. "Let's just get dressed and sell our little hearts out as fast as we can."

We split up. Rory and I go into the girls' room, while the boys go across the hall to change. There's only one stall, so I let Rory go in first. "How do I look?" she asks a minute later. She twirls around and the orange skirt poofs up around her.

"It actually fits you really well," I tell her.

"Still waiting for that growth spurt, I guess," she says. "Okay, your turn."

I go into the stall and try to get changed without my clothes falling all over the floor. I can barely pull the top down past my belly button. The skirt reaches almost to my knees, but won't zip up no matter what I do. I guess this is what happens when your growth spurt comes in first grade.

"So?" Rory asks from the other side of the door.

"Not good," I tell her. "It's a little — well, a *lot* — too small."

"Okay," Rory says. "Wait here, I'll be right back."

So I wait, hoping no one comes in wanting to use the bathroom. She returns two minutes later and passes me a balled-up white and blue striped shirt under the stall door. "Just put that on over your uniform."

I unfurl it to discover a man's button-down shirt. I slip it on, then take it right back off. It would only hide my belly if I buttoned it up, and if I did that, what would be the point of wearing the uniform in the first place? So I wrap it around my waist instead. That way it covers my bare belly in the front and the open zipper in the back.

Rory nods in approval as I step out of the stall. I tighten the knot holding it in place. "Where did you get this?"

"Lost and Found."

I sigh. I'm going to have to take a long shower when this day is over.

As we gather up our clothes, I feel something crinkling in the back of my skirt. A piece of paper is stuck in the small pocket. I reach in to find a forty-percent-off coupon to Applebee's restaurant. "Hey, look what I found." I hand Rory the coupon. "The last kid to wear this must have left it there. Do you want it? I think Aunt Bethany is more of the 'order in' type."

Rory pushes it back toward me. "No, thanks. Sawyer's banned from there for three years."

"*Banned?* Why?"

"Long story involving his bare butt and an elderly couple with very little sense of humor."

I look closer at the coupon before tossing it in the trash. "It expired two years ago anyway." Which makes me realize how long these uniforms have been hanging in the store. My future shower just got longer.

When we meet back up with the boys, I have to cover my mouth to keep from laughing. Rory doubles right over. David and Leo both look like they're wearing their seven-year-old brother's clothes. If they *had* seven-year-old brothers, which I'm pretty sure they don't. David's shirt is pulled so tight across the chest that the sun is utterly unrecognizable. Leo keeps reaching behind him to un-wedgify the back of his shorts. But the worst part might be the hats. With the pointy front and flipped-up sides, they would be at home on either a pirate or the ice cream man. With Leo's curly black hair, the hat makes him looks like a hobbit. Or an elf. I was never very clear on the difference.

Rory is now pointing at them and gasping for air. This makes me lose it.

"Where are *your* hats?" David asks, crossing his arms in front of his chest. When I can catch my breath, I tell them that only the boys' uniforms came with the hats.

Leo scowls. "A likely story. Good thing Amanda isn't here. I'd never live this down."

"If my phone took pictures, I'd send her one," Rory gasps. Still shaking with laughter, she uses our regular clothes to wrap up the cane, which she tucks under the boxes.

"C'mon," David says, picking up the handle of the wagon. "Let's get this over with."

As we walk back into the main room, I ask, "Did I mention there's singing?"

Chapter Twelve

"Should we split up?" Leo asks, looking around the large room. "You know, divide and conquer?"

The rest of us shake our heads. There's comfort in numbers. Four people looking incredibly dorky is a lot better than one. We go over to Bucky Whitehead's couch first, where he's deep in conversation with two other old men.

David clears his throat, glares at me, and starts singing.

"We are the Sunshine Kids. We've come to brighten up your day, no matter how gray the sky, we are here to tell you why . . . why you want to buy our yummy cookies!"

Stunned silence is how I would describe their reaction. I'm kind of surprised, too. David's voice wasn't anything like I'd heard either in the pool hole or at Apple Grove. This time he sang kind of off-key and halting. Was he intentionally trying to be bad? Still, I'm sure it's better than I could do.

I lean close and whisper, "How did you know the song?"

He whispers back, "Connor's little sister used to be a Sunshine Kid. Until she turned seven and realized how uncool it was."

"So . . ." Rory says loudly, "who wants to buy some cookies?" She holds up a box in each hand and waves them around.

"They got nuts in 'em?" one of the old men asks. "Can't eat nuts no more with these new chompers."

"Well, there are four different kinds," Rory says. We each reach into the wagon and pick up a different type of cookie to check the list of ingredients.

"Oatmeal Dream doesn't have nuts," Leo announces.

I scan the side of mine. "Neither does Chocolate-Chip Delight."

David tosses his box of Nutty McNut Clusters back into the wagon without even checking the label.

"Minty Melts are nut-free, too," Rory says. "So would you like any of them?"

The anti-nuts guy shakes his head. "Nah, I don't like cookies."

Rory's face falls.

"I'll take a box of Minty Melts," Bucky Whitehead says, reaching into his pocket. He pulls out two quarters and hands them to Rory.

She looks at the fifty cents sitting in her palm and turns to me helplessly. Guess I need to step in. "Um, I'm sorry," I tell him, "but it's actually four dollars a box."

"Really?" he asks. "Didn't Girl Scout cookies used to be fifty cents?"

"We're Sunshine Girls," Leo says. "I mean, Kids, we're the Sunshine *Kids*."

"That might have been the price a long time ago," I tell him. "But it's four dollars now."

Rory adds, "We totally understand if you don't want them anymore." She reaches over to give him his change back, but he waves it away and digs into his pocket. He pulls out two more quarters, and a roll of dollar bills held together with a rubber band. He counts out three bills and gives them to Rory, who hands him the box in return.

"Thanks, Bucky," Leo says. "I'll bet you won't be able to keep the ladies away when you offer them a Minty Melt."

Mr. Whitehead winks. "That's the plan."

This notion makes the other men guffaw.

"C'mon," David says. "Always best to leave 'em laughing."

So we wheel the wagon toward the next group, and all I can think is *One box down, forty-four to go.*

Rory stops before we reach a group of women playing cards. "I feel kinda bad asking these old people for money," she says. "I mean, they really don't have a lot to begin with."

I look around the room at all the potential cookie buyers. It's not like we're forcing them to buy anything.

But David nods in agreement with Rory. "Yeah," he says, "some of these people probably haven't had jobs in thirty years."

Leo nods too, and I feel like a jerk for being thoughtless. "What else is in the building?" I ask.

"The dance studio is upstairs," Rory says. "Those girls always look hungry."

Leo and David each take an end of the wagon, and we climb the stairs. Class is just letting out, so all the girls are busy untying their ballet slippers and finding their bags. A tall girl with black hair wrapped in a bun hurries over to us and gives Rory a hug. Then she pulls back for a good look. "Did you lose a bet?" She glances at the rest of us. Leo starts to de-wedgify again, then stops himself and pretends he was just scratching his leg.

"Hey, Sasha!" Rory says warmly. "This is my new friend, Tara. We're helping her out." She reaches over and grabs the closest box. In a loud voice she calls out, "Anyone wanna buy some cookies?"

The girls all look at us, and then to the teacher, who scowls and points to the door. We slink out and huddle in the hallway.

"Now what?" Leo asks.

"We're just gonna have to brave the neighborhood," Rory says.

Sasha comes out of the room first, slinging a gym bag over her shoulders. "*Pssst*, follow me," she says, gesturing to the staircase. Once inside, she says, "I'll take five," and presses a twenty-dollar bill into Rory's hand. "My family loves these."

"Really?" Leo asks, clearly finding that hard to believe.

"Especially with ketchup," she replies.

"It also helps if you warm them up," David adds.

"Why, David Goldberg," Rory teases, "are you a secret Sunshine Kid cookie eater?"

"I might be. My mom used to get them from the neighborhood kids."

Sasha picks five boxes from the wagon and says, "You might want to hang out here for a little while. I have a feeling you'll get more business."

She's right! One by one, the ballerinas file down the stairs, slipping us money and taking boxes! The last girl tucks a box of the oatmeal cookies under her arm and warns us that the teacher isn't far behind. We hurry back downstairs and keep going until we're out the front door.

"How did we do?" I ask. The pile in the wagon is considerably smaller.

Our skirts don't have pockets, so we turn to the boys, who had been stuffing the money into theirs. Leo struggles to reach his hand far enough into his front pocket to grab the money, and Rory has another fit of giggles.

"Um, everyone's kinda looking at us," David says.

It's true. We've attracted a bit of a crowd.

Summoning my courage, I ask, "Anyone want to buy some cookies?"

One little boy tugs on his mother's sleeve. "Aren't they supposed to sing?"

David sighs. I brace myself for the same performance he gave inside. Instead, his voice is clear and sweet. People actually clap! We sell two boxes before the crowd breaks up.

"We still have twenty-two boxes left," Rory says. "It's getting late. I have to be home by six."

"Let's all call our parents and see if they want some," Leo suggests.

"Good idea," Rory says, reaching into the wagon for her phone. The three of them start dialing while I busy myself organizing the remaining boxes by flavor.

"Aren't you going to call your aunt?" Rory says to me. "She'll definitely buy some."

How can I explain that even though she's my mom's sister, she's pretty much a stranger to me? "I . . . I'd just feel weird asking her."

"I'll ask her for you," Rory offers.

It's strange that Rory knows my aunt much better than I do. But it's undeniably true. A minute later she hands me her phone. "It's Ray. He wants to talk to you."

I take the phone and turn away a bit, into the shelter of the doorway. "Hello?"

"I'll be stuffed," Ray says in his usual cheerful voice. "Look at you selling biscuits with your new mates!"

"They're cookies."

"I'm glad you gave it a fair go. They're a nice groupa kids."

"Ray? Is anyone else home?"

"Nope."

"All right, well, see you later."

"Hold on. Aren't you going to ask me if I want to buy any biscuits?"

"Do you?"

"You didn't pinch 'em, did you?"

I look over at the boxes. "No, they're all in good shape."

He laughs. "I meant the ol' five-finger discount."

"Huh?"

"Did you *steal* them?"

"Of course not!" My face grows hot.

"Okay, okay, don't fret your freckle. I'll take three boxes."

"Really? Great, thanks!"

"No problem. Cheerio."

"Bye." I hand Rory her phone back. "Ray bought three!"

"Great! My mom said she'd take three, too."

"Two for mine," Leo says.

"No one was home at my house," David says. "But Connor lives around the corner from here, and I'm sure his mom will buy some boxes."

After we set aside the ones we just sold on the phone, fourteen remain in the wagon. We head off to Connor's house, huddling close together. Only once did we have to duck inside a store when Rory saw some girls from school. If I didn't have to return these uniforms to Angelina, I'd suggest we start a bonfire with them.

Connor himself answers the door. A video-game controller dangles from one hand. He's tall and thin, with the reddest hair I've ever seen. He also has a lot of freckles, which makes me think of Ray and "don't fret your freckle." I might actually use that one some day.

Connor lets out a long whistle. "Dude," he says, shaking his head. "Halloween's been over for eight months."

"Yeah, yeah, we've heard it all."

"Seriously, why are you guys dressed like orange and yellow pirates?"

Rory holds up the cookies. "Wanna buy some?"

"Mom!" Connor calls over his shoulder. "Will you buy some cookies from the Hamburglar and his friends?"

A tall, red-haired woman comes to the door, along with an equally red-haired girl, who looks around eight. "Well, now, this is a surprise," the mom says. The girl just giggles.

"Hi, Mrs. Kelly. Hi, Grace," David says, tugging on his shirt. "These are my friends Leo, Rory, and Tara."

At the mention of my name, Connor peers out the door for a closer look. I take a step to the side so I'm mostly hidden behind Leo and his elf hat.

"Nice to meet you all," Mrs. Kelly says. "I'm sure there's a very good reason you're dressed that way."

"What about the song?" Grace asks. "The song's the best part."

David sighs, and launches into the cookie song. "*We are the Sunshine Kids. We've come to brighten up your day, no matter how gray the sky, we are here to tell you why . . . why you want to buy our yummy cookies!"* It's just as good as the one outside the community center.

The three of them clap at the end. Mrs. Kelly says, "Grace, we're going to need some favors for your birthday party next month, shall we get some cookies for everyone?"

The girl considers this. "Okay, let's do it. They must really be desperate to dress like that at their age."

Connor laughs and puts his hand on her shoulder. "That's my little sis. Calling it like she sees it."

I think if I had an older brother, he's the kind I'd want.

Mrs. Kelly goes to get her wallet and Grace follows. "Seriously, Hamburglar," Connor says to David. "What's the dealio with the freaky getups?"

David leans forward and says, "To tell you the truth, I have no idea. Maybe someone would like to tell me?"

I shrink farther behind Leo. Fortunately, Mrs. Kelly returns before things get ugly. "Let's see . . . Grace will be turning ten, and there will be ten girls at the slumber party, so . . . I'll take ten!" She hands David two twenties, and he helps her pick out ten boxes. I sneak a peek at Grace, who has returned. I'm surprised that she's turning ten. She's very small and there's something frail about her. Like she could break if the wind blew too hard.

David carries a stack of boxes into the house and stacks them on the front-hall table. As he passes Grace he says, "Hey, Squirt, you're still gonna be at my bar mitzvah even though it's your birthday that day, right?"

"I'm having my party the night before," she says, "so you're stuck with me." Then she whips out a camera and says, "You've gotta let me get a picture of you guys," and then takes the picture as the four of us each move to cover our faces.

Connor bends down so they can high-five.

In unspoken agreement, the four of us turn and run across the lawn, the wagon bouncing behind us. We regroup at the end of the driveway. "Remind me not to send that girl a birthday card," Rory grumbles.

I take a deep breath and say, "You guys really don't have to do this anymore. It's almost dinnertime and we only have four boxes left. I don't even know how to thank you."

David looks up the street. "Let's just do one more house. I kinda have to use the bathroom, and I don't want to go back into Connor's house and risk having our pictures go up on the Internet."

So onward we trek. The lights are off at the house next door. Then at the next house, a lady peeks out of the curtains beside the door, takes one look at us, and disappears. She doesn't come back.

"Only one more, okay?" Rory says. "I really should get home."

At this point David has started to walk with his legs crossed. Sort of hobbling, really. He nods and rings the next bell. "I've met this lady before," David says. "She's in some kind of baking club with Connor's mom." A middle-aged woman wearing a lot of thick makeup opens the door even before David's finger is off the doorbell.

Her face falls when she sees us. "Oh. I thought you were the deliveryman. I'm waiting for an important package."

"Sorry," David says. "I'm a friend of Connor's, you know, from down the street?"

She peers at him. "You're the one who's always singing out in their vegetable garden?"

David reddens. "Not *always* singing," he mutters.

"So how can I help you?"

David seems stumped for an answer. Leo elbows him, and he launches into a very sped-up rendition of the cookie song.

The woman stiffens. "Is this one of those hazing things at school?" She peeks out to look up and down the block. "Is someone forcing you to do this? I can call the school for you, if you like. No one should be treated this way."

We all go wide-eyed and quickly assure her that no one is bullying us. "We're just trying to sell a few last boxes of cookies," I explain. "For, um, a Sunshine Kid we know who ordered too many."

"All right," the woman says, relaxing against the doorpost. "That's good." She glances at David, who is nonchalantly crossing and recrossing his legs. "I'm Bettie with an *i-e.* Would you like to come in and tell me about the cookies?"

"Thank you," Rory says, wheeling in the wagon. The rest of us follow. The house smells like warm bread.

"The bathroom is down the hall on the left," she says, "if anyone would like to use it."

David takes off without another word.

"So what kind of cookies do you have?" Bettie with an *i-e* asks.

Rory shows her the boxes while I glance around the house. It reminds me of my own, all on one floor and cozy. That's one thing I'll say about my mother: She always tries to make each new house as welcoming as possible. David returns from the bathroom and I'm about to ask Bettie if it's okay for me to go, too, when the deliveryman shows up and she heads over to the door to sign for her package. I decide to just hurry and go while she's busy.

The bathroom is all done in shades of pink and white. Makeup kits full of lipstick and eye shadows and blush and things I don't even recognize fill baskets and bowls and threaten to spill off the shelves. Bettie likes makeup a LOT.

After I wash my hands, I look around for a hand towel or napkin but don't see anything. There's a white basket filled with cotton balls next to the sink. Am I supposed to dry my hands with cotton balls? I lift up the basket, thinking maybe there's a napkin underneath. Nope. I rest it back down. Then I shriek. Twice.

"Tara?" Rory says, knocking on the door. "Are you okay?"

With a trembling hand, I open the door. Rory and the boys and makeup-loving Bettie are standing in the hall, concern creasing their faces.

I hold up the basket by one of its heart-shaped handles. "How much do you want for this?"

Chapter Thirteen

The kitchen table has been transformed into one of the cosmetic counters at the mall that Mom always hurries past. Bettie leans over and dabs my nose with a powder puff. I try not to sneeze as some powder goes up my nose. I needed a basket; she needed someone to test her new line of makeup on before offering it for sale. A win-win, as my dad would say!

The others are seated across the table, munching on the fresh breadsticks that Bettie laid out for us. Rory and Leo have been sending a flurry of texts back and forth while David looks somewhat stupefied. I'm pretty sure Leo has been texting Amanda, too, because every once in a while his phone beeps even when Rory hasn't sent anything.

"One more dab of the forehead," says Bettie, "and we're done!" She holds a round mirror up to my face. "What do you think?"

I think I barely recognize myself under the purple eye shadow, pink lipstick, and red cheeks. "Wow, it's . . . colorful!"

She lays the mirror down on the kitchen table. "I should probably tone it down a bit, now that you mention it. My mother, she was the real artist. She always knew just how to bring out someone's best features, or hide any imperfections." Her eyes get a little glassy and she blinks a few times.

Rory jumps up from her chair. "It looks great," she assures her. "But we've really got to go."

I grab the white basket and follow Rory to the door. Leo trips right over the open box on the floor that was once filled with the makeup that's now on my face. We hear a *riiiip*, followed by "Uh-oh, that's not good!"

Rory tosses Leo his regular shorts. He ducks into the kitchen and comes out a few seconds later holding the orange ones, which are pretty much in shreds. "Ah, I can breathe again," he says.

No doubt I'll be paying Angelina for those.

"Thank you again," I tell Bettie, placing the basket in the red wagon. I still can't believe my luck at finding it.

Bettie beams and turns my chin from side to side, admiring her work. "Thank you for letting me experiment on your face."

"Any time," I reply, because really, what does one say to that?

"Enjoy the cookies," David says, ushering me out the door.

"Bye!" Bettie calls out after us, already opening up her box of Minty Mints.

As soon as the door is closed, Rory's smile fades. She turns to David and asks, "Would it be okay if Leo and I talk to Tara alone?"

David sniffs under his arms. "I don't smell, do I?"

"It'll only take a minute," Rory promises. "It's kind of a girl thing."

"Leo's not a girl," David points out.

"He's standing in for Amanda," Rory replies. "You know they're interchangeable."

"True," David agrees. "Come get me at Connor's when you're done."

"Thanks," Rory says, pulling me down the driveway. I look

back over my shoulder at David standing beside the red wagon in his stretched-out shirt and sun-covered shorts. He tips his yellow felt hat at me and then heads off across the lawn. I can guess what Rory and Leo want to talk to me about, but I'm not sure why they can't do it in front of David.

"We've only known you a few days," Leo begins, bringing my attention back to them, "but do you always go into new places and ask people if you can have their stuff?"

How can I lie to them after everything they've done for me today? I shake my head.

They exchange a glance, and Leo continues. "Amanda and Rory and I have learned that if someone's doing something they don't usually do, or acting really weird, then there's usually something behind it."

"Or some*one*," Rory adds. "Short, with white hair? Duck on her cheek?"

I let what they're saying sink in. They know Angelina! "Do you guys work for her, too?"

Rory shakes her head, but Leo says, "Sort of. Not exactly. It's hard to explain."

I glance at Rory, who doesn't look particularly surprised. I turn back to Leo. "Does the thing with you and Amanda and the blackboards have to do with Angelina in some way?"

He tugs at the collar of his Sunshine Kid shirt as though it's suddenly gotten even tighter. "I really can't say," he mumbles. Which I take to mean *yes*. Then he motions us closer with his hand and whispers, "We're doing this to help Tara."

I gape at him, stunned. "You are? To help *me*?"

Rory's jaw has fallen open, too.

My brain tries to process this, but I'm coming up empty. Emily told me Leo and Amanda had started talking to each other with the blackboards last summer. They didn't even know me then! He must be confusing me with someone else. "To help me with what?" I ask.

Leo sighs. "We have no idea. We're not even totally sure it's about you. I've already said too much. Can we please talk about the more pressing problem of what's happening now?"

He looks so desperate that I feel bad pushing him further. So I turn to Rory. "Then how are you involved with Angelina?"

"I'm not," she insists. "Not anymore. But, Tara, are you done getting stuff from people? The cane, and now this basket?"

I shake my head.

"What else do you need?"

"Well, I sort of have this whole list."

"How many more things are on it?" Leo asks.

I think for a second. "Eleven."

"Eleven!" Rory exclaims. "When do you need to find them by?"

"I have a whole month. Not until July thirteenth."

"Isn't that your birthday?" Leo asks.

I nod.

He and Rory exchange another knowing look. "Angelina has a thing with birthdays," Rory explains.

"Look," I tell them. "This thing with Angelina, it's not such a big deal. It's just a job. She gave me a list of things to find for her store, and she's paying me for it and everything."

"That's all?" Rory asks.

I nod. I don't even feel like I'm lying. Because honestly, except for the element of blackmail involved, it really *is* just a job. "Why didn't you want David to hear our conversation?" I ask. "He's eventually going to ask about this stuff, too, right?"

"It's because we suspected Angelina is involved somehow," Leo says. "So we didn't want to bring it up in front of him."

"Why?"

"It's just not a good idea," Leo says.

I take a deep breath. "I know I haven't had a lot of experience being a part of a group, but I don't want to get in the middle of anything. I don't want David to get left out because of me." I might not know what it's like to be a good friend, but I know what it's like to be a bad one.

"Tara," Rory says gently, reaching for my hand.

This time I flinch. Her hand drops.

I know what to do. I need to go back on the sidelines. "I'm going to do the rest of this alone, okay? It's nothing personal, you guys have been really nice to me. Can you tell David I'll see him later?" I start walking away, willing the tears not to fall. Hopefully my bike is where I left it outside the diner.

"Tara!" Leo says. "Please listen. You can't tell him about Angelina, you just can't."

I keep walking.

I make it to the curb before Leo and Rory appear on either side of me. Rory stops me and says, "Remember when we were at Angelina's store yesterday and David was joking around, saying the store was empty?"

I nod. How could I forget?

"The thing is . . . he wasn't joking."

"What do you mean?"

Rory takes a deep breath and says, "The store really *is* empty."

Okay, they're officially crazy. "No, it's not! I've been in there twice. And you've seen all the stuff through the window."

"It's not empty for *you*," Rory explains. "Or Leo or Amanda or me, or whoever else Angelina wants to let in. But it's empty for *him*. Do you understand?"

"It's empty for David?" I repeat.

"Yes," Leo says. "It is."

My head starts to swim. How can a store look different to different people? And why David, of all people? If I hadn't seen his strange reaction in the alley with my own eyes, I'd never believe what they're telling me. "I need to sit down."

They both reach for me as I half fall, half sit on the curb. Rory sits down next to me. I don't take my eyes off the road.

"Are you going to be okay?" she asks.

I wish I had an answer to that. "I have no idea what to think right now."

"We didn't want to freak you out," Rory says. "It's just that David's a really good guy. He'd want to keep helping you find the stuff you need. But he wouldn't understand why you're getting things for a store that doesn't exist. He'd either think you were crazy or that *he* was, and with him already being so nervous about his bar mitzvah . . ."

"The store doesn't exist. Doesn't exist," I repeat. Nope, doesn't make any more sense the more times I say it.

"It doesn't exist to *him*," she clarifies.

I drop my head into my hands. "Am I . . . ?"

"Are you what?"

"Crazy? Am I the one who's crazy?"

"No," she says. "I promise you're not crazy. Whatever's going on, you just have to trust it will make sense to you one day."

The little bit of food in my stomach is threatening to end up on the street. "Just so I'm totally clear," I whisper, "we live in a world where a store can be empty to one person, and full to others?"

"I don't know if it's like that anywhere else, but in Willow Falls, yes."

We sit there in silence for a few minutes. "It's getting pretty late," Rory says, standing up. "You wait here; we'll go get David."

"What are you going to tell him?"

"As close to the truth as we can," she replies.

I stare up at the dusky sky, now streaked with orange and pink. I don't believe in Friday the thirteenth being bad luck. I don't believe if you make a weird face it will stay that way. I don't even believe that if you make a wish on your birthday candle it will come true. And I'm supposed to believe these things they're telling me?

From the minute I saw Amanda and Leo with those blackboards, I should have known theirs wasn't the only secret in Willow Falls. I just never thought I'd be a part of one myself.

Chapter Fourteen

Even though I'd locked the bike up outside the diner, I'm still relieved to see it there safe and sound. It might not be anything like my bike at home, but right now it's my only way to escape. I wrap up the chain and put it in Emily's squashed basket. The broken basket is my excuse to get inside the shop again.

The alley is even more deserted than it was this morning, if that's possible. The setting sun doesn't seem to touch this street. I shiver, glad I'm no longer wearing the Sunshine Kid outfit. Rory took them home to wash. She said she'd have an easier time explaining their appearance to her mother than I would to my aunt. Supposedly, her mom is used to a lot of strangeness.

No light shines from Angelina's store, either, but as I get closer I can hear dance music. Not normal dance music, but like big-band-orchestra-grandparents kind of dance music. I peek through the cleaned off spot in the window and there she is, dancing. Alone. In the middle of the shop. She's moving a lot more gracefully than one would think the oldest person in town should be able to move. I watch for a minute until she spots me. She stops moving, and the music stops, too. I didn't see her turn any radio off, but that's not even one of the top three strangest things that's happened to me today, so I let it go.

We meet at the door. Hands on her hips, she says, "You know you're only supposed to be here because you have all my stuff. And yet your hands remain maddeningly empty."

"I know but, um . . ." I quickly unsnap the basket from the bike and hold it up. "I need a new one of these. Mine broke carrying home the tape recorder."

She sighs. "I'm going to need the recorder back eventually, you know. That one is my favorite."

"Okay," I promise, even though there's a good chance Uncle Roger has taken it apart by now. "So do you have another basket that will fit the bike?"

She grumbles, but steps aside so I can come in. Before I can ask where to find them, she reaches over and plucks a pink plastic basket from the window display. It has a white plastic flower in the front and is clearly meant for a little girl. Which means, unfortunately, that it's perfect for my bike.

She holds out her hand. "That'll be five dollars."

This time I don't argue. I simply reach into my sock and pull a twenty off the roll. It's still sweaty, and she holds it by the corner when she goes to get change. I take this chance to look around the place, like *really* look. The hardwood floors, the ceiling with long wooden beams reaching across it, all the *stuff.* It's all so . . . real. So solid. I lean against the wall, trying to look casual. Then I give it a little push. Yup, solid. I bet most people wouldn't notice the one thing I saw the very first time I came in here. Or rather, what I didn't see — dust. It's the only thing that makes the place unusual for a secondhand store. But maybe Angelina's just a really good duster.

She returns with my change and a wet paper towel.

"What's this for?" I ask, holding out the towel.

"Your face."

Angelina can be very direct when she wants to be. I wipe the makeup off as best I can. Angelina takes the old basket and the used paper towel, although not happily. Ushering me out the door, she asks, "And when will I see you here again?"

"When I have all the stuff on the list?"

"Exactly," she says, and shuts the door firmly behind me. I don't want to leave yet. I want to ask her how a soul actually solidifies and where it's supposed to be while I'm figuring all this out. Flying in the air above me? Off reading a good book somewhere? I want to ask why David sees an empty store. But I know I'm not getting any answers today. I snap on the basket and walk the bike back up the alley to Main Street.

Dusk has definitely settled on Willow Falls, and I have no reflective padding on me. For a split second, I actually worry that Mom will see me and I'll get in trouble. I start peddling as fast as the little bike will take me until I accept the fact that no one is going to see me. No one I know, at least. Plus, Mom's on the other side of the world. She doesn't even know a store can be empty for one person, and full for another. She'd never believe it anyway. Why should she? I certainly wouldn't have. Dad's the one in our family whose head is always dreaming up imaginary worlds. Mom and I prefer our worlds solid, where the rules don't change.

It feels strange to ride all the way back to Aunt Bethany's house and then turn into David's house, instead. Rory's mom pulls up just as I'm leaning the bike up against the garage door. Amanda climbs out first, the blackboard around her neck. Leo told me she lives all the way on the other side of town, which is probably why I beat them here.

"Rumor has it you had a pretty crazy day," she says.

"Yup, pretty crazy."

"Can't say I'm sorry to have missed dressing up in that Sunshine Kid skirt," she says. "I still have my old one somewhere."

Obviously Leo texted her about the connection between the things I'm looking for and Angelina, but I don't want to ask her about it with David only a few steps away. So as the last car door slams, I quickly say, "Well, if you're ever looking for a secondhand shop to sell it to, I know just the place."

"I'll remember that," she replies.

David's mom opens the front door and says, "Come on in, everyone, I've got grilled cheese grilling and iced tea icing."

I breathe a sigh of relief to see that Rory didn't lose either the cane or the basket. Now that I'm not riding my bike, I really want them back. But I also don't want to insult her, or to reveal that getting all the items on the list might be a little more important to me than I'd let on. So I just smile as she walks into the house with them.

David and I are the last to climb the porch steps. He doesn't seem mad about anything, and I'm curious what Leo and Rory decided to tell him. He gestures for me to go ahead. As I turn around, I see him touch a small rectangular box hanging crooked on the side of the door frame. Then he kisses his fingers. He notices me watching and smiles. "It's a Jewish thing." He points to the little box. "That's a mezuzah. It has a little scroll inside with a prayer in it. You're supposed to kiss it every time you pass by."

"Why?"

He pauses. "Because it's tradition."

"Oh. Like when I ki —" Was I seriously about to say, *like when I kiss Jake Harrison's picture every time I pass it?* Clearly I'm still not in my right mind.

"Do you like tomatoes on your grilled cheese?" Mrs. Goldberg asks me when we get to the kitchen.

I join the others around the table. "I've never tried it that way."

"It's a Jewish thing," David says, setting out a bunch of napkins.

"Oh."

He laughs. "I'm just kidding."

"David!" his mother scolds as she flips the sandwiches over in the pan.

"Sorry, Tara," he says sheepishly. "I promise to be nice. After all, you did let those birds poop on my head yesterday."

"What?" his mother exclaims, nearly dropping the pan. "Get upstairs and take a shower right now!"

"Ma! I took one when I got home yesterday." He turns to me and says, "My mom hates animal poop. That's why we don't have any pets."

"My mom can't get enough of that stuff," I reply. "She can identify almost any animal by its excrement."

"Um, we're trying to eat here?" Rory says, holding up her sandwich.

David's mom points upstairs with the spatula. "I'm not asking you again."

"But I'm hungry," he whines.

She places a sandwich on a paper plate and hands it to him. "Go."

He slinks off and the rest of us dive into our sandwiches. Mrs. Goldberg goes upstairs to make sure David didn't just turn on the shower water while he eats his sandwich and reads a book in his room. According to her, he has a habit of doing this.

When she's gone, I ask, "So what did you guys tell David about why I need to find all the stuff?"

"We told him you lost the money you came to town with," Rory whispers, glancing behind her. "And that a wealthy collector hired you to find some objects for him. I may have let him believe that it's a friend of your uncle's, since he knows your uncle is a collector, too. He said he'd be happy to help."

The surprise must show on my face because Leo says, "Was that all right? You're not mad, are you?"

"It's perfect," I tell them, feeling very pleased with myself. "Because that's really what happened."

"What do you mean?" Amanda asks.

"I mean I really DID lose the money my parents gave me. That's why I went to Angelina in the first place."

Leo scribbles something to Amanda, who scribbles back. Then Leo says, "So you really did go to Angelina first? She didn't seek you out?"

I'm confused. "Why does it matter?"

"We're not sure," Leo says. Then to Rory, "Angelina came to you, right?"

She nods. "She pulled me out of the drainpipe."

"You were stuck in a *drainpipe*?" I ask, incredulous. I mean, Emily had said Rory was clumsy, but wow.

She lifts her chin. "It totally looked like a rock."

"You were stuck in a rock-shaped drainpipe?"

She nods again. "I don't recommend it."

Amanda turns to me and asks, "But what made you go to Angelina?"

"Well, after we found her store yesterday I figured it was the only place in town I could se —" Oops! Can't tell that part. "The only place in town that might hire me," I finish. "She even paid me in advance!" It feels so good to tell them about losing the money. One less secret I have to keep track of.

"Wow," Rory says. "Maybe she's softening in her old age."

"I don't think so. She's pretty tough. She says she doesn't want to see me again until I've got all the items on her list."

"Can we see it?" Amanda asks.

"Let's wait for David to come back," Rory says.

We don't have to wait long. A minute later he shows up with wet hair and directs us down the hall into the family room. Rory grabs the cane and basket, which she had propped up in the corner of the kitchen.

The family room is filled with pictures of David growing up. A bunch from the younger years includes a dark-haired man who I assume is his father. The two of them playing catch, swimming in the ocean, sitting on a porch. Sometimes his mom's in the picture, too, and in the more recent years it's mostly David alone. Other than the photographs, there's no sign of his dad anywhere. No oversized slippers by the couch, no sports magazine by the television.

As soon as we sit down on various couches and chairs, everyone (except me) starts talking at once. Finally David stands up, grabs the cane, and taps it on the floor like a judge with a gavel. Even without the noise, the sight of him holding the duck-headed cane is enough to make everyone stop and laugh.

"Now that I have your attention," he says, "I did some thinking while forced to take my second shower in twenty-four hours." He starts pacing with the cane. "It seems to me, if there are eleven more things on Tara's list, and she has almost four weeks to find them, that's less than three a week. That's not so bad, right?"

"Wait a second," Rory says. "Tara, has your aunt said anything to you about going to the beach this summer?"

I shake my head. "Why?"

"They always go in the beginning of July for ten days. I heard them talking about it last week. They're definitely going, which means you are, too."

"Which *means*," Amanda says, "that we don't have a month to get these things, we have two weeks."

I take a deep breath. Okay, two weeks. Eleven things. Is that even possible? But then a thought cheers me up. "Hey, look how fast I found the first two — maybe they'll all be like that."

"Something tells me the rest won't be as easy," Leo says. "It was probably beginner's luck, finding those first two so quickly."

"Maybe," David agrees. "But I still think it's worth trying to sell the last of the cookies tomorrow. It'll get us into more houses."

I shudder at the thought of putting on that outfit again. "Leo's shorts are in shreds," I remind David. "And what's a Sunshine Kid without his sunshine shorts?"

"So true," Leo says, shaking his head sadly. "So true."

"Well, how else are we going to get inside people's houses?" David asks.

"We could pretend to be walking by and then one of us can ask to use their bathroom," Rory suggests. "You know, if they seem friendly."

Amanda shakes her head. "That might get us in the front door, but it's not like we can wander through their whole house. These objects could be anywhere. What are the chances of finding something else in a bathroom?"

"I think we need to see the list," Leo says, "so we know what we're up against."

I still can't get used to hearing them say "we." I doubt any of the four of them would be volunteering to help if they knew the real reason why I need to get all these objects in on time. But if Rory's right and we only have two weeks, I'm certainly in no position to turn anyone away.

I take the list out of my pocket and unfold it. "It's kind of random," I warn them, laying it on the wooden coffee table.

They all huddle around as Rory reads it out loud. At first her voice is full of enthusiasm, but as the list goes on, she starts to sound more and more defeated. Then she gets to the last one. "Hey, Amanda and Leo! The final item is a bottle of wine brewed by Ellerby-Fitzpatrick Brewers! Is that you guys?"

Amanda and Leo grab the paper to read it themselves. "No way!" Amanda says, laughing. Then she grabs her blackboard and writes, *Did you know our great-great-grandfathers made apple wine together?*

Leo shakes his head and writes, *Nothing those two would do surprises me.*

What surprises *me* is that they know anything at all about their great-great-grandparents! I guess roots in Willow Falls grow deep.

"Can you find a bottle of it?" Rory asks them.

"We'll do our best," Amanda promises.

Unfortunately, the wine is the only item on the list that anyone in the room has an association with. David starts pacing again. "Why would this guy give you such a random list and not tell you where to find everything? What's the point of that?"

"I don't think she knows where they are."

"Oh, it's a lady?" he asks.

I nod, purposefully not glancing at the others in case I shouldn't have given that much away.

But David is persistent. "Why does she want this stuff in the first place?"

"I guess for whatever collectors collect things for. Maybe to resell it?"

"Or maybe to put on display somewhere," Leo suggests. "Like in a museum."

David looks at the cane in his hand. "I'm not sure this is museum-worthy. And that basket looks old, but not, like, old enough to be on display somewhere."

I know Leo is just trying to get David off track so he doesn't think of Angelina's store, but I don't blame David for being confused.

Leo jumps up. "I know what we can do! We can put up a sign in the community center, on that big bulletin board. Everyone reads that thing when they come and go. Or at least the grown-ups do. We can list all the items and ask people to contact us if they own one of them."

Amanda writes *That's a great idea* on her blackboard.

David stops pacing. "And we can post it on the Willow Falls website! Everyone checks that at least once a day."

"Definitely!" Rory says.

"Um, don't take this the wrong way," I say, "but your town has a website that people actually look at?"

They laugh. Amanda says, "Every day, one of the businesses or restaurants in town gives something away to the people who logged on that day. It also lists town activities, things like that. We don't have a town paper anymore — saving the trees and all — so that's where you go to find things out."

"But wait," Leo says. "What if posting the list jacks up the prices? Like when Tara asked for the other stuff, she had the element of surprise on her side. But if people see ahead of time that we want it, maybe they'll ask a lot for it."

Good point, Amanda writes. *But what other choice do we have?*

Amanda and Leo's concerned faces tell me something I should have figured out earlier — they're really worried about what might happen if I don't get all these items in to Angelina on time. I'm worried, too, of course, and now I'm even *more* worried. Could they know something *I* don't? Are there bigger consequences that I haven't suspected?

"Amanda's right," I say. "We're just going to have to take that chance. At least we'll know where things are, and that's the hardest part, right?"

No one answers for a minute. "Just promise me," Leo says with mock sincerity, "no matter what people want us to do, that you'll never make me wear shorts that tight again. I think I'm traumatized. Physically, and emotionally."

"I promise. And whatever happens, whether we get all the stuff or not, I really owe you guys one." I'm pretty sure this is a basic rule of friendship.

"Oh, we already have plans for how you'll repay us," Rory says. "That's why we're helping you."

The flicker of panic her words inspire must show on my face because Rory quickly says, "I'm just kidding, silly!"

I smile weakly. I'll figure this stuff out sooner or later. Let's hope it's sooner.

David lifts the cane above his head like a leader trying to convince a crowd to follow him into battle. In a deep voice he declares, "We will obtain everything on Tara's list. And let us hope we will not have to do anything embarrassing, degrading, or illegal along the way. Onward and upward!"

"Onward!" Leo says, lifting his fist in the air in solidarity.

"And upward!" the rest of us shout.

Outside the family room's large window, a branch creaks, leaves rustle, and the unmistakable *kreeee, kreeee* of two hawks in love fill the room. Only this time it sounds like they're laughing.

Like they're laughing at *us*.

Chapter Fifteen

By the time I let myself into the house, it's almost nine o'clock. I don't think I've ever been out this late alone. I hear Aunt Bethany in the kitchen on the phone, so I duck my head in to let her know I'm back. She waves for me to come in while she finishes up her call. I'm glad I stashed the cane and basket in the shed with the bike. It would be very hard to explain why I have them. I'm going to have to come up with a better hiding place than that, but for now it'll have to do.

Aunt Bethany hangs up the phone and opens her arms. "Tara!" she says, giving me a big hug. I have to admit, it's kind of nice. For a few seconds it allows me to forget the events of the day. "Did you have fun with Rory and her friends?" she asks.

"They're all really nice. Thank you for inviting them over yesterday."

She smiles. "That was your cousin's idea."

"It was?"

She nods.

I haven't seen Emily since that morning. I hope she doesn't think I'm avoiding her. I wonder if I should have invited her along for the pancakes. But if I had, she'd just be dragged into this whole mess, and having her a part of it is just too close to home. I remember all the clothes on my bed. "Oh, I meant to thank you for the clothes; you didn't have to do that."

"I hope they fit."

"I think they will." Although I'm kind of hoping that they won't. After wearing yellow and orange all day, I'm feeling especially fond of my drab browns and blacks.

She gestures for me to sit at the table. "I've been feeling guilty all day," she says. "There's something I didn't tell you."

I stiffen, unable to imagine what I'm about to hear. Whatever it is, it can't possibly compare with all the things I haven't told *her*.

"That e-mail from your teacher? Well, I read it. I didn't mean to, but your mother told me the school would be sending me your homework assignments, so I figured it was your first assignment."

"Don't worry about it," I tell her, relieved that it was something so minor in the scheme of things. "I don't mind. I know Mom told you what happened with the principal and everything."

"Okay, good. I just want you to know that respecting each other's privacy is big in our family."

Of course I'm the one who feels guilty now, for keeping so much from her when she's being so nice to me. And snooping around the rooms upstairs is pretty much the opposite of respecting their privacy. Guilt isn't an emotion I have much practice with. I've gotta say, I'm not a fan. I can't even look her in the eye, so I face the desk and ask, "Can I use the computer to write my teacher back? I didn't get a chance yet."

"If you don't mind me asking, are you going to take her up on her offer to write the essay?"

I nod, forcing myself to face her again.

She smiles. "I thought you might. Be sure to tell them the cabins are drafty and the juice is watered-down."

I laugh, feeling the knot of guilt in my stomach begin to unravel. My aunt is pretty cool.

She leaves me alone to write back. After I accept my teachers' offer, I type in the address for the Willow Falls website. There, on the home page, is my list with the heading *Any of this stuff sound familiar? Taking up room in your house or business? If so, we'd love to talk to you.* David even created a new e-mail address so no one would recognize his regular one. We'd gone back and forth on the wording. David thought writing "love" sounded too mushy, but Rory insisted it sounded friendlier than "we want to talk to you," which was David's initial idea.

It feels weird to have the list be so public like this. I have a flash of regret. What if Angelina gets mad? Is this cheating somehow? She said it didn't matter how I got the items (other than stealing them), so, hopefully, it's okay. Well, it's got to be okay because it's already up on the Internet. And in the morning, Leo will be posting it at the community center. And then we wait.

I'm halfway up the stairs when my phone beeps. I'm so surprised at the noise that I almost don't recognize it as the sound of a text arriving. My first text from someone other than my parents! At least, I assume it's not from Madagascar.

One name is flashing on the short list of contacts Amanda programmed in. *Bee Boy.* I smile. To Amanda, it seems, David will always be Bee Boy. I click on his name, nervous and excited to see what he has to say.

We got a response already!!! Call me!

Call him? I'm supposed to call a boy? Late at night? I thought texting was invented so people didn't actually have to talk to each other.

Emily's door is closed, but some shuffling sounds tell me she's not sleeping yet. I duck across the hall into the bathroom and close the door. Drat that Angelina for making me "be in the game," as she put it! I take a deep breath and click on his number.

He doesn't even ask who it is, just jumps right in. "Bucky Whitehead has the violin! Can you believe it?"

It takes me a second, then I say, "You mean that guy from the community center? The one who bought the first box of cookies?"

"That's him!"

"Wow! Even the second-oldest person in town goes online! My grandparents can't even find the power button!"

"Hey, when there's a chance to win a free spoon rest from the Creative Kids Pottery Studio, people can't pass that up!"

"Was that today's prize?"

"Nope. Today was a free haircut. My English teacher won it. Too bad he's totally bald!"

"You're making that up."

"Maybe. Anyway, I couldn't believe it when I got Bucky's e-mail. He says he can meet at the community center in the morning. What should I tell him? Should we ask him to wait till the afternoon, when school's over?"

"No, don't do that. I'll go by myself."

"Sure?"

"Yup."

"Okay."

And with that, we seem to have run out of things to say. I'm starting to feel weird about talking to him alone, anyway. Like, what if he and Rory *are* a couple? Not that this conversation is in the least bit romantic, but from what I've overheard at school, you don't talk on the phone with another girl's boyfriend.

"Well, I've got some homework," he says, much to my relief, "so just text me after and let me know how it went, okay?"

"Okay."

And that's it. My first phone call with a boy and it wasn't even too painful.

I still hear shuffling in Emily's room. I knock, not wanting to surprise her. She doesn't answer. I knock again, but still no response. So I slowly turn the knob and push the door open.

At first I think she's practicing her fencing moves, but then I notice the wireless headphones on her ears, the laptop on her desk playing *High School Musical*, and the fact that she's leaping and twisting in a way that I'm pretty sure you can't do with a sword in your hand. Or whatever it's called that fencers use. Emily's dancing! And she's really great!

I stand there for another full minute before she notices me. Her eyes widen and she yanks the headphones off, pulling out a few strands of long hair in the process. "Hey. I didn't see you there."

"I didn't mean to sneak up on you. I knocked, but you must not have heard."

"It's all right," she says. "I'm just glad my mother wasn't with you."

"Because it's so late?"

She shakes her head. "Mom doesn't like it when I dance."

"Huh? Why?"

"It's because of Grandma Emilia," Emily says, shutting down the laptop. "I don't know the whole story, but from what I've pieced together, she was a really great dancer and wanted to be a real actress, like on Broadway, and this famous producer was coming out to see her perform in a play here in town. But then my mom was born and Grandma dropped out of the play and stopped dancing and acting. Mom said that she always felt like her mother thought she'd made the wrong decision and was bitter about it. Our moms had to fend for themselves a lot. Once when I was little I said I wanted to be an actress and Mom freaked out. So now I just play around in my room at night sometimes. I know all the words to every one of Jake Harrison's movies!"

"Wow. That's impressive. And you're a really good dancer."

She blushes. "No one's seen me dance except for Rory."

I sit on the edge of the bed. "I didn't know any of that stuff about Grandma. All I knew is that she used to be an actress and that she loved hats. Mom never told me anything about what she was like as a mother." I guess I never asked, either. Thinking of Mom having to fend for herself as a little kid makes me really sad. And to think that now Emily can't even dance in her own house without upsetting Aunt Bethany is really sad, too. I climb off the bed and reach underneath. "C'mon, let's hang Jake's poster. I bet he'd like to see you dance."

. . . .

After Emily performs a special dance routine for me and Jake, and after she works on her math problem again under the covers, she finally goes to sleep. Once again, I wait until her breathing is even before I tiptoe out of bed and into the hall. This is getting to be a nightly routine. I'm so exhausted, but I can't pass up the chance to see if Uncle Roger had found a way to unlock the Collectibles Room.

The handle to the room turns easily, and I push the door open an inch. Hurrah!! Now all I need to do is get the comic from his lab and slip it back in the correct folder. I tiptoe down the hall, happy to hear the gentle snoring coming from the master bedroom. I open the door to the lab to find the desk light on again. Even though it's a waste of electricity, it does save me from trying to navigate all around the piles of junk in the dark. I've just crouched beside the magazine pile when I hear, "Hi, Tara! Couldn't resist the lure of all those wonderful products yet to be invented, eh?"

My heart leaps to my throat. Uncle Roger! I turn to find him standing across the room behind the airplane engine. Or the thing that *looks* like an airplane engine but could just as easily be a giant toaster. "I'm really sorry to barge in like this. I didn't, um, see you back there."

"Not a problem," he says, making his way over to me. "Stopped by for some late-night reading?"

"Yes, exactly." I grab the magazine on top. For a second, I debate trying to find the comic so I can slip it inside the magazine. But I don't have the nerve to try with him in the room. I hold up the first one I picked. "This one looks good."

"Can't go wrong with *Inventors Digest.* You'll come away very inspired." He smiles warmly at me. "I've gotta tell you, it makes me happy that someone in the family might follow in my footsteps. Making things for people that they don't even know they need, things that make their lives easier, or better, well, there's just nothing like it."

"Cool," I say. I'm way too tired to think of anything more intelligent. "Thanks. I better get to bed."

Uncle Roger follows me back out to the hall. He continues to expound on the joys of creating something out of nothing, while all I can do is stare in horror at the fact that I left the door to his Collectibles Room open an inch. If he so much as *glanced* in that direction, he'd see it. I begin slinking away down the hall, trying to block his line of sight. Finally he waves good night and goes back into his lab.

I breathe a sigh of relief and practically leap toward the door in my hurry to close it. I'll have to remember not to be fooled by Aunt Bethany's snoring again.

. . . .

Bucky Whitehead is in the same spot on the same couch as yesterday. Even if he hadn't been, it would have been easy to find him. There's something regal about him that makes him stand out. Even sitting down, it's clear that he's tall and straight.

And his hair is somehow whiter than the other old people's hair. Almost silver.

"Mr. Whitehead?" I say, approaching slowly. It's probably not a good idea to sneak up on someone that old. Instead of a newspaper, he had a blanket folded in his lap today. It's very warm out, so I hope the blanket doesn't mean he's sick or coming down with a cold.

"Call me Bucky," he says. "Mr. Whitehead always makes me look over my shoulder for dear old Dad." He gestures to the chair beside him. "Sit. I'm curious what would interest someone in this ol' gal." He pulls the violin out from under the blanket, which I now realize was protecting it. "She hasn't been played in thirty-five years."

After posting the list last night, we'd practiced what we were going to say if people contacted us. But I'm not sure it applies to an old violin that clearly has sentimental value, along with monetary value. Still, I can't give up now.

Swallowing hard, I say, "Well, I have a friend who collects things, like violins, and if you're not using it, I mean, if it hasn't been played in so long, maybe you'd consider selling it, or bartering for it?"

"A barter you say, eh? Interesting. What would we barter?"

"Well, um, we could mow your lawn, walk your dog, pick up dry cleaning, bring food from the market, any errands really."

"Don't got a lawn or a dog or dry cleaning," he says. "But I could use someone to fetch some things from the drug store, say, once a week for two months?"

"Yes, sure! We could do that."

"Then she's all yours," he says, and places it in my lap.

"That's it?" I ask, stunned. "That's all you want?"

He smiles. "Honey, at my age there ain't no use holding on to things. If I haven't played it in thirty-five years, what are the chances of me playing it now?"

I smile in return. "Thank you. This means a lot to me."

He pats my knee. "I can see that it does."

I sit with the violin on my lap, feeling the grain with my fingertips. It must have been a really special instrument in its day. I can't imagine that Angelina will make any money off it now, but who knows. I turn it over to make sure the silver plaque is there. It is.

"Oh, you might as well take this, too," he says, handing me the blanket. "I lost the case ages ago."

"Thanks!" I begin to wrap it up when I suddenly stop, my hand in midair. The blanket is old, very old, and has long since faded into a nondescript blend of brown, tan, gray, and black. But it clearly has a thick stripe around the border. "Does this look red to you?" I ask, pushing a corner of the blanket as close to Bucky's face as I can reach. "Here, around the border?"

He laughs. "Kid, I'm surprised I can still see the nose on my face in the mirror."

"Sorry," I say, and squint at it again. "I really think it's red. I think this is the blanket on our list!"

"You're kidding," Bucky says with delight. "How wonderful! Two for the price of none!"

I grin. "Let's make it four months of trips to the drug store!"

"Deal!" he says. He reaches into the pocket of his shirt and pulls out a twenty-dollar bill and a folded piece of paper. "Just a few items today. Shouldn't be too hard to find."

I finish wrapping up the violin and set it down next to me. "Will you hold on to this while I go to the store?"

"What if someone else comes in and wants to buy it?" he asks, eyes twinkling.

"Well, then I guess I get to keep whatever I'm picking up for you."

He laughs. It's an old man's laugh, punctuated with coughs, but it's a happy laugh. "Let's hope for your sake it doesn't come to that."

When I get outside the first thing I do is text David. It's hard to type with your thumbs! It takes a lot of backspacing and correcting before I get the hang of it.

Hi david! Tell everyone I got the violin! And guess what. I got the blanket, too! Full story later. We have to go to the drugstore for him for 4 months!

I hop on my bike and ride the few blocks to the store. It occurs to me about halfway there that since I'll only be here for the summer, the others are going to have to uphold the rest of my bargain with Bucky. If things end badly, well, they're really not going to be happy about that.

There's no bike rack near the drugstore so I have to leave it outside and take my chances that no one wants a kid's bike with a banana seat and a brand-new (used) basket. As I step into the store I notice my phone is flashing. David's reply must have come while I was riding.

Mazel Tov! (that means congratulations! You know, another Jewish thing, like the tomato?) Hiding in bathroom stall right now so phone doesn't get taken away. And we got another email! I went to the computer lab and checked. One of the Larrys at the music store says he knows where the wooden key is! Says he gives a lady piano lessons in her house and he's seen it there. Amanda says she's her neighbor! We'll call you at lunch with the deets.

I reply: I know what mazel tov means! I wasn't born under a rock, you know! You are a strange boy who spells out congratulations and not details. Hurrah on the key!

I have to admit, texting is fun. No wonder Rory's bummed about her phone. I pull Bucky's list out of my pocket and read it over for the first time. I quickly fold it back up again, aghast. I'm not one to embarrass easily, but come on! *Bunion cream? Nose-hair clippers? Easy-In, Easy-Out Fiber Suppositories?* I shudder. Getting old is not pretty. The only thing NOT embarrassing on the list is a Valentine's Day card. And even that's kind of embarrassing because I have to ask for one in the middle of June.

I refuse to ask for the first three, so it takes me forever to find them. I'm the only person under sixty browsing these sections. I make a mental note of their locations on the shelf, in case these are recurring purchases. It turns out they *do* have Valentine's Day cards in June, in the sliding drawers below the regular cards.

"No school today?" the clerk asks me as she pulls out a few cards for me to choose from.

"I'm just visiting Willow Falls," I explain as I drop one of the heart-shaped cards into my basket, along with a red envelope. "My school's already over for the year."

"What do you think of the town?"

"It's . . . different."

When she smiles, her olive-colored skin practically glows. "Yes, it is. My family just moved here about a year and a half ago. We're still getting used to it."

Mom's warning about risking a green tongue by talking to strangers is tucked far away in my mind as the woman tells me her favorite place to get donuts and that the shoe store has really good sales in the summer. Not that I'm in the market for donuts or shoes, but she's very easy to talk to. Since she seems to know a lot about the stores in town, I gather my nerve and say, "I was wondering . . . have you ever been inside that store at the end of the alley? Angelina's Sweet Repeats and Collectibles?" I hold my breath as I wait for her reply. I've got to know if it's only David who can't see inside, or everyone else, too.

Her face lights up again. "That's my aunt's store!"

My jaw drops. "Angelina is your aunt?"

She nods. "Technically she's a distant aunt. I've never been entirely clear on how we're related."

"Your *aunt*?" I repeat.

"Wait a second," the woman says, pursing her lips. "Did she say anything to you?"

"Say anything . . . like what?" I'm beginning to think this was a bad idea. I try to put on an innocent face, but she's not buying it.

"Argh! She promised me she wouldn't meddle in other people's lives. She drove poor Rory crazy last year!"

"You know Rory?" I ask, incredulous. Talk about your small towns!

"*You* know Rory?" she asks, equally surprised. "Wait, are we talking girl Rory or boy Rory?"

"There's a boy Rory?"

She nods. "Cute kid. Not the sharpest crayon in the box. Anyway, Rory and Auntie Angelina had a run-in and . . . well, I guess it's not really my story to tell."

I already knew about the drainpipe, but now I wonder what more important things Rory left out of the story. No wonder she thinks Leo and Amanda deserve their secrets. She has her own.

"I better get back with this," I say, swinging the basket, then wishing I hadn't when the boxes on the bottom jostle for attention. I really don't want Angelina's niece to think I have a nose hair problem. Or worse!

"Well, it was very nice to meet you," she says.

"You, too."

"Tell Rory that I said hi. My name's Lynn, by the way. Rory helped me get my first job in town, at the bookstore."

Why doesn't it surprise me that Rory did something nice for someone?

I pay for the four items (not even remotely looking the cashier in the eye) and leave the store. My tongue does not turn green.

On the way back, I stop at the diner to give Annie the money for the cookies. "You sold them all?" she asks, beaming.

I nod, placing the wrinkled dollars and assorted coins into her hands. I don't think it's necessary to tell her I bought the last three boxes myself.

"Well, color me impressed!" she says. "Thank you!"

"I had help," I assure her.

"It's strange," she says, looking over at the umbrella stand by the door, "not seeing that old cane in there. When I was little, my dad used to make up stories for me. You know, about the person who left it here. One week it would be a fugitive on the run from the law. The next it would be a traveling salesman who had just sold his last vacuum cleaner; the next week it was the tooth fairy." She gives me a sad smile, then grabs two menus and leads an elderly couple to a booth.

Now I feel bad about taking it. If I have any money left by the time Angelina puts the cane up for sale, I'm determined to buy it back for Annie.

• • • • • • • • • • •

After I give Bucky his goodies and collect the blanket and violin, I stop and check the bulletin board. Well, you can't miss our flyer. It was Amanda's idea to print it out on hot-pink paper, and I can see why. No one's going to look at the announcement for the next bingo tournament or the offer of a free house cleaning, while ours screams, *LOOK AT ME, OVER HERE!*

About halfway down the list, next to the line about the black leather-bound Bible with the book of Genesis repeated twice, someone scribbled the initials *WC*. Someone named WC has the Bible! I do a quick tally in my head. Cane, basket, violin, blanket, key, and now Bible! We're almost halfway done! In only two days! Maybe there really is nothing to worry about.

My phone rings, and Amanda's name pops up. A few women playing cards nearby give me the stink eye. I hurry back outside and tell her the good news about the blanket and the Bible.

"That's great!" she says. "I don't know anyone named WC, but my parents and Leo's are looking into the apple wine. They don't have any but they're asking some other relatives."

"What's the story with the key?"

"Mrs. Grayson, my neighbor, has it! At least according to one of the Larrys."

"He must hae been looking at it pretty close to read the tiny print on the side."

"It's strange, I know. This could be a total dead end, but we have to try."

We make arrangements to meet later and before we hang up, she asks, "What did Bucky ask you to get from the drug store?"

"Trust me, you don't want to know."

Chapter Sixteen

Mrs. Grayson is not home when we ring her bell after school. She's not home at dinnertime. Nor is she home when I ride all the way over there the next morning. For three days we wait for her to come home, and for more people to write to us. But none do. We've scanned the phone book and the school directory for someone with the initials *WC*. We had high hopes for William Cantor and Wanda Chesterton. But neither of them had any knowledge of a Bible with two books of Genesis. We even tried Rory's idea of knocking on random doors to use their bathroom, but all we discovered is that a lot of people — young or old — have *People* magazine in their bathrooms. But no knife, shawl, fish-shaped candlestick, purple bottle, trunk, or apple wine.

I'm getting a bit jittery with each passing day. To keep myself occupied when Emily's at school, I've been trying to write my essay. It's harder than I thought it would be. After deleting the first five beginnings, I decided I can't say I'm at the camp. It would be disrespectful to all the kids who actually *are* there. All Mrs. Schafer asked for is for me to say what I learned from my experiences, and I'm surprised to see I've learned a lot in the last week. So far I have the following:

I have learned that doing something for the wrong reason will likely backfire on you. It may also backfire on you if you do it for the right reason.

I have learned that when traveling by train always go first class if someone offers you a ticket.

But I have also learned that if you don't want to lose your money or your iPod while traveling on aforementioned train, glue it to your body.

Thanks to Google, I have learned that even though a hawk can fly over 250 miles a day, it's not fast enough to beat a train.

I have learned that some people love math because either the equation works or it doesn't. There is no gray area. If everything in life was clearly wrong or clearly right, I would be much happier.

I have learned that a piece of the Torah (which is like the Jewish bible) is inside a little box on some people's doorways and they kiss it to remind themselves of what it teaches.

I've learned that old men need a lot of upkeep.

I've learned that it's possible to eat from a different take-out restaurant every night and not get tired of it.

I've learned to make sure the lock is not turned before you close a door.

I have learned that there are some towns where special forces are at work, and you can't tell if you live in one of these towns until strange things start to happen to you.

I've learned that if you hide a violin in a storage shed and don't wrap it tight enough, a mouse might make a home inside it and scare you half to death when you find it.

I've learned that Sunshine Kid cookies do *not* taste good. Even with ketchup.

I've learned that if you tell an Australian person that they talk funny, their accent will get even stronger and they'll get all agro on you and start a furphy that you're really a spy sent to town to report back to your home planet.

I'm not sure what I have so far qualifies as an essay yet, but I save it under TARA'S ESSAY anyway. And then, since the whole family uses this computer, I password-protect it.

Finally, on Friday morning, Amanda texts me from the school bus that Mrs. Grayson got home late the night before. I'm supposed to meet them at Amanda's house at noon, since school is a half day because of final exams. I reply that I'll be there and then run upstairs to change out of my pajamas. Today I finally feel ready to wear one of the outfits Aunt Bethany bought me. I wondered during the week if she was going to say something about me not wearing any of them, but she never did. No way could my mom have held off that long. I think Mom would be pleased that I'm picking up on the differences between the sisters. It's like my own little sociological research project. I choose a pink shirt and matching pink shorts. I feel like a strawberry marshmallow.

Ray finds me in the backyard, inspecting my bike tires. "Howdy there, partner. I see you are all up in the pink today. Very sharp."

I look up from the bike. "Why are you talking like that?"

"Like what?"

"Even weirder than usual."

He says each word very slowly and drawn out. "I am trying out for a television commercial and they want an all-American-boy type. So I am attempting to talk like one. How am I doing now?"

"You sound like a robot."

"Yes, but an *American* robot?"

"I guess it could be an American robot," I admit. "So you're an actor, too? Besides a personal assistant and a glassblower?"

"What I really want to do is direct," he says with a wink. Then he points to the front tire. "Got a hole there. Bet Roger's got a patch up in the lab. Want me to check?"

I jump up. "No, I'll go." This is my chance! I'd been afraid to go in there the past few days after running into my uncle. But now I have a reason. I take the steps two at a time, although I know no one else is home.

For one crazy second, the magazine pile appears to have disappeared. In its place is a lumpy green Jell-O-like substance slowly oozing onto the rug. I think it actually *is* Jell-O. Then I see the pile about four feet to the left.

One by one, I thrust the dusty magazines aside. I should have paid more attention to the covers, because they all look the same! I have to shake each one out until finally my *Fantastic Four* reveals itself. To be on the safe side, I stick it back inside the *Inventors Digest* and restack the pile. I turn to go as Ray steps into the room.

"Did you find it?" he asks.

"Find what?" I ask, a little too guiltily.

He glances down at the magazine in my hand. Is it too thick? Is it obvious something is stuck inside it?

"Did you find the patch," he says, enunciating each word. "For your tire."

"No. Robot. Ray. I. Did. Not. Find. It. Yet."

He laughs. "I didn't sound like that."

"You kinda did."

"I think the patch is in here," he says, poking through a big box on the desk. "By the way, totally bonza of you to take an interest in your uncle's work. He's happier than a clam at high tide."

"I'm just gonna go put this in my room," I tell him, not meeting Ray's eyes as I hurry past him. I already feel guilty enough about everything; Ray's "clam" comment just makes it worse. Now I'm really going to have to read one of these magazines.

If Ray hadn't come upstairs, I'd be able to replace the comic in its rightful home right now. As is, I can't take the chance. He always seems to turn up exactly when I don't want him to. I hide the magazine with the comic inside in my suitcase and slide it back under the bed. Then, with a quick kiss to Jake, I rejoin Ray in the lab.

"Found it," he announces, holding up a small plastic bag with a square piece of rubber inside.

Five minutes later I'm munching on an apple while he fixes the hole in my bike. "I could get used to this," I tell him, tilting my face toward the sun.

"Just doing my job," he says cheerily, stretching the tire back around the rim. "All done. You gonna ride or do you want it back in the shed?"

"I'll ride it," I say, hurrying over. I close the shed door as nonchalantly as possible. The four objects we found so far from Angelina's list are all the way in the back in a cardboard box. Rory had offered to store them for me, but I still feel like it should be my responsibility.

I toss the apple core in the bike basket along with a bottle of water and climb on. Amanda's house is a few miles away, and I have just enough time to make it. "Thanks for your help."

"Have a fun arvo with your mates."

"Okay," I say, hoping an arvo isn't a bad thing.

I'm about to start peddling when he says, "Hold up a sec."

I peer around at the back wheel. "What, is my tire still flat?"

He shakes his head. "Nope. Just wanted to ask if you knew anything about a cane, a violin, a blanket, and a basket in a box in the shed?"

I wobble on the bike. Ray reaches out and grabs a handlebar to steady it. When I don't answer due to my throat suddenly closing up, he continues. "Because — funny thing — someone in town seems to be looking for all that stuff. And a bunch more, too. Saw it online."

I try to talk, but it comes out more like a squeak.

"If you pinched those things," he says, sounding more serious than I've ever heard him, "someone out there's gonna spit the dummy."

"I didn't pinch them," I insist, finding my voice. "How did you find them?"

"I was looking around in there yesterday for some pieces of plaster your uncle needed. Stumbled on the box and recognized the stuff from the list on the town website."

"*You* go on the town's website?"

"Won a free pound of bagels last week."

"Why would you think the stuff in the box was mine?"

"Wasn't hard to nut out. In the year I've been here, you're the only person to go near that shed."

My brain spins as I try to figure out how much I can tell him. This secret-keeping business is very confusing. Finally I say, "My friends and I are the ones trying to find the things on that list. It's a real job; like, we're getting paid and everything. Nothing shady, I promise."

"Then what's with the hiding?"

I realize I'm going to have to be even more forthcoming if I expect him to drop this. "I don't want my aunt and uncle to know that I need the money. They'd offer to give it to me, and I wouldn't feel right."

"I see," he says, rubbing his chin. "Well, that sounds commendable. I guess I can help, then."

"Help?" I'm not sure I like the sound of that.

"I happen to know the whereabouts of one of the things on the list."

"You do? Which one?"

"What do I get if I tell you?" he teases.

"Well, I can help you practice for your commercial."

"Okay," he agrees. "It's the knife. But I don't think the dude who's got it is gonna part with it."

"Why not?"

"Well, for starters, last night at the pub he said, 'No way am I handing over this knife to no one. Somebody wants this knife, they're gonna have to take it over my dead body.'"

My eyes widen. "He said that?"

He shakes his head. "No. But he did say it would take three hundred bucks."

I sigh. "That's just as bad."

"He's seriously attached to it. I've seen him pick his teeth with it after wings, then polish it clean."

"He sounds like a great guy."

"You'll really like him. A people person, just like you." He grins. It's hard to stay frustrated with Ray when he flashes that smile.

I check my phone to see what time it is. "I'm going to be late now to meet everyone. Can you drive me across town to Amanda's?"

"I can do that."

"Promise me you won't embarrass me in any way."

"That I can't do."

• • • • • • • • • • •

The others are waiting on the curb outside Amanda's house when we pull up in Ray's beat-up old Ford. We'd practiced his lines for the commercial on the way and he's getting a tiny bit better. He gets out of the car and salutes the group. Then in his best American accent he says, "Hello there, young people of America. Is it not a lovely day?"

"Who's the robot that looks like Ray?" David asks.

I figure I might as well jump right in, so I say, "Ray knows we're the ones who posted the list."

Everyone exchanges worried glances.

Ray makes the locking-mouth-throwing-away-key gesture.

I continue. "The good thing is that he knows where we can find the knife."

The others jump up from the curb. Amanda's and Leo's blackboards both hit them on their chins. They're so used to it they don't even flinch.

Ray shakes his head. "I'm telling you, Big Joe isn't going to give it up for less than three hundred bucks."

"We haven't failed yet," Rory says confidently.

"Let's try to get the key first," Amanda says. "Then we'll worry about the knife."

We turn toward the door, with Ray walking right along with us. I stop. "Um, Ray?"

"Yeah?"

"You're waiting in the car."

"Why? I can be very charming. Ladies love the accent." He winks at Amanda, who blushes.

I roll my eyes. "We shouldn't overwhelm Mrs. Grayson with a lot of people."

Ray grumbles, but turns back around. The rest of us go on, and Amanda rings the bell. Mrs. Grayson opens the door in a red flannel shirt and jeans. Her graying hair peeks out from underneath a sun hat.

"Amanda and Leo! Lovely to see you. And hello, Amanda's other friends."

Amanda and Leo give her a hug, and then Amanda introduces me, Rory, and David.

"Nice to meet you all," she says. "What can I do for you? Seems like you're a little old to be selling cookies." She laughs.

"Way too old," Rory agrees.

"Definitely," David and I say at the same time.

"Can we come in for a minute?" Amanda asks. "We wanted to talk to you about something."

"Sure." Mrs. Grayson backs up and holds the door open for us. We file into the front hall and wait for Amanda to ask for the key. We decided she would be our best chance.

"Have you gone onto the Willow Falls website lately?" Amanda asks.

Mrs. Grayson shakes her head. "I've been away. Why, did I miss something? Or wait, did I win something? I've been eying that five-dollar gift certificate to the bowling alley!"

We laugh. Amanda shakes her head. "Sorry, you didn't win anything this week. But, well, we posted this list up there of a bunch of stuff we're looking for around town, and you might have one of the things on the list. A wooden key? With the words *Made in Willow Falls 1974* carved in it?"

She smiles. "I do indeed have that key. And someone wants it?"

We nod.

"But why? I'm sure it's not worth anything."

"A collector we know is looking for a whole bunch of things from town," I tell her. "We'd be willing to pay you, or run errands, mow your lawn, anything you need."

"That's not necessary," she says. "You can have the key. Perhaps I'll think of something I need later."

"Are you sure we can take it?" Amanda asks.

Mrs. Grayson smiles again. "If you think you can carry it."

We exchange puzzled glances.

"Is it really fragile?" Rory asks. "Maybe we should put it in a box?"

I'm thinking she's probably right, that it's pretty old. I mean, who makes keys out of wood anymore?

"Why don't you have a look for yourselves," Mrs. Grayson says, pointing us toward a room at the end of the hall.

The first thing I see when we enter the room is a piano. The only other things in the room are a couch and coffee table. I figured the key would be in a bowl or on a key chain or something, but all the surfaces are bare. "It's in here?" I ask her, confused.

"Um, Tara?" David grabs my sleeve and points behind me.

And there, on the wall, hangs the world's biggest key.

Seriously. The key is so big the only door it could possibly open would be a castle in Giant Land. It must be four feet long!

We line up and stare at it.

"There must be some mistake," Rory says. "That can't be it, can it?"

We move closer. It says all the right words down the side.

"That's it, all right," Leo says.

"You're sure you want to part with it?" Amanda asks. "There's gonna be a big empty space on the wall."

"That's okay," Mrs. Grayson says. "I wound up with it by default anyway; it was never really mine. Out of curiosity, what else is on the list?"

None of the other people had asked us this. I don't see the harm, though. I fish around in my pockets while the boys climb on the piano bench so they can work on getting the key down.

"Nice outfit, by the way," Rory says to me. "Very colorful."

"Aunt Bethany got it for me. I feel like I'm four years old." I find the list and hand it over.

Rory, Amanda, and I follow Mrs. Grayson over to the couch, where she sits down with the list. A minute later, she abruptly stands up and leaves the room, leaving the list open on the coffee table.

"What just happened?" Rory whispers.

"Maybe we shouldn't take the key," Amanda says, worriedly. "Maybe it means more to her than she let on."

"Um, kinda heavy here?" Leo calls out.

We look over to find Leo holding the full weight of the key. "Sorry," David says, hurrying to lift the other end off the nail. "Got distracted."

They climb down from the bench and stand there, holding it awkwardly. "So what should we do?" Leo asks.

No one has an answer. Finally Mrs. Grayson returns. Instead of being upset, she looks almost, well, *relieved*. Like some burden has been lifted.

"Is everything all right?" Amanda asks. "We can leave the key."

Mrs. Grayson shakes her head. "I want you to have it. And this, too." She hands Amanda a long, skinny box. I know instantly from sorting through Mom's jewelry drawer that it's the kind of box a necklace fits in. Amanda opens the box and lifts out a long strand of pearls. They shimmer in the light.

"You'll note the gold clasp," Mrs. Grayson says. "I believe it's the necklace you're looking for."

"This is yours?" Amanda asks incredulously.

"It belonged to my sister, Francis. She used to be the dance teacher in town many, many years ago. She'd wear that necklace for her performances."

Amanda lays the pearls back in the box and tries to give them back. "We can't take your sister's pearls."

"Yes, you can," Mrs. Grayson says. "They aren't real, if that makes it any easier. Only the clasp is."

The two of them argue back and forth. My breath starts coming faster. How can Angelina ask people to part with their things like this? Just so she can make money reselling them? It's cruel. Did she get all the things on her shelves this way, or did people come in and drop them off? I think it's time for another visit.

While I've been seething, Mrs. Grayson has somehow convinced Amanda to take the key and the necklace, and Rory has told Mrs. Grayson about the knife.

"I'd like to tag along," Mrs. Grayson says as everyone moves out of the room. "That can be the favor you do for me."

Amanda nods in agreement.

"Wait," I say, hurrying after them. "Maybe we shouldn't even try for the knife. Maybe this whole thing isn't a good idea."

But David and Leo are already lugging the key out the door to Ray's car. Amanda and Mrs. Grayson chat as they head toward the garage. No one is listening to me. I literally stomp my foot in frustration.

Rory hangs back and pulls me aside, into Mrs. Grayson's kitchen. I can't help noticing that only one place at the table is set.

"Tara, remember what I said about things with Angelina seeming like they don't make sense? And that you have to just do your best to trust her?"

"Yes, but —"

"I need you to remember that. Amanda and Leo tried to help me last year, and I'm trying to help you."

I feel myself calming down. I'm lucky to have someone like Rory, who cares so much. If I had to do all this alone, I never, ever would have made it. "Okay, you're right. I'll try."

She squeezes my arm. "That's the spirit! Now let's go get some strange guy to give up his favorite knife!"

When we get outside, Mrs. Grayson has already backed out of the garage. I'm surprised to see that her car is a bright orange Jaguar. David and Rory yell, "Shotgun!" and race each other over to it. Ray strides across the lawn toward me. "Hang on a second; how come she gets to go on the next one when I had to stay out here?" He gestures with his thumb at Mrs. Grayson.

Leo answers. "She's got a cooler car."

I nod. "Can't argue with that."

Ray grumbles all the way back to his car. The key takes up his whole backseat, so Amanda and Leo have to go with Mrs. Grayson, too. We lead the way to Big Joe's, and to his credit, Ray is very good at making sure Mrs. Grayson keeps up. We drive past Apple Grove and the mall, to a section of town I haven't seen before. It's more rural here, with some corn and some barns, and the houses are farther apart.

We pull up in front of a small brown house. Piles of wood and half-finished wood carvings of deer and bears fill the lawn. The big NO TRESPASSING sign actually lights up. I peer out the window, not anxious to get out. "This is the place, huh?"

"Yup."

A guy in overalls and boots, who looks to be around Ray's age, comes out of the house, takes one look at the two cars idling in front, goes back inside, and slams the door.

"Well, he seemed nice," I say.

"Oh, yeah," Ray says. "Big Joe's a real sweetheart. London to a brick, this isn't going to go well."

While we sit there debating what to do, Mrs. Grayson gets out of her car and starts up the walk. Ray quickly opens his door and calls out for her to go back.

"It's all right," she says. "I know what I'm doing. You guys stay put."

"No disrespect, ma'am," Ray says, "but —"

"I'll be fine, young man, don't worry." She turns away and marches up the porch steps.

"See? The accent gets them every time," Ray says.

"Uh-huh."

We watch as she opens the screen door and knocks. The front door opens right away, and I can see Big Joe filling the doorway, arms crossed. I can't hear what they're saying but I'm getting nervous. Why are we sitting here? I reach for my phone and call Rory.

"Should we go up there?" I ask when she picks up.

"Mrs. Grayson made us promise to stay in the car. She said, and I quote, 'I got this one.'"

"Okay, then, I guess." I hang up and tell Ray what Rory told me.

"She gets thirty more seconds," he says, "then I'm going out there."

Big Joe disappears into the house. Mrs. Grayson looks very small standing alone on the porch. A few seconds later he returns to the door and hands her something. She couldn't possibly have gotten him to give her the knife, could she? Just like that?

She turns to go, waving good-bye. He waves back and quickly shuts the door again. We all pile out of the cars to meet her. She gives us the thumbs-up, and holds out a knife with a long handle, safely tucked inside a red sheath.

"I'll be gobsmacked!" Ray exclaims. "How did you do it?"

She smiles. "A little trick I like to call 'The Remember Game.'"

"The remember game?" I repeat.

She nods. "As in, remember when I used to be your kindergarten teacher? No one turns down their kindergarten teacher."

We laugh. "Sneaky!" Amanda says, clearly impressed. "Did you know it was him all along?"

Mrs. Grayson nods. "The knife used to be an old keepsake of his father's. He and I worked together at different community events before he passed on a few years back. I admit I was curious to see how little Joey turned out."

"Not so little!" I say.

"And he didn't even want any money for it?" Rory asks.

She shakes her head. "And he's coming for supper on Sunday."

Amanda hugs her. "You're incredible!"

"Nah. You live in this town long enough, you know things. Like the Bible you're looking for? It doesn't belong to anyone named WC. Those letters stand for Willow's Church."

"D'oh!" David says, smacking his forehead. "Anything else?"

Mrs. Grayson turns to Amanda and Leo. "Your great-grandparents' wine. The last bottle is in the historical society. All those school trips and you guys still didn't know that. Tsk, tsk."

Amanda and Leo groan, but the rest of us are cheering. "That just leaves four more," I announce. "The shawl, the trunk, the purple bottle, and the candlestick holder."

"Sorry," Mrs. Grayson says, "can't help you with those." Then, quick as a flash, she tosses the knife to me! The others yelp as I instinctively reach for it. Some deep-seated survival instinct kicks in and tells me I don't actually *want* to catch a knife with my bare hands, so I pull them back at the last second and let it fall onto the street. It lands, not with a *clank* or a *thud*, but with barely a *plop*.

"Oops," Mrs. Grayson says, "did I forget to tell you it's a plastic knife?"

Chapter Seventeen

We all wave good-bye to Mrs. Grayson from the sidewalk in front of the historical society. I'm still a bit shaken by the knife-throwing incident, but am grateful to her for all her help. Ray has taken off, too, with the promise to keep the key and knife in his own room.

Amanda and Leo huddle a few feet away with their blackboards.

"Oh, right," David says, "they don't like going in there for some reason."

"Allergies!" Leo yells out without turning around.

"Creepy stuffed raccoon!" Amanda adds.

"We'll go in and ask about the wine," Rory says. "C'mon, Tara." She's about to push open the door, when Leo says, "Don't bother, they're closed Fridays."

Rory tries the door. "You're right. How did you know that?" She looks all around the door. "It doesn't say it anywhere."

"The only way in is around back," Amanda says.

Rory, David, and I exchange a look, but follow the two of them around the back of the building. Amanda points to a window about four feet off the ground. "There."

I stare at the window. "You're talking about breaking in? Why can't we just wait until they're open?"

"Trust us," Amanda says. "It's easier this way."

"But Angelina told me I can't steal anything." As soon as the words are out of my mouth I realize I slipped up by saying her name. Amanda and I whirl around to look for David. Fortunately he's a few yards away, trying to find something to stand on to reach the window.

"I don't think he heard," I whisper. "But seriously, we can't steal it."

"I know," Amanda says. "It wouldn't be stealing. You're allowed to take something back that belongs to your family."

"Are you sure? How do you know?"

"There's a lot of stuff in there from my relatives, and Leo's, too. We looked into it once. All we'll need to do is leave a note saying we're taking it back."

"But then whoever runs the place will know you broke in."

"That's okay," she assures me. "They won't be too surprised."

The next thing I know, we're all climbing on an old milk crate and squeezing through a half-opened window. We land behind the counter. Leo immediately starts sneezing and we all shush him except Amanda, who just throws him an exasperated look. "Stay low," she whispers, crawling out into the main room. We try our best not to bump into things as we crawl behind her. "Anyone see it?" she asks.

We each face a different direction and scan the room. There are a lot of places for a wine bottle to hide among the shelves of old vases and pictures and jars. I look closer at the jars in the hopes that one might be small and purple, but no luck there. I'm still feeling uneasy about the whole breaking-in thing — it's bringing back bad goat memories.

"I found it!" David calls out, forgetting to whisper.

We all scramble over to him. He points to the top of the tallest bookshelf in the place. The wine bottle is on the top shelf, practically touching the ceiling.

"Figures," Leo mumbles.

All the chairs and tables look too breakable to withstand our weight, and the bookshelf is definitely too fragile. Amanda slips off her sneakers. Without a word, Leo links his hands together. Amanda steps onto them, placing one hand on Leo's head for balance. He lifts her high enough to grab the bottle. As she's being lowered down, there's a point where she and Leo are pretty much hugging so that she doesn't fall. They both turn bright red.

Amanda reaches the floor and holds the bottle up in victory. The white label is almost completely faded except for ELLERBY-FITZPATRICK BREWERS, and the outline of two apples. Amanda and Leo head off to find some paper behind the counter so they can write the note.

"Hey, look at this," David says. He's standing in front of a large map of the town on the wall. It must be a hundred years old. He points to a spot near the top. Rows of tiny trees fill the area. The words *APPLE GROVE* are printed below it.

Rory traces the area with her finger. "My dad used to tell me about how even though it was only half that size by his day, the whole town used to gather there on weekends."

"I think it's really great that Amanda and Leo are starting it back up again," David says. "I like going there."

I watch David's profile while he talks and looks at the map. I like that he says whatever he feels. He turns slightly and sees me watching him. He smiles and I quickly pick up whatever's closest on the shelf as though that's what I was doing all along.

"You're pretty brave," he says.

"Me?" I ask. "Why?"

He points at my hands. "To hold some old guy's teeth."

I look down and see that I am, in fact, holding a set of teeth. I quickly toss them back onto the shelf. Rory giggles. I'm wiping my hands on my shorts when the front door opens and we all freeze. We watch in horror as a short, wide woman with white hair walks in with a set of keys dangling from her wrist. She takes in the scene before her. She looks at Amanda and Leo and their blackboards. Then up at the open window. Then at me, then Rory, then David, where her gaze lingers a second longer than on the rest of us. I sneak a peek at David's reaction, but he's just staring at the duck-shaped birthmark.

Angelina works *here*, too?

Are any of us going to acknowledge knowing her? Is she going to acknowledge knowing *us*? I'm certainly not going to be the first to speak. At least I understand now why Amanda and Leo weren't that worried about breaking in. Their relationship with Angelina — whatever it is — seems a lot deeper than the rest of ours.

Angelina walks over to the counter and places her large black pocketbook on top of it. "We're closed on Fridays," she says firmly.

Amanda holds up the wine bottle in one hand, and gives Angelina the note with the other. Without so much as a glance, Angelina tosses it on the counter and repeats, "We're closed on Fridays."

"We were just leaving," Rory assures her. But before any of us can move, the door opens again. This time it's a very pregnant woman. She's holding something wrapped up in a few layers of tissue paper. She places it on the counter in front of Angelina.

"Sorry to interrupt," she says. "But I was hoping you might have a use for this? I tried to bring it to the secondhand store in the alley, but it was closed down."

I have to force myself not to look at Rory or Amanda and Leo.

"See," David says triumphantly.

"Weren't you all just leaving?" Angelina asks, her voice raised.

The woman unwraps the object and places it on the counter. The five of us gasp. It's the candlestick holder in the shape of a fish!

"I bought this at a garage sale last year," she says. "I don't know if it counts as *historical*, but maybe there's a place for it here?"

"How much you looking for?" Angelina asks, barely glancing down at it.

"Fifty dollars?"

"I'll give you twenty," Angelina says.

I hurry over to the woman's side. "I'll give you twenty-five!"

The woman looks at me in confusion. "You want to buy this?"

I nod. "I, um, collect them?"

"You collect fish-shaped candlestick holders?"

David steps in. "You wouldn't believe some of the things people collect. They have a set of fake teeth here. Like, the real ones, not plastic ones with fangs."

"Thirty," Angelina offers.

She's driving up the price on me! I want to glare at her, but I don't dare.

"Thirty-five," I say.

Angelina waves it away. "Fine, take it."

I reach into my sock for the money.

"I was really hoping for fifty," the woman says. "My husband's overseas and with the baby coming, well, it's a little tough."

Fifty dollars would be a really big chunk to give away. "Um, is there something we could maybe do for you, to make up the difference? Like, carry your groceries? Or anything else you can't do because of . . ." I trail off. It doesn't seem polite to say *because of your huge belly*. But she gets the drift.

"Well, there are a few things around the house I could use help with. But I don't know you." She turns to Angelina. "Do you know these kids? Can you vouch for them?"

Angelina rolls her eyes. "I'll vouch."

"All right." The woman takes a wrinkled receipt out of her pocketbook and hands it to me with a pen. "My name's Carolyn. I live in the town house around the corner. If you write your phone number on there, I'll call you to set something up."

I write my number, then hand her the card and the thirty-five dollars. She leaves the candlestick on the counter. Rory swiftly picks it up and wraps it in the paper.

"Um, thanks for your help," David says to Angelina.

All she says in response? “We’re closed on Fridays.”

David gives her a strange look. The rest of us grab various parts of him and drag him toward the door. “That was nice of her to vouch for us,” he says as we push him onto the sidewalk. “I mean, after we broke in and all.”

No one replies.

“Did you guys see her cheek? She should get that thing removed. It looks like a duck!”

At that, we all crack up. Yup, David calls it like he sees it. At least Angelina didn’t seem angry that the others are obviously helping me find the things on her list. That’s one less thing to worry about.

I call Ray to come pick us up. He’s very surprised to see the candlestick holder. From the backseat Rory says, “Hey, Ray, thanks for protecting us from Big Joe and his plastic knife before.”

“Hey,” Ray says, “I know I’m no Jake Harrison, the swashbuckling hero of all teendom, but I don’t mess around when lives are at stake.”

“Oh, Rory knows you’re no Jake!” David says. “Right, Rory?”

“No comment,” she replies.

I turn around from the front seat. “Wait, do you like Jake Harrison, or don’t you?”

The others laugh. Even Ray. “We’re just friends,” Rory says.

My eyes pop out of my head. “Friends? Like, you *know* him?”

“We all do,” Amanda says.

“I don’t,” David says. I can’t tell, but he almost sounds a little jealous.

"How do you know him?" I ask, breathless. "Are you guys kidding me?"

"Emily didn't tell you?" Rory asks. "Jake filmed *Playing It Cool* here last year."

My jaw falls open. "Are you for real? The one that's opening in August?" How could Emily have left that out?

"They filmed it at our school," Rory says. "We got to be extras in the movie."

"Jake and Rory had a very special relationship," Leo says, elbowing her.

Rory elbows him back. "Yeah, one based on him laughing at me all the time."

"Rory," Amanda says, "a movie star doesn't e-mail you every week because he likes laughing at you."

Rory blushes.

I can't believe it! Rory and Jake Harrison! I don't know which is crazier, Angelina's now-you-see-it-now-you-don't collectibles store, or *this* news!

David has to do some bar mitzvah practicing and the others have to study for their last final exams next week, so we call it a day and make a plan to go over to the church tomorrow morning.

Ray drops me back at the house, then goes off to practice his American accent with his mates down at the pub. Aunt Bethany and Uncle Roger are still out. Emily is going to be home in a few minutes, but she always goes straight into the kitchen for a snack first. That will give me a solid ten minutes to return the comic before I need to worry about her coming in.

I grab the comic from my suitcase and run down the hall. My ears are locked in on even the smallest sound. I push open the Collectibles Room and make a beeline for the comics. I drop *The Fantastic Four* into one of the folders and push the bin back on the shelf. Twenty seconds later I'm back in the bedroom. Thirty seconds after that, Emily walks in and catches me dancing around the room.

"At least someone's in a good mood," she says, tossing her book bag on the bed. It falls onto the floor and she steps right over it.

"What's wrong with you?" I ask, still too euphoric to stop smiling.

"I got a ninety-nine on my math final," she says, a hollow sound to her voice.

"That's great!"

She glares at me. "I missed a really easy question, which makes it even worse."

"You're upset because you got a ninety-nine?"

She sighs. "I wouldn't expect you to understand. No offense."

"None taken." Sort of. "Hey, not to change the subject, but why didn't you tell me Jake Harrison made a movie in Willow Falls? And about him and Rory?"

"Oh, I didn't? Yeah, he filmed a movie here and he and Rory are friends."

"Yeah, thanks, got that now."

She kicks her book bag and says, "Want to go for a walk? I'm not really allowed to wander by myself yet."

"Sure," I reply, surprised. Every other day after school she's had one activity or another. We haven't actually left the house together since my arrival.

"Where do you want to go?" I ask as we head out the front door.

"Let's just walk through the neighborhood," she says.

We walk for a while through the streets, mostly in areas I haven't explored on the bike before. Emily is quiet for most of the time but perks up when we turn into an area with some smaller houses. She chatters about school and the other Emilys, and about how much fun the beach will be, and how she's going to miss Ray when his visa's up and he goes back to Australia at the end of the summer. She slows down as we approach a house with a teenage boy washing a dog out front. She keeps glancing over at him shyly, while pretending not to be. The boy is a bit plump, with a baseball cap pushed half over his eyes. The dog shakes some water off his coat and the boy tilts his head back to avoid being splashed in the face. He catches sight of us.

Emily tries to speed up, but he's already calling out to her. "Hey," he says, "aren't you the kid who lives in that big house? The one who always orders two large pizzas with extra cheese on 'em?"

She nods.

"Thought so," he says. "I never forget the good tippers."

She smiles and grabs me. "Okay, bye!" she calls out as she hurries me past the house.

"See ya," he replies, going back to his dog washing.

Clearly we didn't just wander onto this street by accident. My little cousin knew exactly where she was headed. When we're out of earshot I say, "He's a little old for you, don't you think?"

"It's not like that," she says, turning around to make sure he definitely can't hear us. "He's the head of the high school math team."

I can't help laughing. "You have a math crush?"

She sighs. "I guess so. Don't tell Mom, though. She'll never let me pay for the pizza again."

"My lips are sealed." Then I realize something. "Hey, is that why you wouldn't let me wait for the pizza guy with you?"

She blushes and nods. "Sorry about that."

My phone rings as I tell her not to worry about it. I pull it out of my pocket. It's David calling. My heart speeds up a little and I glance at Emily. She's smiling. "You should answer that."

Now it's my turn to blush as I walk a few steps away.

"A lady wrote about the little purple bottle!" David tells me without even a hello. "She says she's not a hundred percent sure it's the one we're looking for, though."

"Is it two ounces? Does it have a silver stopper?"

"She didn't say. But she told me we can go over there to check it out."

"Great. When?"

"That's the thing," he says, "she's leaving later tonight on vacation for a week! So we need to get there in the next hour or so."

"Where does she live?"

He rustles some papers, then says, "12 Tanglewood Trail. It's about a half mile from our houses. I can't leave, though. I have a live webcam session with the rabbi in a few minutes."

"I'll take this one," I tell him.

"You're sure?" he says.

"Yup. Good luck with the rabbi."

"Okay, good luck to you, too. Let me know how it goes."

We hang up. Emily grins and says, "A little old for you, don't you think?"

"No, he's exactly my —" I catch myself before I get myself in any deeper. Emily is sneaky indeed.

"So you DO like him!"

"I do not!" I say, doing a quick check that David isn't still on the other end.

"You do!"

"I don't, but it doesn't really matter because he likes Rory."

"Maybe he used to," she admits. "But that was before Jake. Trust me, David and Rory are just good friends."

Desperate to talk about something else, I ask if she knows where Tanglewood Trail is. She points down the street. "It's about four blocks that way. Why?"

"David asked me to pick something up for him."

"Okay," she says. "Let me text Mom and tell her we'll be back a little late."

A response arrives half a block later. "Mom says we're having pizza again tonight, so let's not take too long, okay? She doesn't tip as well as me. I don't want him not to come back!"

As we speed walk through the neighborhood, I ask Emily if she knows what the story is with David's father. I'm not used to thinking about other people's lives. But recently, they've become a lot harder to ignore.

She shakes her head. "I don't know too much. I was only in

first grade when the Goldbergs moved here, so I didn't really catch too much of what went on. I think maybe he got really sick or something."

"Did he . . . is he . . ."

"I think he's alive," she says. "But maybe in some special place? Like a hospital or something? I really don't know."

I feel a rush of sympathy for David. What must that be like for him? I wonder if he was ever going to tell me.

Emily stops walking. "Here we are. Tanglewood Trail."

"Already?"

She nods. We walk a few houses down until I find number 12. I'm tempted to ask Emily to wait outside, but it's not really our neighborhood anymore and she's still only eleven. "When we get in there, just act cool, okay? Let me do all the talking."

"Aye, aye, Captain," she replies, saluting me.

I push open the small white gate in front of the walkway and lead her up to the front door. The bushes and flowers on either side of the door are kept up really nice. The screen door is closed, but the front door is wide open. I'm not sure what to do. "Knock, knock!" Emily says loudly.

I shush her, but a woman's voice inside calls out, "Come on in. I'm just zipping up my suitcase."

I go first, and when I'm sure everything's okay, I motion for Emily to follow. We find the woman sitting on the floor on top of a blue hardback suitcase. She's putting all her weight on it in an attempt to get the zipper to shut.

"Um, we're here about the glass bottle?" I ask.

“Here, give me a hand, will ya?” she scoots over and lets go of the zipper. “I’ll push, you zip.”

I do as she says, and the suitcase closes.

“Thanks,” she says, blowing a piece of her long dark hair away from her face. She’s very pretty, probably around my parents’ age. The sight of oversized LEGOs and picture books scattered on the floor tells me there are little kids around somewhere. “So you’re looking for the purple bottle?”

“Yes. My friend said you had it?”

She stands up and grabs a little white bag from the table. “Here,” she says, handing it to me. “I’m not sure it’s the exact one you’re looking for, but it seemed to fit the description.”

I carefully pull the bottle out of the bag. It fits in the palm of my hand. I mentally check off the requirements. It could definitely be two ounces, but I’m not good with measurements. It’s glass. It’s purple. It has a silver stopper. “It sure looks right to me,” I announce. “What can I offer you for it?”

She’s sitting on the next suitcase, trying unsuccessfully to close it. I kneel down and zip again while she pushes. “You can just have it,” she says, as the zipper slowly makes its way around the side. “I don’t have any good memories attached to that thing.”

“Are you sure? I mean, I can pay you something, or barter. Like I could water your flowers while you’re on vacation or something? You know, if it doesn’t rain?”

“Wait a sec,” she says, and reaches for my arm. “Okay, I’ll barter with you. I’ll give you the bottle for your bracelet.”

I see Emily immediately grab her own wrist, and her own bracelet. I hesitate. Our friendship bracelets have actually started to mean something to me. "I . . . I don't know. It's not valuable or anything."

"That's all right," she says. "There's just something about it."

"Here," Emily says, slipping hers off her wrist. "Take mine." She rests it in the woman's palm. "We've gotta go, though, Tara. Pizza waits for no man."

"Your name's Sara?" the woman says. "So's my daughter's."

I shake my head. "It's Tara, with a T."

"Oh. Close, though."

I want to tell her *No it's not close, it's a totally different name*, but really, what would be the point? She tucks the bracelet into her pocket and we quickly finish zipping the suitcase. Emily is already waiting outside, tapping her foot.

"Thank you for the bottle," I say.

"Thank your friend for the bracelet," she replies.

I'm about to tell her Emily is my cousin, but I realize that she's both. So I just say, "I will."

"Mommy!" a little voice calls out. "The dog is eating my Play-Doh!"

The woman gives me a quick smile then closes the door.

I try to keep up with Emily as she jogs toward home and her pizza-delivering math crush. "You didn't have to give that lady your friendship bracelet," I tell her. "Maybe she would have taken me up on the flower watering."

"That's okay," she says. "I don't need a bracelet to know we're friends."

I smile. "Me, neither."

• • • • • • • • • • •

At eleven the next morning, David and I walk up the steps of Willow's Church. "This is going to be weird," David says. I was thinking the same thing. Just the two of us? We've never done anything alone before. Then he says, "I've never been in a church before. And I've only been in a temple once or twice."

Okay, so he wasn't talking about us at all. It's a good thing I'm walking a step ahead and he can't see my face.

The inside of the church is larger than it looked from outside. Stained-glass windows line both sides, with rows of pews that go straight across. The only people we see are a few women talking about a bake sale. "Are you here for the youth ministry meeting?" one of them asks us. "It doesn't start until noon."

We shake our heads. David has retreated into quiet mode, so I say, "Actually, we wanted to speak to someone about a Bible?"

"The minister is in his office," she says, pointing to a hallway off to the side. "I'm sure he'd be happy to talk to you."

"Thanks," I tell her. David doesn't move, so I have to push him down the hall. "He won't bite, I promise."

"You don't know that," he mutters.

The door is open, so we walk in. The minister is around fifty, with very little hair and a friendly smile. "How can I help you?"

There's no way David is going to say anything, so I step forward. "This is going to sound —"

But David steps in front of me and blurts out, "How do you know if you're doing something because it's what everyone did before you, or because you really believe it?"

Well, *that* was a surprise.

The minister leans back in his chair. "Ah, young man, that's the age-old question, isn't it? The simple answer is that you don't know . . . until you do. Know, that is. Does that make sense?"

"Um, I'm not sure," David says.

"Children are generally brought up to believe what their parents believe, right?"

David nods.

"Then at some point, when they're old enough, they start to question it, as you might be now."

David nods again.

"And then at some point further down the road, they'll decide what's right for them. But you'd be amazed at the power of tradition. When something is in your bones, it's pretty hard to ignore."

"Thank you," David says. "I'll think about that."

"You two have a lovely day now," he says, turning back to the papers on his desk.

David turns to go. I grab on to his shirt. "Um, actually, we have another question."

He looks up expectantly.

"This is going to sound weird, but you wouldn't happen to have a copy of the Bible with two books of Genesis in it, would you?"

"Actually, we do!" he says, clasping his hands together. "It's been in our storage closet in the basement since I was around your age!" He chuckles. "We used to bring it out and try to make the old minister think he was going senile. Hmm, that doesn't sound very godly of me. Forget I said that!"

"And you still have it?" I ask.

He nods. "Indeed. No one wants to throw out a copy of the Bible, even if it IS missing the book of Exodus! It's a dilemma. Can't use it, can't throw it away."

"Then this is your lucky day," David says. "We can help you by taking it off your hands. We know someone who's looking for it."

"Is that so? And what would this person be doing with it?"

"I can honestly say I have no idea," David says.

I'm glad David answered that one, since I have a pretty good idea I know exactly what Angelina's planning on doing with all this stuff. If she can find room on the shelves.

The minister pushes back his chair. "Well, who am I to keep a Bible out of someone's hands who's asking for it? I'll go get it for you."

He leaves us in the office grinning at each other. "Nice work," I say.

"You, too."

We keep grinning until David's phone rings. "Am I supposed to answer it in a church?"

"I have no idea."

"It's pretty loud. What if people are trying to pray?"

"Good point. You better answer it."

He pulls it from his pocket. "Hello? Uh-huh. Really? No way! What are we going to do? What are the odds? Crazy! I've gotta go, we're still in the church. I may be sinning right now.

No, I'll tell her." He hangs up the phone and shakes his head. "You're not gonna believe this. That was Leo. He said we got an e-mail from someone who has the steamer trunk! The lady says we'd be doing her a favor by carting it away!"

"That's great. Why wouldn't I believe it?"

"Because it's your aunt!"

Chapter Eighteen

"What about Connor?" David suggests. We're sitting on a park bench, splitting our third hot pretzel. After a flurry of panicked texts and phone calls between everyone, we've decided the best way to handle it is to let someone else handle it. Someone Aunt Bethany wouldn't connect to me.

"Would he do it?"

"I think so," David says. "If I can wrestle the video-game controller out of his hand."

"Okay, let's try him."

David goes off to call Connor while I text Rory to let her know. As I'm sending off the text, my phone rings. I don't recognize the number.

"Hello?"

"Tara? Tara, it's Dad!"

I jump up from the bench. "Dad! Where are you?"

"We're in Madagascar, honey, remember?"

I laugh. "I know, but where are you calling from?"

"The top of a baobab tree! You should see the view!"

I laugh again. I didn't realize how much I missed hearing his voice until now.

"Okay, I'm actually calling from the base camp."

"How are the lemurs?"

"Pretty cute. Mating habits? Not so cute. Many people here believe in the supernatural, though. I'm getting a lot of great material for my next book."

"Do *you* believe in it?" I ask, half hoping he says yes. But the connection gets garbled and I miss his reply. Then I hear, "How are you enjoying my hometown?"

I plop back down on the bench. "Everything's . . . really different than I thought."

"Different good or different bad?"

"Good, I think. Mostly. I've met some really nice people and seen some . . . really strange things."

He laughs. "That's Willow Falls for you!"

"I know Mom said people get busy and stuff, but didn't you ever want to come back here?"

It's quiet for a few seconds, and I fear the call dropped. But then he says, "For whatever reason, your mother felt strongly about never going back. I didn't want to push it. By the time we were out of college, Grandma Emilia had passed away and the rest of your grandparents had retired to Florida anyway."

David's still on the phone with Connor, so I move a little farther away and ask, "Hey, do you remember a lady named Angelina D'Angelo?"

"Short, white hair, duck-shaped birthmark?" he asks.

I gasp. "Yes! That's her."

"Sure, everyone knew her. She was a fixture in town. At one time I think she was the chaperone for all the school dances up at Apple Grove." He laughs. "She used to make sure you could fit a ruler in between the boys and the girls during a slow dance."

"Sounds like her."

"Don't tell me she's still alive? She was old when *I* was a kid."

"Still alive and kicking."

"Who else have you met?"

"Well, there's —"

"Honey, sorry to cut you off, Mom wants the phone and we only have a minute left."

"Wait, Dad!"

"I've gotta hand over the phone. Miss you, honey."

"I miss you, too," I say, truthfully.

"Here's Mom."

I take a deep breath, trying to prepare myself to talk to her.

"Tara?"

I attempt to say hello, but a lump has formed in my throat and I can't seem to speak. It's a lump made of anger and frustration and confusion and trying to act grown-up and keeping secrets and missing her all wrapped into one.

"Tara? Are you there?"

"I'm here," I manage to squeak out.

"Is everything okay?"

I force myself to pull it together. "Yes."

"Are you sure? I've been frantic here, not being able to talk to you."

"Really?"

"You're surprised?"

I swallow hard. "Well, you've been so weird and angry, and you sent me away."

"Okay, I see your point. But you're okay? You're meeting people? Nothing bad has happened?"

"Yes, I'm meeting people. And nothing . . . too bad has happened."

"Tara, they're telling me I have to hang up. Stay strong. We'll call again next week. And, Tara, I'm really sorry."

She hangs up before I can ask which of her recent behaviors she's sorry for.

"Your parents?" David asks, sitting back down next to me.

I nod.

"They're still in Africa?"

I nod again.

"That's far."

"Yup. And things with my mom have been weird lately."

"Sometimes that happens with me and my mom. It's hard not to take it personally, but I've sort of figured out that mostly, it has nothing to do with me. Something at work could be bothering her, or she'll get a call about my dad that will upset her."

I figure this is as good a time as any, so I say, "You haven't mentioned your dad before."

He looks off into the distance, past the kids playing in the sandbox and the man selling pretzels, and into some place I can't see.

"He's in a special facility about three hours away from here. He has a condition called dystonia. It started to get bad when I was four or five. He used be at home but now he has to be someplace where he can be monitored and taken care of correctly. He can't control a lot of his muscles or even talk anymore."

David's hand is gripping the edge of the bench as if he needs to feel the solidity of it. I remember doing that as I sat on the curb outside Bettie's house after Rory and Leo told me about Angelina's store.

As though someone else is taking control of my body, with absolutely no conscious thought whatsoever, I rest my hand on top of his. After a full minute of sitting like that, I start to obsess over the fact that our hands are touching and that I started it and that he didn't pull away. Should I take my hand off his now? What if he wants his own hand back but doesn't want to be rude and move it first?

Then he whispers, "It's genetic. It might happen to me, too."

I stop thinking about our hands. "Might? How will you know?"

"I just have to hope I get lucky and the gene doesn't turn active." Then he smiles. "Good thing I've got a good luck charm now." He flips his hand over while it's still underneath mine.

David and I = Two People Officially Holding Hands.

I feel full. Like I could burst. It's an absolutely perfect moment. Right up until my phone rings and the pregnant lady who sold us the candlestick holder asks me to come over and clean her cat litter.

• • • • • • • • • • •

"That's Muskrat Suzy," Carolyn says, pointing to the hugely fat orange cat currently hissing at David and me from the porch. "Don't mind her. She about to have kittens and she's very protective of her space. Muskrat Sam is around here somewhere. He's the expectant father."

We make a wide circle around the cat and step into the house.

"Sorry about the mess," she says. "Bending down isn't what it used to be."

I've gotten so used to Emily's room that the few books and clothes scattered around don't even faze me. Still, I find myself picking them up as she walks us over to the litter area.

"You're not supposed to clean cat litter when you're pregnant," she explains. "Something about a disease they carry in their . . . well, in the stuff they leave behind in the litter box. My neighbor had been doing it for me, but she's on vacation for a week. There's kind of a lot in there."

"It's not a problem," David says, plucking the little plastic shovel off the shelf. "We'll be happy to do it."

I nod in agreement.

"You two are very cheerful for people about to clean out cat poop."

I blush and grab one of the plastic bags next to the box. "This is nothing. I've seen a lot more poop in my day than this."

"You have?" she asks, amused.

"I once spent a whole summer helping my mother label which animal it came from."

David stops, mid-scoop. "There's a lot I don't know about you."

That's for sure.

While we work, Carolyn sorts through some boxes of clothes that someone must have sent her. Every few seconds I'll see her touch her belly, or rest her hand on it briefly. I've never been this close to someone as pregnant as she is. It's totally bizarre actually.

I must not be the only one stealing glances at her belly because she asks, "Would either of you like to feel the baby kick?"

My eyes widen. I quickly shake my head. "I'm sorry, I didn't mean to stare."

David jumps up so fast he almost knocks the litter box over. "I do! I want to be a pediatrician one day."

Clearly, there's a lot I don't know about David, either.

David steps over to the sink to wash his hands. But when he approaches Carolyn, Muskrat Suzy positions herself directly between them and hisses, daring him to approach.

Carolyn laughs and gently shoos the cat away. "She's protecting me. Us two pregnant gals gotta look out for each other." She places David's hand on her belly.

"Wow!" he exclaims, his eyes wide with excitement. "C'mon, Tara, you've got to feel this!"

I really don't want to put my hand on a near-stranger's belly, but David seems to have no problem with it. So I wash my hands and join him. When I first lay my hand there, I'm surprised at how rock hard it is. Nothing like a regular stomach. A second later it feels like a tiny fist is punching my palm. I yank my hand away in surprise.

Carolyn smiles. "Now you've met Milo."

"Isn't it amazing?" David asks.

Carolyn beams. "And the thing I didn't expect was to love him so much, before he's even born. Like there's nothing I wouldn't do for him."

She starts singing a lullaby to her belly, and to my horror, David joins in, voice cracking and all.

"You'll make a really good doctor one day," Carolyn says, smiling up at him.

After another round of "Twinkle, Twinkle, Little Star," we resume cleaning the litter box and generally straightening up the place. David keeps chatting about this and that, but I can't focus. All I keep thinking about is how my mom protected me like that, how she loved me like that, and how we can't even talk to each other anymore.

. . . .

"Are you all right?" David asks on the walk home. He hasn't tried to take my hand again, which I'm grateful for. I think all of this voluntary touching of other people in one day has overwhelmed my system.

"I'm fine," I tell him, feeling better now that we're on the move again. And soon we'll get to cross one more thing off the list. "We better hurry. Connor's going to be at your house any minute."

We pick up the pace. "I guess we shouldn't have stayed there so long," he says. "It just seemed like she didn't get much company."

"Probably not," I agree. "She'd have to be lonely to let a strange kid like you touch her belly."

"Who are you calling strange?"

"If I ask you something, will you promise not to get offended?"

"Interesting way to start a question."

I start walking even faster, looking ahead instead of at him. "How come when you sing, sometimes it's really good, and sometimes it's, um, not so good? Don't get me wrong, it's still much better than anything I could do."

"When is it good and when isn't it?" he asks, sounding like he really wants to know.

I think back to all the times I've heard him sing, both good and not-as-good, and am surprised that there's actually a pattern. "This is going to sound strange, but when you sing outside, you're really good."

He only hesitates for a second before answering. "It's because outside is where I feel him the most."

I stop walking. "Feel who? God?"

He shakes his head. "My dad."

. . . .

Connor is sitting on David's porch when we arrive, playing a handheld video game. "Hey, Hamburglar," he says, standing up. "Hey, new girl."

"Hey," I reply.

David takes out his key and ushers us inside. "Did anyone see you?" he asks Connor.

Connor laughs. "You didn't tell me to wear my trench coat and sunglasses."

"Forget those things," David says. "I shoulda told you to wear a cap. You could see that red hair from clear across town."

"So exactly what is this top secret mission?" Connor asks. "And more important, how much am I getting paid?"

"Five bucks?" David suggests.

"Ten!" Connor says.

"Deal," I agree. "And you know what to do?"

"All the Hamburglar told me was I'm supposed to tell your aunt I'm here for the trunk."

"That's right," David says. "Don't start chatting, don't ask for a snack, just get in and get out."

"Got it, boss," Connor says.

"I should go home first," I tell David, "that way we're not arriving together."

"Okay." He pulls the Bible from his backpack. "I'll hold on to this."

"Dude! You're changing religions? Pretty gutsy move three weeks before your bar mitzvah."

"Just don't mess this up," David says, ignoring the religion comment.

"Oh, ye of little faith," Connor says. "I'll be the best trunk-picker-upper this town has ever seen."

I leave them and race across the street. Everyone's in the kitchen gathered around the computer. Even Ray. My first reaction is that they're looking at the list we posted. That can't be good. I'd have to pretend I don't know what it is. But then Aunt Bethany says, "See, Em? Watch what she does with her left foot." They're watching a video of a fencing match. I breathe easier.

Emily sees me first. "Hi, Tara! Want to come to the match with us? We're leaving as soon as I put on my uniform."

I try to figure out if it actually matters if I'm here or not when Connor comes. I guess it really doesn't. "Sure," I say.

"Great," says Aunt Bethany, "we're all going, then."

I open my mouth to say *What about the trunk?* but shut it as soon as I realize I can't possibly say it. Let's hope Emily takes a long time getting her uniform on. I try to send a telepathic message to David to get Connor over here fast. Thankfully the doorbell rings before Emily even comes back downstairs.

"That must be the people coming for the trunk," Aunt Bethany says, heading out of the kitchen.

"What people for what trunk?" Uncle Roger asks, fast on her heels.

Ray throws me a sharp glance. I can't very well fill him in now, though.

"The old steamer trunk of my mother's that I've been trying to get rid of for years," she says as we all follow her down the hall. "The one in the attic."

I didn't even know there *was* an attic!

"But why are you getting rid of it now?" he asks.

"Because the guy wanted it," she says. "Honestly, Roger, it's no big deal."

"But why does he want it?" Roger presses. "Maybe it's worth something."

"I don't know why he wants it," she says, reaching for the door. "Why don't you ask him?"

My heart stops. There weren't supposed to be any questions! Easy in, easy out.

"Hi," Connor says, smiling a bit too wide. "I'm here for the trunk."

"And what exactly would you be wanting with it?" Uncle Roger asks, peering out at him.

Connor's smile slowly shrinks. He glances at me for a second, but there's nothing I can do. "Um, I need a place to store my video game collection?"

"Good enough for me," Aunt Bethany says. "Come on in. Ray, will you grab it from the attic? It's the black one with the gold latch. Not real gold, Roger," she adds.

"Okeydokey," Ray says. Then he winks at me and says, "Still practicing my American."

"No one says 'okeydokey' anymore," I tell him.

We stand around awkwardly while Ray bounds up the stairs. "Wait a second," Connor says. I cringe. What is he doing? "Are you Roger St. Claire? The inventor?"

Uncle Roger's face lightens a bit. "Yes, that's me."

"Oh, wow! It's an honor, sir. I'm a huge fan of the Sand-Free Beach Towel. Genius!"

"Is that so?" Uncle Roger says, sticking out his hand. Connor shakes it. "Well, well, what do you know? I have fans!"

"I want to be an inventor when I grow up," Connor says. "I've got every issue of *Inventors Digest* since I was eight."

Uncle Roger steps over to me. "Well, you should meet my niece, then. She's interested in the field, too."

"I didn't know that," Aunt Bethany says.

"It's, um, kind of a new interest."

"Good to meet you," Connor says, shaking my hand.

"Yeah, you, too," I mumble.

Ray brings the trunk down and lays it in the middle of the foyer. Roger glances at it, touches the scraped-up yellow latch and the dented sides, and turns back to me and Connor. "Tara, what do you say we show Connor my lab? Show him where all the magic happens?"

"Um, I'm sure he has to go."

"No, I can stay," Connor says. "I'd love to see your lab."

I'd kick him if I could get away with it looking like an accident.

"Roger," Aunt Bethany says, pointing to Emily descending the stairs in her fencing outfit.

"Oh, right. Well, maybe Tara should stay and show the boy my lab."

Aunt Bethany puts her hands on her hips. "You're suggesting we leave our thirteen-year-old niece with a strange boy you only met five minutes ago based on the fact that he doesn't like getting sand on his beach towel?"

Uncle Roger shrugs. "You wanted her to make friends. Here's a nice boy with the same interests."

"I can keep an eye on 'em," Ray offers.

"You're sure?" Aunt Bethany asks.

"What about my match?" Emily asks, pouting.

Uncle Roger puts his arm around her shoulder. "Tara can come to the next one. You'll understand when you get older."

She looks over her shoulder at me as Uncle Roger guides her out the door. "But Tara likes . . ."

If she completes her sentence, I thankfully don't hear it.

Aunt Bethany reminds Ray to offer us lemonade and says they'll be back before dinner. She takes one last glance at the steamer trunk, and shuts the door behind her. I plop down next to the trunk in relief. "Gotta say, Connor, I'm impressed! How did you know just what to say to get him to trust you?"

"I didn't! I'm really a huge fan!"

"Seriously?"

"Yup!"

I sigh. "Ray, would you mind taking him up to the lab? I want to tell the others we have the trunk."

"Okeydokey."

"I think I liked you better when I didn't understand you."

The two of them go upstairs and I'm alone with the trunk. It's easy to see why Uncle Roger wouldn't want it. Angelina must not know the kind of shape it's in or else she probably wouldn't want it either. The latch is unhinged, so I push up the lid to make sure nothing has been left inside. Good thing I did, because it's filled to the brim with what looks like old costumes. Long skirts, white peasant blouses, vests, and shawls. Even clunky black shoes in various sizes.

Wait, a shawl! I pull it out and keep turning it until I find the initials *ER* sewn into the corner. This is it! The last item on the list! I'm done! I can't believe it! Now I can give Angelina all this stuff and be free and clear of her. Debt all paid off with three weeks to spare! I have enough money left to buy David a really nice gift, too.

I put the shawl aside and dig through the rest quickly. I wonder if Aunt Bethany knew all this stuff was even in here. Or if it would have made any difference. I dig through the clothes until I get to the bottom, which appears to be lined with old papers. I reach in and grab a few. They're pages of a play. I push the clothes aside until I can get all the pages, along with a thin, stapled playbill. The cover of the booklet is torn and wrinkled, but still I can still read it.

THE WILLOW FALLS
COMMUNITY PLAYERS PRESENT:
FIDDLER ON THE ROOF
Friday, July 13, 4 pm
Tickets on sale now at the
Community Playhouse Box Office
Come see this once-in-a-lifetime performance!

My middle school put on the same play last year, and everyone had to see it or it counted against your grade. I remember sleeping through the dialogue and waking up for the songs. It's weird enough that the play was performed in Willow Falls on my birthday, but the weirdest thing is that the woman on the cover, in the white peasant blouse and long skirt, is Emily.

Chapter Nineteen

I hold the playbill on my lap. Yup, still looks like Emily. I hold it up to the hundreds of bulbs in the chandelier above me. Still her. I know it can't be. And the girl in the photo is at least fifteen years older. But it's really uncanny.

I open the playbill and see Emily's face again. Only this time there's a name underneath the picture: *EMILIA MAY ROSE AS TZEITEL.*

The next two pages are filled with black-and-white photos of the other actors and scenes from the set. On one of them Emily/Emilia is sitting on top of the same black trunk I'm leaning against right now! It looks much shinier in the picture and not so dented. In another picture, a man with a white beard is dancing around a barn. *AVERY PITTMAN AS TEVYE.* I'm about to turn the page when a giant key leaning up against the corner of the barn catches my eye. A giant key! How many giant keys are there in the world? I look at another picture. A scene in a kitchen. And there, on the table, is my basket with the heart-shaped handles! My head is starting to swim. Picture after picture. There's the knife on the table next to a long roll of bread. There are the pearls around an old woman's neck. There's the violin in the Fiddler's hands! And on and on!

There is no denying it. Angelina had me collect all the props from *Fiddler on the Roof*! I sit back on the hard floor, utterly flabbergasted. Why? Why on earth would she do that? Is it her idea of a joke? Deep down, even though she had called them trinkets and bric-a-brac, I had hoped there was some significance to her choices, some greater plan that made it worth separating the items from their owners. But there wasn't. They were just props in an old play. What are the others going to think? It's humiliating.

I thrust everything back in the trunk except for the playbill, which I fold up and tuck in my pocket. What I really want to do is gather all the items so I can dump them on Angelina's counter and storm out of her shop. But it would take too long to gather them up. I don't even want to take the time to go upstairs and tell Ray I'm leaving. So I call instead while I get out my bike.

"You're seriously calling me from downstairs?" he asks as he picks up.

"Yes. I have to run back into town for something. Can you ask Connor to bring the trunk to David's? I'll deal with it later."

"Okey —"

"Don't say it."

"Dokey."

Ugh. I hang up and pedal my heart out until I reach the alley. I leave the bike leaning up against the watch-repair shop and run down the street, only half aware of the effort it takes not to twist my ankle on the cobblestones. The store, of course, is dark inside, but that doesn't fool me. I walk right in and stand in the middle of the room. I wait. I watch the last slant of late-afternoon sun come in from the top of a small side window. It hits a glass figurine of a dancer, lighting her up for a moment like fire, then letting her die out to ice as a cloud passes.

I wait some more.

Finally, the door to the back office opens. "Hello, Tara," she says, placing a small box under the counter. "I thought we agreed I wouldn't be seeing you here until you have everything on my list."

"I do have everything." I am calmer now, and glad for it. I want to keep my wits about me.

"All thirteen?" she says. "Wonderful! And so quickly! Where are they?"

"I have to round them up from a few different places. I wanted to ask you a question first. Why? Why did you do it?"

"Why did I do what, exactly?"

"Why did you have me collect thirteen props from *Fiddler on the Roof*? Was it just a test? To see if I'd actually do it?"

She bursts out laughing. "*Fiddler on the Roof*? The old play? What are you talking about?"

That wasn't the reaction I had been expecting. I step back a foot or so. "The props . . . in here." I unfold the playbill and show it to her. "The objects from your list . . . they're all in there."

She looks down at the playbill and then hands it back to me. "Didn't you use the list on the tape recorder I gave you?"

"Yes, of course I did. And those are the objects on the list."

She shakes her head. "Not on my list. You must have listened to the wrong side of the tape." Then she mutters to herself, "Should probably erase those old tapes one of these days."

"But it was your voice I heard, I'm sure of it."

"Probably was," she admits. "I used to help out over at the theatre. Had a little crush on one of the musicians, to tell you the truth. So charming and dapper."

A cold dread washes over me. "So what you're saying is that I — along with people who trusted I was doing something important — just spent the last week convincing strangers to give up their things based on the wrong list?"

"Sure sounds that way from where I'm standing."

"But . . . but you saw me buy the candlestick holder at the historical society. Why did you let me buy it if it wasn't on your list?"

She shrugs. "I figured you liked it. Can't keep up with young people these days and their trends."

I just shake my head in disbelief. "But my debt is still paid off, right?"

She shakes her head. "Not until you finish the job."

"But there's no time. I can't possibly find thirteen more things!"

She taps her chin in thought, then scratches behind her ear. She's simply *got* to let me off the hook. She's got to! Finally, she says, "Seems to me there's only one choice . . . you must put on the play!"

My heart drops. "*Put on the play?* Are you serious?"

"Why not? You have all the props. Now all you need are actors, a director, a choreographer, an orchestra, a propmaster, hair and makeup people, costumes, and let's see, what am I missing . . . oh, yes, a fiddler!"

My voice flat, I say, "You want me to put on a production of *Fiddler on the Roof*."

"Yes."

"Here, in Willow Falls."

"That's right."

"Why? Why should I do this crazy thing?"

"Well, to pay off your debt of course, but more importantly, because if you do this, you will understand why you're here in Willow Falls."

That makes no sense. "I know why I'm here."

"Do you?" she asks.

Something in her tone tells me not to bother trying to explain about the punishment. "Look, I don't know what you're talking about, but obviously the people in Willow Falls already did this play, like, decades ago."

She shakes her head. "No. They didn't."

In response I wave the playbill in my hand.

"I was there," Angelina says. "The show never happened. The star pulled out at the last minute, the big Broadway producer coming to see it changed his mind, and it all fell apart. Dashed many people's dreams that day."

"And me somehow getting this play to finally go on, that will magically fix things?"

"I'm not saying that at all. I'm saying only one thing . . . if you put on this play, you will understand why you're here. And if you don't figure that out, well, you risk reaching your thirteenth birthday without a complete understanding of who you are. And we all know what happens then."

"Let me guess. My immortal soul gets trapped outside my body? Doomed to wander the earth without me?"

"You said it, not me."

"And when am I supposed to do this impossible thing? I'm only here for the summer."

"Oh, you won't need that long." She reaches over and pries the playbill from my clenched hand. Holding it up she says, "Got a perfectly good date right here."

"My *birthday*?"

"That's right!" she says. "What a perfect coincidence!"

Rory's words come floating back to me. *There are no coincidences in Willow Falls.* I grit my teeth. "Fine." I can't believe I'm agreeing to this.

"Wonderful," she says. "I'll be the first in line to buy a ticket."

"I have to sell tickets?"

"Of course!"

"And where am I supposed to have it? My aunt's backyard has a pool hole in it!"

"Now, Tara, you didn't have any problem getting all these people to help you with my little project, I'm sure you can get them to pitch in again and help you with all these pesky details."

"But I didn't get them to do anything. They wanted to help."

"Either way, I'll see you Friday the thirteenth at four P.M. I'll be in the front row singing along." Then she starts twirling around the room singing:

"Matchmaker, Matchmaker,
make me a match,
find me a find,
catch me a catch.
Matchmaker, Matchmaker,

look through your book,
and make me a perfect match."

Well, it is catchy, gotta say that for it. "Angelina?"

"You still here?" She stops singing, but keeps humming the tune.

"Does Amanda and Leo not talking have anything to do with me?"

She stops humming. "Everyone is on their own journey in this life. You have yours and they have theirs."

"Thanks for clearing that up."

"Any time."

As I trudge toward the door, she serenades me with another song from the play:

"If I were a rich man,
Daidle deedle daidle
Digguh digguh deedle daidle dum
All day long I'd biddy biddy bum.
If I were a wealthy man!"

I can't get out of the store fast enough. I'm only three steps away when the feeling of being watched washes over me. I look back at the store, thinking maybe Angelina followed me out and is planning on launching into another song. But the store is dark again.

I turn back around and find myself face-to-face with David. I'm so surprised to see him there — to see anyone at all in the alley — that I instinctively back up and lose my balance on an uneven stone. He catches me right before I hit the ground.

"Sorry," he says, "I didn't mean to scare you."

"You just surprised me," I say, catching my breath. "What are you doing here?"

"Connor brought the trunk to my house and you weren't with him. He said you told Ray you had to run off downtown somewhere. I'd been so curious to hear about how it went with the trunk, but you just left without even texting me."

"I'm sorry, it all . . . it all happened so fast. What made you look here?" I ask, wondering what he sees when he looks at the store behind me.

"I saw your bike on the corner. Why were you inside that empty store? I'm surprised the door was even open." He steps forward and reaches for the knob. I want to stop him, but an even bigger part of me is curious to see what's about to happen.

"It's locked," he says, jiggling it a few times. "But weren't you just inside?"

When I don't offer up any explanation he says, "Look, I've been friends with Amanda and Leo and Rory for a while now. I know there are things going on in Willow Falls that I'm not a part of. After all, everyone's on their own journey."

Now *that* sounds familiar. When I don't comment, he continues. "But if you're going to involve me, it's not nice to just leave me hanging."

"You're right," I say, edging away from the store. Being this close to Angelina and David at the same time is making me anxious. "I should have texted you before I left. I don't really have much practice at it. Is it okay if we talk about this on the way home? This alley is giving me the creeps."

While we make our way to Main Street, I sneak a peek at his face. His mouth is still set in a firm line. I guess I don't blame him for being upset. The truth is, it's not just texting that I'm not in the habit of. It's thinking of other people at all. I should tell him that. Then I won't have to worry about disappointing him. Or any of the others.

Then he reaches out for my hand, and that idea goes right out the window.

Chapter Twenty

"*They were props? For a play?*" *Amanda and Rory* cry out, halting their forks in midair. Leo stops chomping on his chocolate-chip pancake, but only for a second. David said if you want something from someone, make sure they have a full belly. So I'm treating everyone to a post-final-exams pancake and telling them the news that I told David yesterday. I haven't told anyone about using the wrong list, though. I plan to take that info to the grave.

I nod. "*Fiddler on the Roof*, to be exact."

Amanda and Rory stare at me like I've just announced that aliens have landed at the diner. "You gonna eat that?" Leo asks, spearing my chocolate-chip pancake before waiting for a reply.

"So what does that mean?" Amanda asks. "Why would . . . the person who hired you make you find all the props to a play?"

"Maybe she really likes *Fiddler on the Roof*?"

"Oh, no!" Rory says, looking from me to David and back again. "You're not going to say we're putting on the play are you?"

"We're putting on a play?" Leo asks, coming up for air. "Can I write it?"

"It's *Fiddler on the Roof*," David says. "Someone wrote it, like, fifty years ago."

"Oh, right."

I pull out the playbill and lay it on the table.

Rory gasps. "That's Emily! How is that possible?"

"Actually, it's our grandmother, Emilia. Emily was named after her."

"I've seen people in town stop her and say how much she looks like her grandmother," Rory says, peering closely at the photo. "Now I see why!"

"Might as well tell them the kicker," David says.

I take a deep breath and say, "And we have to do it kind of fast."

"How fast?" Amanda asks.

I point to the date on the front of the brochure.

"Of *this* year?"

I nod.

"But there's no time," Rory says. "That's less than three weeks away. And it's the day before David's bar mitzvah."

"It's okay. I've been practicing long enough," David says. "If I don't have it by now, I'm never gonna get it."

"What about the beach?" Rory asks. "You're supposed to be going for ten of those days."

"I know. I'm hoping if Emily agrees to star in the play, then Aunt Bethany will let us put off the trip."

Rory shakes her head. "Emily would never agree to it. She's never performed in public before, and I don't think her mom wants her to."

"I know. But look" — I slide the playbill across the table — "she was born to play this part." I'm sort of surprised that Rory is the one throwing up roadblocks. She almost seems angry. Usually she's so quick to want to help everyone.

Rory looks at the playbill and sighs. "Maybe you're right. Can I talk to you alone for a second?"

"Um, okay." I start sliding off the bench.

"Girl stuff," Rory explains to David and Leo as she climbs out.

"Hey, I know all about girl stuff," Leo says. "My best friend has been a girl for thirteen years. Well, twelve, if you count the year she hated me. Either way, I know more about girl stuff than I ever wanted to."

Amanda elbows him in the ribs.

"Maybe you can teach me some," David says.

This seems like a good place to exit the conversation. Rory leads me to the other side of the diner, next to the old jukebox. "I'm sorry," she says. "It's not you I'm mad at, it's Angelina. Did she tell you something would happen if you don't put on the play? Or that something *will* happen if you do?"

"Something like that," I admit, hoping she doesn't ask for specifics.

"I don't want to know what it is," Rory says, to my relief. "It's just that I thought you'd be done with all this once you finished with the list. I was hoping, for your sake, that it was over."

"I know. I think it will be, after this."

Rory sighs. "Well, then, I guess we have a play to put on."

"Thank you," I tell her, "for everything. For even caring in the first place."

She grins. "That's what friends are for."

"I'm learning that," I say, not really intending to say it out loud. Maybe she didn't hear me over the clattering of dishes as a busboy clears a table nearby.

But she must have, because she says, "Before last year, I really only had two friends — Annabelle and Sari. Definitely not any friends who were boys. So I'm still learning, too."

"Girl talk over?" Leo says when we return to the table.

"Just beginning," Rory says, and we share a smile.

David says, "If we're going to do this, we have to start right away. I think the first thing we need to do is get a script and find a crew. Costumes, sets, music, all that stuff. And actors, of course."

"What happened to the playhouse anyway?" I ask. "I think this was the last play they tried to put on."

"It was?" Amanda asks.

I tell them what Emily said about my grandmother and the Broadway producer and then I add how the play never went on, although I don't tell them it was Angelina who told me that part.

"I bet I know who could tell us what really happened," David says.

We all turn to him expectantly.

"Any of the people who had the props."

"You're right," I say. "I hadn't thought of that. They must have been involved in the play somehow. Where do we start?"

"How about the lady who did your makeup?" Rory suggests. "She lives right around the corner from here."

We shovel in the last bits of pancake, and then I take the check up to the front counter to pay. "How's that cane working out for you?" Mr. Milazo asks, taking the bill.

I reach down to my sock to get the money. "Haven't used it yet," I tell him. "Soon, though."

"They have this newfangled device called a wallet," he says as he hands me my change. "You should try one."

. . . .

When Bettie with an *i-e* sees that it's us again, she opens the door wide. Rubbing her hands together excitedly, she says, "Oohh, you brought me two more models!"

Amanda and Rory look uneasy as they step inside.

"Sorry, Bettie," I say. "We just wanted to ask you a question about that basket you gave me last time?"

"Oh, okay," she says, obviously disappointed. "What about it?"

"Do you remember where you got it from?"

"It was my mother's," she says, glancing at a photograph on the wall of an elderly woman sitting on a lawn chair. "She had dozens of baskets. She used to carry her makeup in them when she did her rounds."

I pull out the brochure and show her the picture of it in the play.

"That's right," she says. "She used to work at the playhouse, doing the actors' makeup. She must have lent it to them for the play."

"Do you remember this one? *Fiddler on the Roof*?"

"I was just a girl," she says, "but Mom used to bring me to

all of them with her. That was the last one they did. Must be about thirty-five years ago. The playhouse closed down after that. Lost their funding or something."

"Do you remember the woman who starred in it? Emilia Rose? She was my grandmother."

"Of course I remember Miss Rose. She was famous in town. Headed for greatness, they said." She glances down at the playbill and says, "That was going to be her big break, if I recall correctly."

"But what happened?" I ask.

"I don't really know," she says. "She pulled out of the play a week before opening night, and it all fell apart after that. Oh, there were rumors. Some thought Miss Rose and the director fell in love and were going to get married, but then Miss Rose accepted another man's proposal. I was too young at the time to be interested in that part. Sometimes people, when they're on the brink of getting what they really want, they decide they don't want it anymore."

It's a different version from what Emily told me. I wonder if we'll ever know the real story.

"And no one wanted to start up the playhouse again in all these years?" Leo asks.

"The town bought the playhouse building and turned it into the library," she explains. "Willow Falls used to have to share a library with River Bend, you know."

"Why can't there be both a library and a playhouse?" Leo asks.

Bettie shrugs. Then she says, "I just got some great eye shadows in the mail, you sure I can't try 'em out on ya?"

Ten minutes later, we've secured a makeup artist for the play, and Amanda and I have purple, pink, and green striped eyelids. Rory claimed to be allergic to a lot of different kinds of makeup, which is an excuse I wish I'd thought of myself. The next stop is the library, to check if they have any of the theatre's old stuff. Once we're inside, it's easy to see how it could have been a playhouse once. It's strange to think of all the time my grandmother must have spent in this building so many years ago. When Rory tells the librarian what we're looking for, she says, "We do have most of the plays, but not all. The Willow Falls Historical Society has a lot of them."

"We'll hope for the best," Rory says firmly.

"Yeah," says Amanda, "we wouldn't want to bother the nice old lady that works at the historical society."

The librarian shrugs and points to the shelves all the way in the back. "Good luck."

The shelf is stuffed full of scripts and playbills and memorabilia from decades of plays. And my grandmother's name is on the front of a lot of them, beginning when she was a kid.

"Here it is!" Leo says, pulling a copy of *Fiddler on the Roof* out of the middle of the pile. We crowd around as he flips through it. Every other page has a handwritten note in the margin. "This must have been the director's copy," he says.

"The play is really long," I say, frowning. "How can people learn all this in such a short time?"

"What if we just do the songs?" David suggests. "Like, tell the play through the music?"

"Do you think that would be okay, Tara?" Rory asks.

"I don't see why not. That's the best part anyway."

"Hey, look!" Leo holds up the script. Handwritten on the back cover is a list of the crew. "Recognize some of these names?" he asks.

Most of the names don't mean anything to me. Then I get down to props. "Look! It's Big Joe!"

"Can't be," Amanda says. "He's way too young."

"Didn't Mrs. Grayson say the knife was his father's?" David asks. "It must be Big Joe Senior!"

"Speaking of Mrs. Grayson," David says, pointing to the script. "It says here she and her sister were the choreographers."

"And look at the next one," Leo says. "'Fiddler . . . Bucky Whitehead'!"

"Bucky!" we all exclaim.

"When he gave me the violin he said he hadn't played it in thirty-five years!"

"Did he say why?"

I shake my head. I don't want them to know that I didn't even think to ask. I'm sure any of them would have. "Do you think he'd be willing to do it again?"

"I guess it depends on why he stopped," Leo says.

We take the script up to the librarian and ask her if we can make a copy of it. "It would probably be easier to download it from the Internet," she says. "It wouldn't cost too much."

"We'd really like this copy," I say.

She suggests we take it down to the copy shop since it's so long and have them do it. We get outside and decide to split up. David's going to get the play copied and then see the best way to fit the songs together. Leo is going to talk to Bucky, and Amanda to Mrs. Grayson. Rory's going to ask her friend Annabelle to do costumes, and her friend Sari apparently loves nothing more than doing people's hair. And I get the fun job of convincing Emily to perform in front of the whole town. Or the five people who'll probably show up. Either way, it won't be easy.

• • • • • • • • • • •

"Not a chance," she says, not even lifting her eyes from her math notebook.

"But look, it's you, you're the star." I place the playbill on the notebook so she has no choice but to look at it.

"It's not me," she says, pushing it aside. It falls off the desk.

I pick it up and pace back and forth with it. "But it could be. This could be your big chance. You'd get to show everyone how good you are."

"Isn't the Fiddler the star of the play anyway? You know, since it's named after him?"

I shake my head. "Nope. He's just some guy who plays the violin on a roof. Technically, I guess the guy who plays the father, Tevye, is the star, but this is the biggest female part."

She scribbles a few more numbers. "Mom would never let me do it. You know how she feels about all this stuff."

"I don't think we'll ever really know what happened with Grandma and the play. But that was her journey, this one's yours."

That gets her to at least put down her pencil. "Why does it matter if it's me? Why can't someone else do it? I'm sure a lot of girls in town would want to."

"I don't know," I reply honestly, looking down at the playbill. "There must be some reason you can do the same things

Grandma could. And you look so much alike. It would be like finishing something she started."

She nibbles on the end of her pencil for a minute, then says, "I just don't think I can."

"Will you think about it?"

"Okay, but don't hold your breath."

I lie down on the bed wondering if there's anything else I can do to convince her. My phone rings, making both of us jump. It's Rory.

"Did you talk to Emily yet?" she asks.

"Yup. She said she'd think about it." Then in a loud voice I say, "I know, she'd be perfect!"

"Not gonna work," Emily calls out from her desk.

Rory laughs. "I heard that. Okay, I have a plan. Have Emily open her laptop. I'm going to send her an e-mail in ten minutes."

"And you think it'll work?"

"If this doesn't, nothing will."

Ten minutes later her computer dings.

"I really have to work," Emily says. "Is this gonna take long?"

I don't answer since I have no idea what Rory's e-mail says. We open it up to find a link with the words *Click Me.*

We click. A small video box opens, then gets larger. The video starts up and first thing we see is waves crashing on a beach. It's a little shaky and grainy, like someone filmed it with their cell phone.

"Um, this is pretty and all," Emily says, "but how is this supposed to convince me to take the part?"

I'm wondering the same thing. Then the camera pans away from the water. A boy with sandy blond hair and bright white teeth waves at us from a tall beach chair.

"Hi, Emily! I heard that you might play Tzeitel in *Fiddler on the Roof.* If you play Tzeitel, I'll play the tailor, whatever that guy's name is. The one who wants to marry Tzeitel."

Emily looks up at me, gaping. "Is that . . . is that Jake Harrison talking to me?"

I would answer but I think I'm having an out-of-body experience. I grip the back of Emily's chair. "So what do you say?" Jake continues. "I'm going to be in Willow Falls that weekend anyway — turns out the producer wants to have our premiere there two weeks before the official opening. You know, to thank the townspeople and all. I know I can't wait to see it myself. Especially the part where Rory walks into a locker!" He starts laughing and his blue eyes twinkle. "Don't tell her I said that. Okay, I've gotta go, they're calling me to the set. Look forward to meeting you, Tara. See you on stage, Emily!" He waves again and walks away. The camera lingers for a second on the name *JAKE HARRISON* painted on the back of the tall chair, then pans back to the ocean.

"Jake Harrison just spoke to me," Emily says, pronouncing each word slowly. "He said my name. And Rory's name. And *your* name. With his mouth. Jake did. Jake Harrison. He wants to play my husband."

"I know! How crazy is that?"

"I'm *totally* doing this play."

"Totally!"

We jump around the room and squeal for ten minutes straight and then watch the video over and over until we've memorized it. If Rory can get Jake to not only agree to be in the play, but to film a video and get it to us in ten minutes, well, I can see why Rory isn't a fan of Jake's anymore. She's much more than that. And I couldn't be happier for her.

. . . .

The first person to arrive at the First Official Meeting of the *Fiddler on the Roof* Cast and Crew is Rory's friend Annabelle. She runs into the back room at the community center and gives Rory a hug. I decide that the pang of jealousy I feel is a good step for me.

"Hey! Remember when we took our babysitting class in this room?" Annabelle asks, pushing her long blond hair out of her eyes. "And that teacher? She was like, 'You must be prepared for any situation. You never know if the child under your care might spontaneously combust!' "

"She was pretty scary," Rory agrees. "You haven't babysat since!"

"True," Annabelle says. "But that's because you got the best gig in town with Emily. I'd get the kid who covers the house in peanut butter, then jumps off the roof in a Superman costume."

Pointing at me, Rory tells Annabelle, "This is Tara. She's Emily's cousin and the reason you're going to be in a play with Jake."

Annabelle rushes toward me and gives me a big hug. "Thank you, thank you!" I don't know if I'm supposed to hug her back, so I sort of movc my arms up and down and say hello. She's almost as tall as me, which is a rare thing. Even though she's gorgeous and bubbly, I decide I like her.

When she finally lets go, she says, "I'm totally excited to do the costumes, but what part do I play?"

"Leo's bringing the cast list," I tell her. "I slept through most of the play when I saw it last year."

"No one's gonna sleep through this one!" Leo declares, coming in the door with his arms full of folders. He drops everything onto one of the round tables in the center of the room. "I've got scripts, lists of characters, props, everything. The director is going to have a really easy job."

Rory and I look at each other. "Uh-oh," she says. "We forgot about a director. Leo, do you want to do it?"

He shakes his head. "Can't. Too risky. I might wind up talking to Amanda without realizing it. I'd be telling her character to take a step to the right and then all would be lost."

"What would be lost?" Annabelle asks casually.

"You know I can't say."

"Hey, can't blame a girl for trying." She looks at me and rolls her eyes. But not in a mean way.

"Okay," Rory says, "so that rules out Amanda, too. It should really be someone who knows what they're doing."

"I know!" I tell her. "I'll go make a call."

"Hurry, though; the meeting starts in ten minutes."

"Okay." I run from the room, pulling out my phone as I go. I wave to Bucky Whitehead as he walks toward the room with his violin cradled in his arms, a look of anticipation mixed with uncertainty on his face.

The phone rings forever, and just as I assume I'm going to have to leave a message, he answers. "Were you serious when you said what you really wanted to do was direct?" I ask Ray. "Because this is your lucky day!"

Chapter Twenty-one

"G'day to you, too," Ray says.

"Seriously, what do you think?"

"What do I think about what?"

"Would you like to direct a production of *Fiddler on the Roof* that some people I know are putting on?"

"People you know . . . would those be your mates?"

"Yes, fine, my friends. I have friends. And some grown-ups, too. So what do you say?"

"Is this out of pity because I didn't get the commercial?"

"Is saying no more likely to get you to agree, or less?"

"I'm not sure," he says. "Try me."

"Okay, then no, I just think you'd be great at it. Everyone likes you, and you're good at doing a lot of things at once."

"I *am* a good multitasker. So sure, I'll give it a burl."

"That's a yes?"

"Too right!"

"Can you make an effort to speak American as much as you can in your role as director?"

"Don't fret your freckle," he says. "I'll try my best."

"And can you get down to the community center in ten minutes? We're in the last room at the end of the hall on the first floor. I'll give you all the details then."

I can hear him opening and closing drawers. He was still in his pajamas when I left. "Do I get paid for this?" he asks.

"No . . . but you get to boss people around and get your name on the playbill."

"Good enough!"

I hurry back inside and tell Rory the good news. "Great!" she says. "Now all we need is a place to put on the play, and a star. What about Emily, has she told your aunt yet?"

"They went out to breakfast and she said she's going to tell her then." At least I hope she is. I look around the room, which is quickly filling up with both familiar and unfamiliar faces. Emily has been trying for two days to get up the courage to tell her mom about the play. I offered to come with her, but she said she wanted to do it on her own.

David comes in the room next, dragging the red wagon behind him. He has all the props piled on there, except for the trunk, which is still at his house. "Guess what?" he says, hurrying over to us. "I know where we're having the play!"

"Where?"

"Here!"

I look around the room. "We'd have to move the tables out, but I guess this would work."

"Not in this room," he says. "Out there, in the main room. On the stage! Since my bar mitzvah party is here the next day, the owner of the center said he'd already have rented all the chairs. All we'd have to do is set them up in rows. And we have to promise to take all the sets and props down at the end."

In my head, I'd pictured something a lot smaller. A real live stage is even more pressure to make it good. Besides Emily and David, most of the people who've agreed to be in the cast can't actually sing or dance, although no one has seemed willing to admit that out loud.

Rory beams at him. "Good job, Hamburglar!"

"What did Bee Boy do now?" Amanda says, coming in with a girl I haven't seen before. She's wearing a green and yellow shirt that says WILLOW FALLS GYMNASTICS TEAM with a cartoon of a girl doing a backflip.

"He found us a way to hold the play here on the stage," Rory says.

"I did not look like a bee!" David insists.

"Yes, you did," Amanda says, turning away from him. "Tara, this is my friend Stephanie. She volunteered to be one of the daughters in the play."

Stephanie reaches over and pinches Amanda's arm. "You volunteered me, is how I remember it."

"That's one way to look at it," Amanda admits.

"What's the play about?" Stephanie asks.

"Good question," Amanda says, looking at me.

"Um, well, I didn't catch all of it, but basically, it's about this milkman guy named Tevye from a long time ago in, like, Russia I think, and he has all these daughters, and some of them want to get married to people he doesn't want them to. And they're Jewish, and their whole community is being driven from the town. And there's dancing and, um, singing."

Stephanie faces Amanda. "I have to *sing*? If you weren't my best friend, you'd owe me big time for this. In fact, you *do* owe me big time for this."

"All right, everyone," Ray's voice booms through the room. "The director has arrived. Let's all take a seat."

Clearly he's got the bossy part down. He must have broken a few speed limits to get here.

"Where's Emily?" Rory whispers as we find seats.

I'm about to reply that I'm sure she'll be here any second when in she walks. She scans the room until she spots me. Her eyes light up as she makes her way over and sits down next to me.

"I did it!" she says, unable to keep her voice down. "I asked Mom if it was okay and she really didn't want me to and I asked her, 'Why, just tell me why?' and she said it's because she doesn't want me to get hurt like Grandma did, to feel that all my self-worth was tied up in an acting career, and I was like, 'Mom, I want to be a mathematician, not an actress,' and she still wasn't sure, so I showed her the Jake video and she was like, 'Okay, you should totally do this!' So now we're going to go to the beach after the play instead!"

"That's great, I —"

But Emily has noticed Rory on the other side of me and has lunged out of her seat to tackle her. "Thank you, thank you, thank you!"

Rory peels Emily off of her and laughs. "It's okay. Jake really wants to do it. But I think Ray is going to fire you if you don't sit down and pay attention."

"Are we ready to focus, Miss St. Claire?" Ray asks, peering down at her.

She slinks back to her seat.

Ray walks back and forth, hands clasped behind his back, eying everyone like he's a drill sergeant inspecting the troops. I'm not sure what a real director would look like, but Ray looks like someone who wandered in from an afternoon hike. He even has a water bottle strapped to his waist. Finally he says, "Okay, folks. I run a tight ship. There will be no mollycoddling of anyone in . . ." He looks at me and asks, "What play is this again? *Grease*? *The Wizard of Oz*?"

At the mention of *The Wizard of Oz*, Amanda visibly shudders. I'm not a fan of the flying monkeys either.

"It's *Fiddler on the Roof*," I reply in a loud whisper.

"That's right, *Fiddler on the Roof*! That classic tale of tradition, love, and family. At least I think it is. I've only seen the movie and you know how they change things. Anyway, as I was saying — cast, crew, you're all the same in my book. And judging by the number of people in this room, you actually *are* the same. Okay. Now let's go around the room. Tell me who you are and what you're doing here. Keep it short. My brain's already crowded."

Leo pops up. "I'm Leo. I'll be playing the part of Perchik, a student in love with Tevye's daughter Hodel." He picks up his folders and begins distributing them. "I've made each member of the cast a folder that will include the lyrics to the songs that you will be performing. Each member of the crew also gets a folder with your assignments. I did my best to figure out the costumes and sets, and as many of you know, we have a lot of the props already. Since we have only a little more than two weeks to get this show ready, it'll be pretty bare-bones. We had to cut out a few of the less essential songs, and we only have seventy-five dollars to spend on incidentals. So look over the lists in your folders and see what you have from home or can borrow."

He continues handing out the folders and I glance over at Amanda. Her face is glowing with pride. She leans over to me and whispers, "And to think my mom said Leo always has his head in the clouds." She gets up next and offers to write the cast and crew list on the dry-erase board in the front of the room.

Director: Ray

Producer: Tara

Tevye, the milkman: David

Tzeitel, his oldest daughter: Emily

Hodel, his second-oldest: Stephanie

Chava, his third-oldest: Rory

Golde, his wife: Amanda

Motel, a tailor, in love with Tzeitel: Jake

Perchik, a student, in love with Hodel: Leo

Yente, the matchmaker: Annabelle

Lazar Wolf, the butcher: Connor

Fyedka, a Christian, in love with Chava: Vinnie

Shprintze and Bielke, Tevye's youngest daughters: Grace and Bailey

Fiddler: Bucky Whitehead

Choreography: Mrs. Grayson

Set design and props: Big Joe

Costumes: Annabelle

Makeup: Bettie

Hair: Sari

There are only three people on the whole list who I don't know — Vinnie (who came in a baseball uniform) is a friend of Leo's. His ears turned pink when he saw Annabelle so I'm sure there's a story there somewhere. Then Connor's sister, Grace, brought her friend Bailey, and Rory brought her friend Sari to do everyone's hair. Considering Sari's own hair is a collage of colors, she and Bettie will no doubt get along swimmingly. Seeing the list in big letters makes it feel so real. This is seriously going to happen. Maybe my immortal soul won't bounce from cloud to cloud after all!

Sari asks loudly where Jake is, and Rory explains to everyone that he isn't going to be here until the day before the play, but that he knows his song already. After a few murmurs of disappointment that they won't be seeing him today, the cast huddles in one corner with their song sheets, while the crew meets with Ray to talk about what supplies they'll need. Seeing my name up there as producer feels very strange. The first hurdle is done, though — we have the cast, crew, props, and a stage. As the producer, it's my job to find an audience while everyone else works on putting the actual play together. If Angelina hadn't said I needed to sell tickets, I would have been fine simply having everyone bring their families.

I wander through the room listening to different conversations. Since choreographing the dances is the hardest part of all, Mrs. Grayson has roped Big Joe into helping her. She has him standing in the center of the room while she flits around him, humming the words to "Matchmaker, Matchmaker" and taking down notes on how the dance should go. Fortunately a lot of the notes on the original script we got from the library were actually hers, so she only has to redo it with the new cast.

I wait until Ray finishes assuring Grace and Bailey that, as the younger sisters in the play, their role as background dancers is very important. Then he tells them to go see Bettie and Sari about their hair and makeup, and that perks them right up.

"Nice work," I say.

"I was born to direct," he says, thumping his chest. "It's all about people skills."

"Since we know mine are lacking, do you need me here?"

He shakes his head. "Go produce. Or whatever it is producers do. I got it covered."

I reach into my sock and hand him the seventy-five dollars I volunteered to contribute.

He tucks it in his pocket. "I will use it wisely," he promises. As I turn to go, he stops me and says, "It's gonna be a ripper play. You'll see. People will talk about it for years."

As I leave the room, I hear Annabelle tell Ray that in order to fully embody her role as the matchmaker in the play, she has the perfect woman to set him up with. That's the spirit.

Instead of biking straight home to work on the flyers for the play, I take a detour over to Angelina's shop. I want to update her on the progress of the play and ask if I really need to sell tickets. As usual, the store looks dark from the outside. But this time when I turn the knob, it doesn't open. I look up to see a sign posted on the door. GONE FISHING.

Somehow I can't picture Angelina standing by the banks of a river casting a fishing line.

I decide on the bike ride home that selling tickets at the door, instead of ahead of time, will be fine. I use the computer in the kitchen to make up some really simple flyers announcing the time and place, and put down that tickets are all six dollars. I figure if it turns out really bad, people won't have lost too much money. The flyers don't say anything about Jake, which is how Rory said he wanted it.

Aunt Bethany comes home as I'm printing out the flyers and says, "We can do better than that." In ten minutes, she designs some really professional-looking flyers. I hadn't really stopped to think about where she went each day, but it turns out she volunteers at different organizations around town, helping them with fundraising projects. She sends a copy of the flyer to all her e-mail contacts, posts it on the Willow Falls website, and then drives me into town to do it the old-fashioned way — with tape. We put the flyers in the window of the diner, the music store, the dress shop, the toy store, the library, and nearly every store in between. Each time another flyer goes up, this whole thing gets more real. If I think too much about it, I'm afraid my head will explode.

During the first week, everything moves along steadily. The cast practices their songs, Big Joe works on the sets, and Annabelle has gathered together (or made) almost all the costumes we'll need. Emily's very good in rehearsals, having quickly gotten over her shyness. Leo is a very confident performer, too. The others . . . well, at least they seem to be having fun.

I like watching David stomping around the stage belting out *"Tradition! Tradition!"* in his black bar mitzvah pants, white shirt, and black vest that is doubling for his character's costume. It's one of his two solos, and then he has two more songs, one with Amanda and one with Connor. I haven't seen the one with Amanda yet, but he and Connor spend most of their routine trying to land on each other's feet. David's still the best singer in the play, but it's nothing compared to when he sneaks over to the pool hole in the evenings. I've been sitting by the back door where he can't see me so I can listen. I'm going to miss hearing the Hebrew songs when his bar mitzvah is over next week. Even though I'm keeping my eyes open for the perfect present for him, I haven't found it yet. Considering that the need for a gift was the thing that started all this, I really better find something great. And soon.

With only a week to go before the performance, the producers of *Playing It Cool* decide to announce that not only will they be holding the premier at the Willow Falls Movie Theatre the evening of Saturday, July fourteenth, but that Jake Harrison will be playing the role of Motel in the Willow Falls Community Playhouse production of *Fiddler on the Roof* the day before. Suddenly the movie and the play are all anyone in town can talk about, and some of the cast are freaking out. Apparently, it's also awkward for Stephanie and Leo to be singing together because Amanda doesn't see Stephanie as much as she used to now that Leo is back in her life. Ah, middle school drama. Exactly the kinda stuff I avoided back home. Here, though, it doesn't seem so much like drama. More like, well, like *life*.

With only three days to go, my parents call again. This time I'm able to talk to my mother without feeling a lump in my throat as big as Texas. This one is only Rhode Island–sized. I tell them I'm involved in the play in case Aunt Bethany mentions it, but I don't tell them how it's only happening because of me. I can tell they're shocked enough that I have any part in it.

The next night, the doorbell rings around seven o'clock. Aunt Bethany and Ray are out picking up refreshments for the play while Emily and I are upstairs in our room practicing. Well, *she's* practicing. I'm working on posters for the ticket table. Rory's voice calls out, "Hello? Anyone home?"

"Come on up," I hear Uncle Roger call out from his lab. "The girls are in their room."

A minute later Rory appears in our doorway. But she's not alone. I jump up so quickly that all of my art supplies go flying onto the floor.

Jake Harrison = STANDING SIX FEET AWAY FROM ME.

"I thought you weren't coming until tomorrow," I say, then immediately want to bite my tongue. I'm actually meeting Jake Harrison, THE Jake Harrison, who is just as cute in person, and those are the first words out of my mouth?

Emily, who had been practicing twirling in one spot, doesn't move for a few seconds. Then she yells, "Hey, what's that?" and points to a typical pile of random stuff in the opposite corner of the room. They both follow her gaze. She then leaps over to my bed and grabs at the corner of the Jake poster hanging on the wall above it. As soon as I realize what she's doing, I grab the other end. We manage to wrestle it off the wall and into a ball on the floor before they turn back around.

"What are we supposed to see?" Rory asks.

"Um, nothing," Emily says. "I've just always wanted to say that."

If Jake knew what just happened, he didn't show it. "So you're my fiancée?" he asks Emily with a big smile.

I think she may actually be rendered speechless for the first time ever. Finally she says something that resembles the word *yes.*

"And this is Tara," Rory says. "She's the reason we're all doing the play."

"Hi," I manage to say, amazed that both Emily and I have managed not to squeal yet. "Thank you so much for offering to be in it."

"It'll be fun," he says. "I've wanted to branch out from the whole teen movie genre for a while now. This could be my big break!" He smiles again and we all laugh. Like anything he does in our little town could actually be anything other than a blip in his career.

"Sorry to barge in like this," Rory says, "but Jake came a day early and we thought we'd get some more practice time in."

No doubt beckoned by the sound of a male voice, Uncle Roger appears in the doorway. Rory introduces them, and Uncle Roger grips Jake's hand a little longer than necessary. "You're fifteen now, right?" he asks.

"Yes, sir."

"Rory's only thirteen, you know. She's like a second daughter to us. We take her well-being very seriously."

Rory shuffles over to where I'm standing and hides her face with her hands.

"Don't worry," Jake assures him. "Rory's father already made me sign something saying we won't officially date until she's in ninth grade. Seriously. He had it notarized and everything."

Emily finally squeals. I reach out and squeeze Rory's hand. She squeezes back.

Jake turns around to Rory and smiles. "Unless she's forgotten all about me by that time."

• • • • • • • • • • •

For the next two hours, Rory and I watch Emily and Jake twirl around the living room. Uncle Roger moved all the furniture out of the way so there's plenty of room. Emily is a really good teacher and Jake picks up the dance steps very quickly. He has to use the sheet music for the lyrics, though, because it's a really long song. *"Wonder of wonders, miracle of miracles,"* he sings over and over, but who could get tired of that voice?

Emily doesn't have any lines in this one, she just twirls with him and basks in his adoration as he sings about how it's such a miracle that they're allowed to be together. The best part is when Jake has to do a backward somersault and then keeps getting stuck halfway over.

Uncle Roger mutters, "It'll be a miracle of miracles if that kid doesn't break his neck."

Ray and Aunt Bethany return and Emily says, "This is my husband, Jake Harrison." Everyone laughs. Then Jake stands off to the side while Rory and Emily practice the song they have together: "Matchmaker, Matchmaker." Emily really belts it out, but Rory does this half-talking, half-singing thing, clearly uncomfortable. Throughout the routine, Aunt Bethany keeps wiping under her eyes with her finger. Her makeup is a mess but no one mentions it. I wonder if she's thinking of her mother, too, and how she used to sing the same song.

Jake gives them a standing ovation. "Bravo, bravo!"

Emily curtsies and blushes.

"I think I'll stick to being an extra," Rory says.

"Who knows," Jake says, twirling her around. "Maybe once the world sees your debut in *Playing It Cool*, they'll demand more of Rory Swenson."

"I'm pretty sure they'll demand less," she replies.

Uncle Roger points out that it's getting late, so Jake and Emily plan to meet up the next day at the community center to keep rehearsing. As they leave, I get a text from David asking me to meet him in the backyard.

I go out through the laundry room and find him sitting at the patio table. The outside lights allow me to see the box wrapped in newspaper on the table in front of him. "Looks like you had company," he says.

I feel a little weird telling him who it was, but he probably knows. I nod. "Rory brought Jake by to practice with Emily."

"What was he like?"

"He was really nice," I admit. "Not at all movie-starry." I leave out the cute and charming and funny and a good singer and dancer part. He really doesn't need to know that.

"Cool," he says.

"How'd it go with the rabbi?" I ask, eager to change the topic.

"It was good. We went over the speech I have to give after the service."

"You have to make a speech on top of all the other stuff?"

He nods. "It doesn't have to be long. I'm pretty sure I know what I'm going to say."

"Cool," I say. We sit there in silence for a minute until I say, "Sooo . . . what's in the box?"

"This little thing?" he jokes. "I just found it here."

"Really?"

"No. I brought it for you."

"Oh! What is it?"

He pushes it toward me. "Friday's going to be so crazy with the play and then I have to go do bar mitzvah stuff at night. I might not get to see you much on your birthday."

"You got me a gift?" I don't think I've gotten a birthday gift from anyone other than a relative in years.

"It's a small thing. But I just thought, when you go back home at the end of the summer, you could take this with you."

I feel a pang of something like the homesickness I felt when I first got here, only the reverse. I focus on unwrapping the newspaper and on ignoring the clenching feeling in my stomach. I put it aside and find that I'm holding a CD case. I hold it up to the light and read *Sounds from the Bottom of the Pool.*

"Your uncle lent me some seriously old tape recorder and then I transferred the recording onto my computer."

"Thank you," I say, clutching it in my hands. "It's the best birthday present I've ever gotten."

He laughs. "Man, I hope that's not true."

"I thought I heard noises out here," Uncle Roger says. "You're not planning on climbing into the pool hole this late, are you?"

David shakes his head and stands up. "I've had my last practice session. Thanks for lending me the tape recorder."

"No problem," Uncle Roger says. "You can keep it."

"Um, I really need that back," I say. "I have to return it to the woman who . . . oh, never mind, just keep it."

David shrugs. "Okay. You never know when a giant tape recorder might come in handy."

"My sentiments exactly," Uncle Roger says, beaming.

"Well, good night," David says to me.

I glance at Uncle Roger, who doesn't seem to be leaving any time soon. "Good night. Thank you again."

"Happy early birthday," he says, pausing for a minute at the edge of the patio. He glances at Uncle Roger, too. The man is clearly not going anywhere. David gives me a final wave and walks out the gate.

Uncle Roger puts his arm around my shoulder as we head back into the house. "Am I going to have to make that boy sign something, too?"

"Very funny," I reply. But I know it wouldn't matter anyway. By the time we're in ninth grade, he'll have forgotten all about the girl who lived across the street for a summer.

Chapter Twenty-two

It seems like everyone in town has suddenly found a reason to stop by the community center. By the time I arrive Thursday morning, I have to push my way through the crowd to get to the back room, which is not easy with a big box in my arms. Big Joe is standing in front of the door, his arms crossed. He motions with his thumb to a sign on the door. PRIVATE — CAST AND CREW ONLY.

"It's me, Tara," I say. I gesture to the big box in my arms. "Playbills? Heavy?"

When he doesn't budge, I add, "I'm the producer?"

Rory opens the door and grabs for my arm. "It's okay, Joe, it's her."

He grunts and moves aside. "You kids all look the same to me."

"What's going on?" I ask when I finally get inside. I plop the box on the floor. Putting the playbills together gave me six different paper cuts, but I think they came out really well.

"That's what's going on," Rory says, pointing to the corner of the room. Jake is sitting at one of the round tables with about ten journalists with tape recorders and notebooks surrounding him. A guy in a suit and tie hovers protectively, making sure that no one gets too close. I'm pretty sure that's his manager. He looks familiar from pictures I've seen of Jake at movie premieres and stuff.

"I don't know if I can do this," Rory says quietly. Her usually bright eyes have dimmed.

"The play? You can totally do this. It's just one night. It's a half hour, really. And then tomorrow we have the bar mitzvah and the movie to look forward to, right?"

She shakes her head. "I didn't mean the play. I meant Jake. How can I have a relationship with someone when the whole world watches his every move? How would that even work?"

"I don't know," I admit.

"Any minute I keep thinking he's going to wake up and wonder why on earth he likes me."

"There's a million reasons to like you," I tell her.

Jake looks up at that moment. His face changes when he sees Rory watching. It softens from the stiff smile he'd been giving the reporters, to a genuine one. I see her smile in return, despite her worries. I never thought I'd say it, but I don't envy her right now. Jake seems great, but in a spotlight that big, there's nowhere to hide.

• • • • • • • • • • •

Everyone's on edge by the end of the day, and Ray treats us all to pizza. While we're eating, he says, "All right, anyone need to whinge about anything? If so, now's the time."

"*Whinge* means 'complain,'" Jake translates. "I did a movie-of-the-week in Australia when I was younger."

"Hey, me, too!" David calls out.

Everyone laughs, including Jake.

"*My* last movie-of-the-week was in Greenland!" Annabelle says. "Pretty cold up there, but my trailer was heated really well!"

Sari raises her hand.

"Let me guess," Ray says. "Movie-of-the-week in the rain forests of Brazil?"

"Nope," Sari says. "I have a complaint. How come all the women have to wear their hair either in a bun or under a scarf or a bonnet? Where's the fun in that?"

"Well, that's how they did things back then," Ray says. "Can't rewrite history."

"Still," Sari says, "everyone would look much prettier if I could actually do something with their hair. Maybe some color . . . or a barrette or two?"

"Bonnet and buns, baby."

Sari grumbles.

"Anyone else?"

No one replies. "All right, then. Big day tomorrow. Go home, get some rest. Be here at two P.M. for hair and makeup. Crew, we'll be setting up the chairs and prepping the stage."

Everyone says their good-byes and I get the same kind of pang I did last night with David, that I'll really miss everyone. It actually physically hurts my stomach. On the sidelines it never hurt. Or if it did, it was a different kind, an easier kind.

Emily talks nonstop from the time we get home until the time we turn out the lights. I know she's excited and nervous, but I really just want to be alone. Eventually I put my head under the covers and make a tent, like she does with her math books. It's peaceful under here, and cozy. I can still hear her, but it's very muffled. She finally drifts off and I bring my head back out. I think I was about to run out of oxygen anyway.

I awake in the morning to find Emily and Aunt Bethany standing at the foot of my bed, watching me. "Happy birthday!" they cry out.

"We thought you were going to sleep your birthday away," Aunt Bethany says.

I grunt and curl up on my side. I'm officially thirteen now. Apparently I have twenty-four hours to become a complete person. I wonder how likely that will be to happen if I stay in bed all day.

Aunt Bethany tugs on the covers in an attempt to turn me over. "You're not supposed to dread birthdays until you're my age."

"Don't you want your presents?" Emily asks.

I open one eye. Emily holds up two gift bags in each hand and swings them back and forth. I open the other eye. She drops one pink bag next to me. "Open mine first," Emily says. I sit up, dig through the tissue paper, and pull out a framed picture of me, Emily, and Jake sitting on the living room couch the night he came over. I hadn't even seen anyone snap a picture.

"To replace the poster," she explains, grinning. "I have a copy, too."

My eyes get watery and I have to blink a few times. "I love it."

Aunt Bethany hands me two more bags. "These are from Roger and Ray." The first holds an issue of *Inventors Digest* with a card announcing I'll soon be receiving my first of twelve monthly issues. The other is a copy of *The Dictionary of Aussie Slang, 3rd Edition.* Easy enough to figure out which gift came from which guy.

"And last but not least," Aunt Bethany says, handing me the smallest of the bags. "I took the liberty of putting David's CD on it, I hope you don't mind."

I turn the bag upside down on the bed, and out plops a brand-new iPod. "I can't believe it," I say, picking it up. "This is amazing! Thank you guys." I reach out and give them both hugs, which feels really great.

The two of them leave me to get dressed and the first thing I do is turn on the iPod. Soon enough I'll be turning it over to Mom as a replacement for losing hers. But it's all mine for at least another month! I recognize the name of the song that David sang at Apple Grove and put that one on. Then I lie back down and close my eyes. It's just as beautiful as it was then. So much so, that I can swear I feel the earth spinning again below me.

• • • • • • • • • • •

Emily and I arrive early at the community center. A bunch of teenage girls are already hanging around outside. I hear them talking about what they're going to say to Jake when he arrives. At this point, if there's anyone in town that doesn't know about the play this afternoon, they've been living under a rock.

Almost everyone is already there when we get to the back room, including Jake! After spending the last few days around him, he almost seems like any regular kid. Almost.

"How did you sneak by those girls?" I ask.

"I have skills," he says with a wink.

Rory rolls her eyes. "I snuck him in through the fire exit."

"Yes," Jake says, "but I had the *skills* to follow you." He sweeps her up and swings her around like he does to Emily in the play. She laughs and holds on tight. I'm not sure they're going to hold out on that not-dating thing till ninth grade.

Ray reminds everyone what their jobs are, and shoos us out the door. While the boys are moving the card tables and couches out of the way to set up the chairs, I pull a small table over to the entrance and tape my poster to the front of it. Aunt Bethany gave me a cash box and a calculator, so I'm all set for my job as ticket seller. I pull out the playbills from the cabinets where I'd stored them the day before and pile them up. Even though everything is going according to plan, I'm very glad Opening Night is also Closing Night.

Big Joe starts putting up the sets, and I go over to watch. I'm amazed at what he's been able to do in such a short period of time. He even painted a backdrop of a forest. Ray has it organized so that each song takes place on a different part of the stage, and Big Joe is setting up according to a chart that Ray drew. There's the outside of Tevye's house, the kitchen and living room, the forest, and a roof for the Fiddler to sit on. Even though Big Joe isn't the easiest to talk to, I can't help but ask him how he learned to make all these things.

"My father taught me everything he knew," Big Joe says as he crosses the stage to set up another prop. "He did all the plays in town."

"I didn't know that," I say.

He nods and lifts the huge wooden key as if it weighed

nothing. "This one he made for a secret admirer. He said it was the key to his heart." He laughs. "Guess my pa had a pretty big heart to make a key that big!"

Aw, Big Joe really is a softy.

His voice turns gruff again when he says, "Don't got no place for these two," and hands me the duck-headed cane, and the small purple bottle.

"Really? They're not on the prop list from the script?"

He shakes his head and points to the poster board. I scan the list of which props go in which scene. The basket, candlestick holder, and wine bottle go on the kitchen table, the knife on the counter, the gray blanket is for a picnic scene. Tevye carries the Bible, the necklace is on a few different sisters in different songs, Tevye's wife wears the shawl, and the giant key is in the barn. But nothing about a cane or a purple bottle anywhere.

"I guess I'll hold on to them," I tell him. He shrugs and gets back to work. I stash them behind the ticket table to deal with later.

I go to the back room to see if anyone needs my help and have to try really hard not to laugh. The cast has changed into their costumes, with their hair and makeup done. All the girls look like how I did when I left Bettie's house that first day. Even the boys are wearing blush and black eyeliner.

"It's a theatre thing," David says when he sees my expression. He puffs out his chest and says, "I think I look very dashing for a milkman."

"Yeah, the eyeliner really makes your eyes pop."

"I'm actually afraid to look in a mirror," he says.

I stand back to admire him from afar. "I do like the suit and the floppy hat."

He tilts the hat a bit. "It was my dad's. My mom gave it to me last night."

"It looks really nice. Very Russian milkman-ish, while still being stylish."

"How do *I* look?" Rory says, joining us.

"Um, did they have green eye shadow in Russia in 1905?"

"I talked her out of the glitter," she says, "so be grateful for that. If I break out in hives, you'll have to toss me my allergy medication!"

Emily joins us, all dressed in her top and long skirt, a blue and white bonnet covering the top of her head. Annabelle had to hem the skirt a little, but everything else was in Grandma's trunk from when she played Tzeitel. They really could be twins. Emily keeps pushing the bonnet back up on her forehead.

"How do you feel?" I ask.

"Like the whole town is about to watch me sing and dance with Jake Harrison, which can't possibly be true because how crazy does that sound?"

"You'll be great," I assure her. "And it'll be over before you know it."

"Six minutes and sixteen seconds," she says. "That's how long my two big numbers are, combined. The rest of the time I'm just in the background." She wanders off, pushing her bonnet away from her eyes and whispering "*Six and sixteen, six and sixteen.*"

"Do you think she'll be okay?" I ask Rory. "You know her a lot better than I do."

"I think she'll be great," Rory says. "I may know her longer, but I've been trying to get her to dance ever since I saw how good she was. It was the very first night I babysat for her. Remind me to tell you that story one day; she was such a little sneak. Anyway, she'd never do it for me. And you've got her starring in a musical! Hey, you should really go sell tickets now before they bust down the door."

"Break a leg," I tell her.

"I just might," she says. "Go!"

Rory was right, people are pressed up against the doors outside, waiting to be let in. And it's not just girls wanting to see Jake. People of all ages are out there, many with cash in their hands. Before I can even sit behind the ticket table, people begin thrusting money at me. No one complains about the price. Some people don't even ask for change from a ten-dollar bill because they're in too much of a hurry to get a seat! I guess six dollars to see a movie star is pretty low. I could have asked for double. Or triple!

The cash box fills up quickly and I have to rummage through the Lost and Found cabinet to find an old gym bag to stuff the money into. Dollar bills are flying everywhere as I hurry to give people their change. David comes out to help, which is really nice of him considering he has the biggest role in the play and is wearing eyeliner.

Eventually the room is filled to capacity, with people standing in the back and kids sitting cross-legged in the front of the stage. Angelina has somehow managed to plant herself right in the front row, just as she said she would, even though I definitely didn't see her come through the ticket line. I join the rest of the crew off to the side of the stage where Ray had been smart enough to reserve seats. Aunt Bethany and Uncle Roger are right behind me. It's warm in the room now, and a lot of people are fanning themselves with their playbills.

Ray — who in slacks and a button-down shirt is more dressed up than I've ever seen him — has to shout three times before the crowd quiets down. "Welcome, everyone, to the new Willow Falls Community Playhouse production of *Fiddler on the Roof*!"

The crowd cheers. I'm just grateful he called the play by the right name. He continues, "Thank you for coming out today and supporting the arts here in Willow Falls. We hope you enjoy the show!"

All I can think is, in half an hour, this will be over. I'll be a whole and complete person, or whatever Angelina said I needed to be before the end of my birthday. But then the curtain parts. David stands center stage, in his black suit and floppy hat and milkman's jug, and all other thoughts fly out of my head.

He takes a deep breath and says the only line in our version of the play that isn't part of a song: "Without our traditions, our lives would be as shaky as a fiddler on the roof!" The curtain parts farther, to reveal Bucky Whitehead sitting on the fake roof. As Bucky starts playing his violin, David starts belting out *"Tradition! Tradition! Tradition!"* And the crowd starts clapping and hollering. They quiet down just as quickly, though, when they realize we never considered the whole need-for-microphones thing.

"Matchmaker, Matchmaker" is up next, with Emily, Rory, and Stephanie as the three oldest daughters. Emily glides across the stage, her voice pure and strong. Rory and Stephanie, well, they're not really singing, so much as *talking* the words. And the dancing is more like, well, *walking*. Grace and Bailey run around after the older sisters trying to be silly and get their attention. The lyrics are pretty funny as the sisters basically beg the matchmaker not to match them with a total loser, and the audience is cracking up. At one point Stephanie completely forgets the choreography and does a cartwheel followed by a back handspring instead. Mrs. Grayson drops her head into her hands, but the audience cheers! By the end, Emily's bonnet has fallen over her eyes so many times that she winds up ripping it off and tossing it inside the black trunk.

David then appears in the make-believe barn and launches into "If I Were a Rich Man." At this point, everyone in the audience over fifty starts singing along with him. Seriously, like, two hundred people are singing and David just goes right along with it.

At the end, Connor joins him on stage. He's wearing a fake beard and a pillow stuffed under his shirt. He's supposed to look rich, so he's wearing a fancy suit that used to belong to Mrs. Grayson's late husband. He and David sing "To Life," which is a really rowdy, upbeat song. They totally ham it up, tripping over each other, throwing up their arms, yelling, "*L'chiam!* To life!" At the end they fall to the ground, kicking up their legs, and get a standing ovation. They exit the stage, bowing repeatedly. The curtains close. When they reopen, Jake

Harrison is standing in front of the forest with Emily by his side. The audience jumps back up and goes crazy, whistling and yelling. Ray has to come out and shush them so the song can begin.

Jake does an amazing job with "Miracle of Miracles," swinging Emily around as they weave in and out of fake trees, singing with such love and confidence. It's easy to see why he's a star. Bucky's violin sings right along to Jake's words. When it comes time for the backward somersault, Jake gets stuck in exactly the same place as in our living room, and Emily gleefully pushes him the rest of the way over. The audience chants for an encore, but there are still four more songs left to go. Leo is really good in his number with Stephanie, and Annabelle is funny as the gossipy matchmaker. Rory and Vinnie — who I haven't gotten a chance to talk to at all — pretty much give up in the middle and make up their own lyrics. In the last song, Amanda's shawl gets tangled on a fake tree branch and David has to untangle her before she chokes. Other than that, the play is a rousing success!

By popular demand, Jake and Emily come back out and do their whole number all over again. Behind me, Aunt Bethany weeps openly. She must have used up a whole memory card with all the pictures I heard her taking throughout the play.

Ray bounds out on the stage when they're through. "Good on ya, everyone!" he says, slipping back into Aussie. "Bonza job today!" He gestures for the whole cast to go back on stage to take their bows. The audience stands and claps and yells *Woo-hoo* and takes pictures. Another new emotion fills me —

pride. But not pride in myself, pride in people that I care about for being so amazing. I close my eyes, waiting for whatever's supposed to happen to me to happen. I don't know what I'm expecting, a voice to come down from heaven? A telegram revealing some big secret?

Jake's manager whisks him off the stage pretty quickly, but the applause continues for everyone else. When everyone's convinced that Jake isn't coming back out, the clapping peters out, and the room starts to clear. The rest of the cast runs off the stage to wherever their families are waiting. Emily gives me a high five, and runs into her parents' arms. A tall, thin man in a black T-shirt and jeans heads toward us. I don't think he's from around here. I saw him talking to Jake's manager before. He walks up and introduces himself as a Broadway producer from New York City. "You should try out for my new show," he tells Emily. "You could have a future on the stage."

Emily smiles and says, "Thanks, but my future's going to be solving the world's greatest mysteries through math."

"Are you sure, Em?" Aunt Bethany asks.

Emily nods. "It was really fun, but this was Grandma's dream, not mine. Except for the Jake part, which was totally mine!"

The producer shrugs and says, "Well, if you change your mind, here's my card." I'm sure he's not used to people turning him down.

The two other Emilys pull my Emily away, and I drift to the edge of the crowd. Even with all the excitement of the play still rushing through me, an emptiness is rushing in with it. Like, the opposite of what it should feel like when your soul attaches to your body. Was I a fool to believe Angelina when she told me all the stuff that would happen if I did the play?

I watch Rory and Amanda and David find their families, and wish for the first time that my parents could have been here. I know it's impossible, but at least it would make this hollow feeling a little less painful.

I try to keep busy by gathering up the stuff I left in the cabinets behind the ticket table. All the money (which, thankfully, is still there in the gym bag) and the cane and bottle. I figure I'll give the money to Ray to figure out what to do with. I spot Angelina still in her seat and head over to her first. I don't have a plan of what to say, so I'm hoping something comes to me before I get there.

Nope. Nothing. I sit down next to her and wait for her to speak.

"Ah, my cane!" she says, plucking it right from my hand.

"This is *yours*?"

She nods. "I must have left it somewhere the other day."

"The other *day*? It's been in the diner for thirty-five years!"

"That long?" she says, shaking her head. "Time really flies."

"I'm confused. If it wasn't a prop in the play, but it was on your list, doesn't that mean that I wrote down the right list after all? You said since I completed the wrong list, I had to put on the play in order to repay my debt. Not to mention the whole thing about finding out why I'm in Willow Falls. Whatever *that* means."

"You kids, always talking in circles. What is it that you're asking?"

"Was this the right list after all?"

She shrugs. "What does it matter?"

I throw up my arms in exasperation. "It matters! I mean, the whole play —"

"Wasn't it wonderful?" she asks, beaming. "Consider your debt repaid!"

"But I still don't understand! Why did I have to put on the play in the first place?"

She shrugs. "It's one of my favorites." Then she taps the end of the cane on the floor and starts singing "If I Were a Rich Man."

I know there are people milling all around us, laughing and talking, but all I can focus on is Angelina, like we're in our own little pocket of the world.

Speaking slowly, I say, "So you're telling me I did all this because you wanted to see the play and didn't get a chance to thirty-five years ago? That's *it*? You said something special would happen for me afterward, but nothing did. Nothing." If I were in a cartoon, steam would be coming out of my ears.

"Nothing happened?" she repeats calmly. Pointing at Emily, she says, "You got that girl to do what she loves in a way that surpassed her wildest dreams. And the boy, the movie star, he got a chance to prove he's more than just a pretty face." She points to Bettie. "She always felt hidden in her mother's shadow. You gave her a chance to shine." Then she points the cane at Bucky, who is shaking hands with the Broadway producer. "That man stopped playing the violin the night your grandmother bowed out of the play. And look at him tonight. He's radiant!"

She points to Ray. "There's enough money to start up the theatre group again. They're going to need a director, and who do you think they'll ask? You got a whole community to come together to celebrate the theatre — something that hasn't happened in thirty-five years. And your friend over there?" She points to David, who is tossing his hat in the air and trying to catch it on his head. "Did you see his face during his first song? He's not confused about tradition anymore. He knows exactly what his role is when he stands up there tomorrow for his bar mitzvah. *You* did all that for everyone, and more. You — the girl who only wanted to sit on the sidelines."

"How . . . how do you know all this about everyone?"

"Oh, I get around," she says, her birthmark wiggling.

I look around the room at my friends. Big Joe is twirling Mrs. Grayson around the stage and she's giggling like a teenager. Angelina is right about everything she said, except for the last part. I look down at my hands. "But you know I didn't do any of this for them. I did it all because you told me there was something I needed to know that I could only find out after putting on this play. I never stopped to think what anyone else needed, or wanted, at all. I can't take any of the credit."

She laughs. "Of course you can! Are you so self-centered that you think the universe cares what your motivations are? If a wealthy businessman donates ten million dollars to build a new hospital, would it matter if he only did it to get a building named after him? Not to the people inside it. If everyone waited to do something good until they had purely unselfish motivations, no good would ever get done in the world. The point is to do it anyway. To do it at all."

The point is to do it at all. I'd never really done anything big before today. "I never thought of it that way."

"And soon enough," she adds, "it will be easier to see what people need, and how to help them. Only the rarest of young people have that gift from birth."

I think about Rory, and how she's always one step ahead of everyone else. "I don't think I'd be very good at it," I admit.

She shrugs. "It won't happen overnight. Don't be so hard on yourself."

The crowd is thinning now. It's mostly cast and crew and their families. A few older women are setting up card games, and a group of moms are giving their kids snacks, and chatting. I turn back to Angelina. "So I guess all that stuff about me finding out why I'm here in Willow Falls was just to get me to put on the play?"

She doesn't reply.

"Angelina?"

She just twirls her cane, the duck's head twisting toward me, then away, toward, then away. I have to grit my teeth to keep from yelling in frustration as my earlier anger creeps back in. Rory was wrong this time. Angelina doesn't always come through in the end. I grab the gym bag full of money, and the purple bottle. "Here," I say, holding out the bottle as I stand up. "This must be yours, too. There was no place for it in the play."

She shakes her head. "It's not mine."

"Why was it on the list, then?"

"It's for you," she says.

"Me? What am I supposed to do with it?"

She shrugs. “If you don’t want it, why don’t you give it back to the person you got it from? She’s right over there.”

She gestures with the tip of the cane toward the group of women with their toddlers. She’s right. The woman *is* here.

“Fine, I will.” I stomp off toward the woman, then force myself to calm down. It’s not like it’s her fault that Angelina is once again not being straight with me.

I tap her on the shoulder. “Excuse me? I’m sorry to bother you.”

“You’re the girl with the bracelet,” she says. “You don’t want to trade back, do you? I don’t have the bracelet anymore, and I’m not bringing that bottle back into my house.”

I lower the bottle to my side. “Oh. Are you sure?”

“I’m sure. I only have bad memories associated with it.”

I open my mouth to say okay, but something stops me. I don’t know whether it’s because the conversation with Angelina is still fresh in my mind, or whether I really care, or whether her last word stretched out a tiny bit too long indicating she has more to say, but I ask, “Why?”

She immediately asks one of the other moms to watch her daughter, then pulls me onto one of the couches. I’m already wondering if this was a mistake. Ray said he’d take me to the mall to get a gift for David. Then later, Rory, Emily, and Amanda said they’re planning a girls-only night for my birthday. But I’m sitting here now, so I might as well listen.

“No one asked me about that bottle for twenty-five years,” she says. “Until the day you rang my bell. I was so eager to get rid of it that I didn’t tell you anything. I’ve felt a little guilty about that ever since. The owner of the bottle should know its story.”

"I should?"

She nods. "What do you know about the bottle already?"

I turn the jar around in my hands. "Um, it's small. And purple. It's pretty?"

"That's it?" she asks.

I nod, wondering what else I'm possibly supposed to know. Was it forged in a volcano on Venus?

She glances back at the group of kids and moms, and then leans close. "I haven't told anyone about this, ever." She takes a deep breath. "Okay, here goes. When I was in eighth grade, so around your age, I had a crush on this boy. I knew my best friend liked him, too. The eighth-grade dance at Apple Grove was coming up and everyone was going to be there. I thought that would be my night. We would dance, he would pledge his undying love, that sort of thing."

I nod, wondering when we get to the part about the bottle.

"I was always pretty fortunate in the boy department, and kind of suspected that he liked me. But I didn't want to take any chances. My grandmother — may she rest in peace — knew this old woman on the other side of town who specialized in, shall we say, *unusual* things. My grandmother brought me to her house, and I told the woman my problem. I know this is going to sound crazy, but she sold me a love potion. In that very bottle."

Well! I wasn't expecting that! I look down at the bottle again, as though seeing it for the first time.

The woman rushes on. "It cost me all the money I'd saved over thirteen years, but all I'd need to do is get the boy to drink it, look into my eyes, and he'd love me forever. Somehow, though, and I still don't know how, I lost it. One day it was in my desk drawer, and the next day it was gone. I searched everywhere. My grandmother offered to give me the money to buy another batch, but the old lady refused to sell it to me. She said she never made the same potion twice."

As interesting as her story is, I can't help noticing my friends glancing over at us. Ray even points to his watch, but what can I do? I turn back to the woman.

"Anyway, I went to the dance, determined that I'd still find a way to get the boy to like me. But when I got there, my best friend was dancing with him. And there, on the table beside them, was the little glass bottle, empty."

"Wow," I say, looking down at the bottle again. Talk about your middle school drama!

"I took the bottle and left the dance. From that day on, Molly and James were inseparable. She and I never spoke about it. In fact, we never spoke from that day on at all."

My head springs up. "Did you say Molly and James?"

She nods. "They had this storybook romance. Wound up getting married, having a kid, the whole thing. I couldn't stop thinking how it should have been me. How she robbed me of my life."

A roaring sound fills my head. "You . . . you must really hate her."

"I did. For a long time." She looks over at her daughter, who is currently demonstrating to Rory's brother, Sawyer, how she can touch her nose with her tongue. "But seriously," she says with a laugh, "who marries the guy she dates at thirteen? I look back at it now, and I'm sure James wouldn't have been the great love of my life. I got married in my late twenties, and had Sara four years ago. If that potion had worked, she wouldn't be on this planet. How could I hate Molly after that? More than losing the guy, though, it was the loss of my best friend that was the hardest to accept." She shakes her head, like trying to shake the memory loose. "So, when I saw that someone was interested in the bottle, I realized I was ready to let go of it, and the bitterness that it represented. Thank you for that."

The hand holding the bottle starts to shake, and I have to cover it with my other one. That doesn't help to stop the shaking.

"Are you all right?" she asks. "You look a little green."

The roaring sound keeps getting louder, threatening to drown out our conversation. "Just out of curiosity," I ask, my voice shaking as much as my hands, "the old woman who sold you the potion, did she have a birthmark on her cheek? Shaped like a duck?"

"Yes, how did you know that?"

"A lucky guess," I tell her. I stand up, gripping the bottle so tightly the bottom digs into my palm. "Thank you for telling me your story."

"Thank you for listening. It felt good to get it out." She touches my arm lightly, and I watch as she goes behind her daughter and gives her a squeeze.

By this point, all the extra chairs have been put away, and the tables and couches have been returned to their usual spots. Angelina is nowhere to be seen. I spot Ray taking down the last of the sets and hand him the gym bag. "You should stay and celebrate," I tell him. I focus on keeping the rising hysteria out of my voice so he doesn't question me.

Before he can reply, I run out of the community center. The GONE FISHING sign is up on both the antique store and the historical society, which does not surprise me. I take off toward Emily's house, trying to outrun the emotions that threaten to unravel me. Anger, hurt, betrayal, shock. They keep hitting me, one after the other. My mother, the one who never does anything wrong, the one who always says how important it is to have friends, this is the woman who did such a terrible thing to her own best friend? Not to mention tricking her own husband into falling in love with her? Poor Dad! My heart aches for him. All these years he's been so smitten, and it wasn't even his choice! Maybe he would have picked the other woman if he'd been allowed to decide. It explains why he's always put her on such a pedestal, always looking at her as though he's the luckiest man in the world to have her.

I feel sick. It's like my whole life is different from what I thought it was. I wish I could just call Mom and confront her with this, but it could take days for the message to reach her.

I'm *totally* not giving her my new iPod!

It feels like I've been running forever. By the time the house comes into view, I'm ready to pass out. I'm halfway up the lawn before I notice the shapes of two people sitting on the porch steps. One very tall, one short.

My parents.

Chapter Twenty-three

"Surprise!" Dad yells.

"Happy birthday!" Mom shouts.

They jump up and throw their arms around me and I'm too stunned to do anything other than stand there, panting from the run. "What . . . what are you doing here?" I manage to choke out.

Dad laughs. "Aunt Bethany told us about how you were really running this whole play. We wanted to show up and surprise you, but we missed it by twenty minutes. So we figured we'd wait for you here rather than disrupt the activities."

"But how?"

"The lemurs were very accommodating in the mating department," Mom says, still holding on to me. "We finished the study earlier than expected."

She finally pulls away. "Let me see you. You look so grown-up!" Her eyes fill with tears.

"And so colorful!" Dad says.

I look down at my white shorts and blue top, courtesy of Aunt Bethany.

"Why don't we go sit down?" Mom suggests, stroking my hair like she used to when I was little. "You seem a bit shell-shocked."

Hand shaking, I pull the glass bottle out of my pocket and hold it up to her. It takes a few seconds to register, but then her very tanned skin drains of all color. She physically backs away from it.

"What's that?" Dad asks, taking it from me. "It's pretty. Did someone give it to you as a birthday gift?"

"Not exactly," I reply. "Mom? Maybe you'd like to tell him what it is?"

She drops down onto her knees, right on the grass.

"Molly!" Dad says, rushing to her side. "Are you all right?"

"Where did you get that?" she asks. Her voice sounds like it's coming through a very long tube. "Did Polly give it to you?"

"I don't actually know her name," I tell her.

"Long brown hair? Very pretty? Probably hates me?"

I nod. "That's her."

"Your old friend from school?" Dad asks, kneeling beside her. "I know you two fell out of touch, but why would she hate you?"

Mom looks at him, her eyes bleak. "You never noticed that we stopped talking once you and I started dating?"

He shrugs. "Not particularly."

She stares at him for a minute, then rolls her eyes in my direction, as though I'm supposed to commiserate with her on the cluelessness of guys. I don't show any expression, and she stares back down at the grass.

"I knew one day we'd have to have this conversation," she says. "It might as well be now. My guilt has only been getting worse."

Dad reaches out to take her hand. *Now* I roll my eyes. Wait till he hears that he only wants to comfort and love her because she tricked him into it.

"Whatever it is, Molly, you can tell us," he says.

She gently pulls her hand away from his, and takes a deep, shuddering breath. "One day, back in eighth grade, I was at Polly's house after school. I overheard her grandmother on the phone, bragging about how her granddaughter was about to snag a boy. I remember she said good genes run in that family. They're tall and sturdy. Good stock."

The corners of my mouth twitch at that one, but I quickly stop myself.

"Anyway, she said how Polly had bought something from Angelina D'Angelo. A love potion." She cringes as she says the words, unwilling to even look in Dad's direction. He starts to laugh, but Mom's story is about to get a lot less funny. "I knew exactly who Polly would be using it on, and I knew exactly where she'd have hidden it. A few days later, I snuck in when I knew no one would be home — no one locked their doors in Willow Falls back then. Probably still don't. Anyway, I took the bottle."

At this point in the story, Dad looks down at the bottle he's still holding. "This?"

She nods miserably. "Then at the eighth-grade dance, I brought the boy I liked a cup of juice and he drank it." She pauses here and waits for Dad to catch up. I watch as realization dawns on him, slowly at first, then with a sudden burst of understanding.

"Me?" he asks, letting the bottle slip from his grip onto the grass.

Mom bites her lip and forces herself to look at him. "Saying I'm sorry doesn't cut it, I know. I couldn't risk Polly snagging you."

He rocks back on his heels. "Polly liked *me*?"

She nods. "And I knew you liked her. And I trapped you into a lifetime of loving someone you didn't want to love. At first, when we were young, it didn't bother me much. Then as we got older, and Tara came along, the guilt started to eat away at me. What right did I have to play with people's lives like that?"

No one answers her. She reaches out for me and tries to pull me down. I stay standing. She sighs and says, "But on top of all that, and maybe the worst part, is that Angelina knew I'd taken it. She chaperoned the dance that night, and she saw me pour the purple liquid into a cup. She didn't try to stop me, or to make me pay her for the potion, but she warned me that if we had a child one day, that child would pay the price of my betrayal."

My knees buckle and I join them in the grass. *"What?"*

"She said that when our child turned thirteen, he or she would have to come work for her to pay off my debt. *Alone.* I agreed, because when you're thirteen, how can you even conceive of having your own child? It seemed a lifetime away."

I place both hands on the ground, willing myself not to topple over.

Mom grips Dad's leg. "That's why I didn't want to come back here after college. I thought if we moved away, Angelina would forget about all this. And for a year or two, I put it behind me as we settled into our life. Soon Tara was born. I was so in love with this baby, I actually congratulated myself on stealing the potion. Otherwise I wouldn't have her.

"I had one month of pure joy with the man that I loved and the baby who I treasured more than anything on the planet, until a silver rattle arrived from Willow Falls. The card inside the gift box said simply, *Looking forward to meeting Tara in thirteen years.*

"So we moved again. And again, she found us. So we just kept moving. I always made sure our phone number was unlisted. I made sure our address wasn't online anywhere. I tried to keep Tara close, never letting her be with strangers, always making sure I knew where she was and how to reach her. But somehow, Angelina kept tracking us down. I thought we'd finally shaken her this last time, but then that telegram arrived and —"

Dad sits up straight. "That wasn't about your job?"

Mom shakes her head. "It was my final warning. Tara was almost thirteen and it was time to pay my debt. But how was I supposed to get her to go to a place we'd never even taken her before? And to send her alone, when I'd barely let her out of my sight for thirteen years? I called Bethany — who of course knows nothing about the love potion, or my arrangement with Angelina — and she said she'd love to have her for the summer. So that was a relief. Then I booked the train, since she had to arrive alone. But I still had no idea what explanation to give." She turns to me. "And then you handed me the solution on a silver platter. You got suspended from school. So I bumped up the dates with Bethany and told her you'd had a bit of trouble and would be arriving early. I changed the train, and, well, here you are."

My whole body is literally shaking with disbelief and shock at all the things she'd kept hidden for so many years. Out of all the things she just told me, one shines like a beacon through the thick web of lies. "So it was you? *You're* the reason I'm here in Willow Falls?"

Mom doesn't say anything. She doesn't have to. "I can't believe it!" I cry out. "She was right after all!" The last thing I want to do is laugh, but I can't help it. It's just all so crazy.

"What's funny about this?" Mom asks. "Who was right about what?"

"Angelina! She said after the play I'd find out why I was here, in Willow Falls. I told her I knew exactly why, but she said I didn't. Guess she was right about that!" Then I fall silent again. The whole story doesn't make sense. Angelina didn't come find me and make me do work for her. *I* was the one who went into her shop. I think back to the order of things. The chain of events started because I needed money. If I'd kept the money my parents had given me, I wouldn't have needed to sell anything. But how could Angelina be sure I'd need money? There was only one person who had the opportunity to take my wallet. She was short, she was wide, and she wore a ton of makeup that would cover any blemishes or birthmarks shaped like talking animals. How could I not have seen it before? "The woman on the train!"

Mom nods miserably. "I almost fainted when I saw her. It took a few seconds to recognize her under all that makeup and the dark wig."

"Wait," Dad says, "you're talking about the woman with the first-class ticket?"

"She stole my money!" I say, in amazement. I didn't lose it after all. Or my phone, or Mom's iPod! "That's how she got me into her store. She made it seem like it was my choice, when it never was."

"Tara, I'm so incredibly sorry about everything. I know I've disrupted your life over and over with the moves, and by being so overprotective. But I love you so much and I only wanted to keep us all together. Has your time here been awful?" Mom cringes in anticipation of my answer.

I consider telling her yes, but what good would that do? "It was really hard in the beginning. But I made some good friends, and that made it better."

Her whole body relaxes. It relaxes to the point that tears start pouring down her face. "You can't imagine how relieved I am to hear that."

"Well, then," Dad says, wiping away Mom's tears with his giant hand, "you're going to be relieved to hear this, too. Polly was a nice girl, and pretty of course, as you said. But I only liked her because she gave me her math homework."

In between gasps of breath, she asks, "Really? You're not just saying that?"

"I'm not just saying that," he says.

She attempts a smile, but it slips away. She looks down at the grass again and waits until she can get her tears under control.

Then she says, "I'm glad I didn't make you lose out on being with Polly. But there's still no excuse for what I did. And don't say you love me in spite of it, because that's just the love potion talking. We'll never know if you ever would have loved me without it."

"That's true," he says. "If I actually drank it."

"What?" we both yell.

"I was a thirteen-year-old boy! You think I'm going to be seen at a dance drinking bright purple juice? It would stain my teeth! I was trying to impress the ladies."

"But . . . but I saw you drink it!"

"You saw me take it, then you saw me point out the full moon, then you saw me drink an empty cup."

"But . . . what happened to the potion?"

He shrugs. "I poured it into the fountain."

Now it's Mom's turn to have the full-body shakes. She actually looks like she's convulsing. Dad and I both reach out to her and she collapses in our arms, sobbing. I start crying, too, and Dad joins in. We're crying so hard that I don't register the opening and closing of car doors until Uncle Roger says, "Now, *that's* what I call a family reunion!"

The three of us look at each other and start laughing so hard we start crying all over again.

• • • • • • • • • • •

After I change my tear-soaked clothes, I stand in front of the bathroom mirror. There's no denying it. I feel different. I even *look* different. My dark eyes have more depth to them, like I can see further inside, and further outside, too. Knowing the true story of my life — and my mom's life — changes everything. My anger's gone; I think I cried it all out. All that's left is the understanding of what Mom tried to do for me for all those years. And it's nice to know that she wasn't always so perfect — far from it. I might have tried to steal a stuffed goat, but she stole her best friend's future husband!

Aunt Bethany stores some of her extra makeup in the medicine cabinet, and for the first time in my life, I think it might be nice to put some on. After watching Bettie, I know what to do. Or I thought I did, until the mascara winds up on my nose instead of my eyelashes. I wash everything off except for the shimmery lip gloss that makes my lips feel really soft.

Mom's waiting for me in the hall when I get out. She's wearing fresh clothes, too. Her face is still very blotchy. She lifts my arm so that the red bracelet slips down a little toward my elbow.

"I thought that looked familiar," she says.

"What, this old thing? I've had this forever."

She smiles. "Have you, now?"

"Okay, it's yours. I found them when I was looking for jewelry for Aunt Bethany. Emily had the other one but then I had to trade it . . . actually, it was for the bottle. Polly took it."

She looks alarmed. "Polly?"

I nod. "She saw it on Emily's wrist and asked for it."

"Huh," Mom says, letting my arm fall. "I wonder what to make of that."

"What do you mean?"

"They used to be ours. Mine and Polly's. They were friendship bracelets. After the, ah, *incident*, she slipped hers into my locker."

I shrug. "I'm sure she didn't know it was the same one. She doesn't know I'm your daughter."

Mom's eyes fill with tears again. "It was terrible what I did to her. And she wasn't the only one who lost out; I lost my best friend. How many of those does someone get in a lifetime? Not many, I'll tell you. That's why I always tried to tell you how important friendship is." She sighs. "I know moving so much didn't give you much of a chance to find that out."

"Hey, if it makes you feel better," I tell her, "Polly doesn't hate you anymore. She said once she got married and had Sara, that she —"

"Wait, *what*? She has a daughter named Sara?"

"Yes. She's four years old, I think."

"I can't believe it," she says, and the tears spring back again. But this time she's smiling, too. "When we were little girls we loved it that our names rhymed. We promised when we had our own daughters we would name them rhyming names, too." She laughs. "And we did!"

"That's really weird."

"What a strange coincidence," she says, shaking her head.

"There are no coincidences in Willow Falls," I tell her.

She smiles. "Maybe not." Then she says, "What's that? Is someone singing?"

I listen for a second, and then I hear it, too. I motion her back into the bathroom with me and we look out the window.

"It's David, in the pool hole. His bar mitzvah is tomorrow, and he likes to practice down there."

"It's really beautiful," she says, opening the window wider.

I step next to her and look out. "I know."

She turns to look at me. I can see her smiling from out of the corner of my eye, but I don't turn. "The lip gloss looks pretty," she says.

I smile. We stand there listening for a few more minutes. As great as he was in the play today, it still doesn't compare to how he sounds in the backyard. It's too bad the bar mitzvah isn't outside. And then it hits me! Why *can't* the bar mitzvah be outside? Could I possibly pull it off in time? "Mom, I have to go make some calls, okay?"

"Of course," she says, closing her eyes as David slides effortlessly into Shalom Rav.

Emily has changed out of her costume and is already back at her desk like she didn't just star in a play and have a Broadway producer invite her to audition. I have to laugh. "That was fast."

She turns around and I laugh again. She hasn't taken off any of her stage makeup. She grins at me. "I'm planning on keeping it on for the bar mitzvah tomorrow and the premiere."

"I don't think it works that way," I tell her. "You'd have to sleep sitting up!"

"It's not like I haven't done *that* before."

"True! Hey, I know you and Rory and Amanda were planning something for my birthday tonight, but I have another idea. . . ."

• • • • • • • • • • •

It's almost eight o'clock by the time we pull into Apple Grove. The sun is still lingering above the horizon, turning everything grainy, like a sheet of gauze is stretched over the world. Emily climbs out of the backseat easily, only because she's used to it and knows the best angles. Dad turns off the engine. "A thing of beauty," he says, stroking the dashboard.

"You heard what Uncle Roger said. Don't get too attached."

He sighs.

"Are you sure you can get out?"

He had to move the seat back as far as it would go in order to fit in the first place. Mom took Aunt Bethany's SUV to Polly's house. She said she was going to stop at the diner first to get bubblegum ice cream to bring with her. Apparently the smiley-face tradition started with them.

Dad tries three times before he figures out how to shift his body in the right position in order to get out of the tiny sports car.

"Jimmy!" Rory's dad calls out, striding over to us. They shake hands, then embrace.

"Wow," Rory says, "your dad's tall!"

"Yup." I look around the grove while the men slap each other on the back. "Where's Amanda?"

Rory points to the end of the row of trees. Amanda is kneeling behind the last tree, which is also the largest tree. And by large, I mean it's taller than my waist, but not as tall as my shoulders. "It's impossible for her to be here without tending to her trees," she explains.

"Hey, Tara," Dad says. "Did I ever tell you I used to be in a band?"

"Some other time, okay, Dad?" I pull Rory away and we run over to Emily, who is climbing on top of what I can only assume is a huge stack of folding chairs. I lift the blue tarp. Yup, folding chairs!

"All of these fit in the back of your dad's truck?" I ask, looking over my shoulder at the truck with the words A PUZZLE A DAY KEEPS THE BLUES AWAY printed on the side.

"We took two trips. And Leo's dad dropped off the podium. He snagged it from the conference room at his office." She points to a large wooden podium, which looks like it will be big enough to hold all the things David will need. Before we drove out here, I'd checked online to see what you need for an outdoor bar mitzvah, and learned there has to be a Torah, a rabbi, ten people over the age of thirteen, and something called a *tallit*, which I found out is like a white shawl with fringes that the bar mitzvah boy wears, and a yarmulke, which is that little round hat like a beanie that I know David has because he wears it sometimes when he's practicing. The ten people part is easy, and I'm assuming the rabbi will have all the other stuff.

Amanda comes over and hands a rake to each of us. "This is for loose grass, dirt, things like that. I wish we had time to plant more grass. . . ."

"It's going to be fine," I promise her. "Once the chairs are out and the podium's set up, and we've cleaned the fountain, and the lights are on the trees, no one will notice the ground."

"Still," she says, her face crinkling with concern. "I want it to look perfect for Bee Boy."

“Hamburglar,” Rory and Emily insist.

“David!” I exclaim.

“David’s a boring name,” Amanda says, “it’s Bee —”

“No, I mean David’s *here*!”

They whirl around and we all watch in horror as David strolls up the path from the mall. I can see his mom’s car parked in the closest parking lot, which is where all the guests will park tomorrow. I had tried to call her before we left the house to tell her our plan, but there was no answer. David sees us and stops short in surprise. Then he hurries over. “What’s going on? What are you guys doing here?”

The others look at me to respond. I hand Rory my rake and pull David aside. They go off to begin the cleanup.

“It was supposed to be a surprise,” I tell him, suddenly nervous. This could have been a huge mistake. What if he didn’t want to have his service at Apple Grove? Who am I to think I know what’s best for him? What if his mother gets mad? I swallow hard, unable to continue.

He takes in the surroundings. The stack of chairs half hidden under a tarp, the podium, the girls frantically raking. Then he turns back to me and whispers, “Is this for my bar mitzvah?”

I nod meekly. “Just the service. The party would still be at the community center. I mean, if you even want the service here. And we were going to put up a webcam so your dad could see and, well, I just thought, you know, how you said singing outside makes you feel closer to him and —”

“Are you sure you’re not Jewish?” he asks, cutting me off.

I shake my head. "I've learned a lot about my family today. That probably would have come up. Why do you ask?"

"Because of what you're doing." He reaches out and takes hold of my arms, just above my wrists. "You're doing *tikkun olam*. You're repairing the world."

"I am?"

He nods. "It's what I'm going to talk about in my speech tomorrow, after all the Hebrew stuff. It's about how the world is broken up into pieces, and how it's up to everyone to help put it all back together. It's about recognizing the spark of life in everyone and everything, and gluing these shards back together."

"And I did that? How?"

"Supposedly when you reach thirteen, you can see the different pieces better. There's an old teaching that says that, at thirteen, your soul gets stuck into your body. I've been thinking about that a lot lately."

"Me, too," I say softly.

"Really?" he asks, tilting his head at me.

I nod and whisper, "I think it might be true."

"Me, too," he whispers back.

We stand there in silence for a minute, him still holding on to my wrists. I'm suddenly acutely aware that my dad is watching us. "Um, see that tall guy over there giving us the stink eye?"

He glances over his shoulder. "The guy with Rory's dad?"

"That's the one."

"Who is he? Did he help bring the chairs or something?"

I shake my head. "That's my dad."

"Not in Madagascar anymore?"

I shake my head. "And if we stand here any longer he's going to come over and say something really embarrassing, inappropriate, or both. Probably both. So if you care about me at all, you'll say something like 'Let's go hang up the lights, Tara, before it gets totally dark.' "

"Let's go hang up the dark, Tara, before it gets totally light."

"Close enough, let's go."

• • • • • • • • • • •

Thankfully, Emily's presence in the backseat means that Dad can't grill me about David. We make a quick stop at the community center to put up signs directing bar mitzvah guests to Apple Grove. David's mom (who, fortunately, is willing to go along with the last-minute change but is probably not my biggest fan right now) also said she'd try to reach as many people as possible.

As soon as we get back to the house, I dash out of my seat, ignoring Dad's claim that the car has shrunk and that he is now stuck. I trust Emily will help pull him out.

I run up to the bedroom, hoping to get a minute or two alone. I haven't gone into my suitcase in at least two weeks, as most everything has been moved out by now. Everything but the hatbox of letters sitting on top of the bag of glass, which is what I have come for. When I pick up the hatbox to move it out of the way, I can tell right away that something feels different. It's much lighter! I yank off the cover and gasp. It's completely empty except for a yellow Post it note on the bottom. I lean in to read it.

Hope you don't mind, I mailed these.
And if you do mind, well, it's too late now!
Love, your cousin and friend, Emily

I sit back, letting the hatbox cover slip from my hand. All those years. All those letters. What is Julie possibly going to think when she gets those? I wonder if she'll write me back or if she'll think I'm just totally insane. In a way, though, it feels kind of freeing to have my past winging its way across the country right now. Like it's freeing me up for the future. I stay on the floor until the initial shock wears off, and then I put the hatbox back together, and leave it on Emily's desk. Looks like my little cousin is doing her own part to repair the world.

I carefully pick up the bag of glass and head back downstairs. At the bottom of the stairs I peek around the corner to make sure the coast is clear. It sounds like everyone is in the kitchen, so I creep down the hall toward Ray's room. Hopefully he's in there. The radio's on, which is a good sign.

I knock. "Ray? It's me, Tara. I need your help."

. . . .

Even in the bright sunshine, the tiny lights we strung on the trees and along the edges of the podium glitter like diamonds. A chair right in front of the podium holds a laptop that Connor rigged up not only to broadcast David to his father, but to bring his father to David, too. About a hundred people have come to watch David become a man.

Mom and Dad are sitting next to me, in borrowed clothes that are about a zillion times more glamorous than anything they own. Mom hasn't let go of Dad's hand once. I think finally knowing how he really feels about her has been the best gift he could ever give her. I have a feeling the jewelry boxes will stop flowing in now. The rabbi starts talking about love and responsibility, and the worst thought creeps into my head — what if Dad lied last night? What if he hadn't actually spilled out the juice? Isn't that exactly what someone who was in love would *say* they did to make the other person happy?

I look over at their hands, so tightly entwined it's hard to tell whose fingers are whose. Well, it *would* be hard if Dad's weren't twice as large as a normal human's. Maybe it doesn't matter how their love began. Still, I wish I knew for sure.

There are so many people in suits and dresses that the service is almost over before I notice Angelina sitting in the back row, wearing that same purple scarf around her head that she wore on the train. I've gotta hand it to her. Root canal and painkillers. The woman knows what she's doing. I still don't know how she managed to steal my stuff.

Our eyes meet. She mouths something, and as clear as if she was sitting next to me, I hear her say, "Look in your bag."

Confused, I reach under my seat for the beaded purse Aunt Bethany loaned me. I was going to bring the little backpack Dad gave me for the train, but one look at Aunt Bethany's horrified face this morning and I knew that wasn't going to cut it. I open the drawstring to find a small package with a note wrapped around it.

Happy Birthday to the girl who thought she wanted to sit this one out.
Tell your mother her debt is repaid.

After I read the note, I turn around to find Angelina's seat empty. Figures. I open the package as quietly as I can, and find Mom's iPod with the headphones still wrapped around it. I lean across Dad and place the iPod on her lap as though I just remembered I had it.

"Oh, that's okay," she whispers, putting it back on my own lap. "I was going to let you keep it anyway."

Sigh. That figures.

David starts singing Shalom Rav and I wouldn't be surprised if every apple tree in the place started to bloom. I'm so focused on listening that I don't notice the birds until the whispering around me finally catches my attention. Max and Flo, the two hawks, have landed on the edge of the fountain, only a few feet away from David and the rabbi. They sit and listen to him sing, heads tilted toward each other, talons entwined.

Dad suddenly squeezes my hand to get my attention. He and Mom are silently laughing so hard that their faces are bright red and their eyes are bulging. "The birds," Dad gasps. "I think they drank the love potion!" My eyes almost bug out of my head. He's right! Leo had said Max and Flo had been around since our parents were teenagers. They are the proof that my dad didn't lie. He really *didn't* drink it!

Halfway through the song, David is joined by Bucky on the violin and Mrs. Grayson on the keyboard. By the time it's over, there's not a dry eye in the grove.

David's mother had the caterers bring the appetizers here to keep people busy while the chairs and equipment are on their way back to the community center. Everyone mills around talking about how wonderful a job David did, and how they didn't know he could sing like that.

I nosh on a pizza bagel and sneak over to the table full of presents. I want to make sure mine is still on top so it doesn't get crushed. With Ray's help, I had made a picture frame out of the shards of glass. I finally understood why I hadn't been able to part with them. They were just like the shards that David had told me about, like little pieces of life. Ray showed me how to glue them back together in a funky kind of design. Then I printed out one of the pictures Aunt Bethany took at the play last night and stuck it inside the frame. David spent so much time helping me with everything this month that he hasn't gotten to spend any real time with Connor, who had been the one person to reach out to him when he first moved here. So the picture I chose is one of David and Connor stomping around the stage singing "To Life" and being really goofy and joyous, pretending to toast each other with fake wineglasses.

"Nice dress," Amanda says, joining me at the table. "It fits you perfectly."

"Please thank your sister again for me," I tell her, smoothing down the light blue silk skirt.

"That would imply I'd asked her in the first place."

"I better not spill anything on it, then." Amanda's wearing her blackboard on top of a really pretty pink dress. "Couldn't you leave that home today?"

She shakes her head and starts chewing on a fingernail. I've never seen her do that before. She looks around to make sure no one can hear us, then says, "Today's the day. We can't take any chances. Especially because we have no idea what we're doing."

My eyes widen. She's never talked about all this before. "You know I have no idea what you're talking about."

"I wish I could tell you," she says. "But you know when Angelina is involved there are things you can't talk about."

"I sure do." One day I'll tell them all about everything with my parents, and about why I'm really here in Willow Falls, but I want to keep it to myself for a while.

"The weirdest thing?" she says, standing even closer to me. "Is that for the longest time, we figured whatever was going to happen today had to do with David. Then we thought it was about you, but that doesn't feel right anymore either. So we're totally lost."

"I don't understand."

I can see the gears turning in her head as she decides how much to tell me. "When a full year passes without Leo and me talking, something's going to happen. I can't tell you what, but it will give us a chance to fix something. Or do something. Or undo something. We really have no idea."

"And that day's today?" I ask.

"Yup."

One of the servers comes by with a tray of mini hot dogs and holds it out for us. I take one. Then another. I feel so grown up. Amanda says she's too nervous to eat.

Leo and Rory join us, and judging by all the crumpled-up napkins in one hand and pile of mini hot dogs in the other, Leo doesn't have the same problem. His blackboard is slung over the shoulder of his blue suit.

"Hey, has either of you seen Connor?" Rory asks. "He was going to take down the computer and we don't want to mess anything up."

We shake our heads. "I saw him earlier setting up," I tell them. "He was here with his whole family."

"I saw them, too," Amanda says. "Grace said, 'Hi, Mommy,' when they walked in because she was my daughter in the play yesterday. It was pretty funny."

"So where are they?" Rory asks. "They shouldn't be this hard to find. They're the only family in Willow Falls with bright red hair."

We're about to spread out in four directions, when Emily comes hurrying over to us. "Are you still looking for Connor?" she asks.

"Yes," Rory says, "do you know where he is?"

"David's mother just told me the whole family had to leave right before the service started. They had to take Grace to the hospital! She doesn't want to worry David, so she told him they had to leave for a family wedding that Mr. Kelly had forgotten to tell them about."

Leo chokes on his hot dog and spits it out. The rest of us jump back to avoid the bits. He and Amanda grab their boards, yank them off their necks, and start furiously attacking them with the chalk. White dust flies everywhere. They've been intense before, but nothing like this.

"Did they say what was wrong with Grace?" Rory asks Emily.

Emily shakes her head. "I've never heard of a kid being rushed to the hospital before."

"I haven't either," Rory says, "except for a broken bone, or the flu or something like that. But she couldn't have broken anything sitting in a chair, and she seemed fine last night."

I look from one to the other. "What do you mean? About kids not going to the hospital?"

"We get really bad colds sometimes," Rory says, "and rashes and bronchitis. I even knew one kid with asthma. But we don't get *hospital* sick."

I can't imagine that's true, but it's not like I can argue it.

"And it's Grace's birthday today, too!" Emily says. "She told me at the play."

"That's right!" Leo says, turning white.

He and Amanda share one last look. "Please tell David we're sorry to miss his party," Amanda says, slinging her board over her neck, "but we've got to go."

"Where?" Rory asks. "What about the premiere tonight?"

But they're already running through the crowd. Amanda turns around and shouts, "Tara, will you explain? We really have to go."

"But I don't understand, either," I shout back.

Leo replies instead. "It wasn't about you after all! It's about Grace!"

"Grace?" I shout in response. But they're too far away now to hear, all the way on the other side of the grove. We watch them run over to Ray, who is manning the drinks table. A few seconds later the three of them run toward the path that leads to the mall parking lots. As Leo passes the last server, he grabs a handful of whatever was on the platter. Amanda smacks him with her board.

Emily shakes her head. "Told you those two are weird," she says and heads off to intercept her math crush, who is apparently making a few bucks on the side by working the bar mitzvah.

"Spill," Rory says.

I tell her everything Amanda had said earlier.

After I'm done, she says, "Well, if Amanda and Leo have been planning for this day for a whole year, they must know what they're doing, right?"

I don't answer. I know she doesn't need me to remind her of how things with Angelina don't usually turn out like we expect them to.

David is still swarmed by relatives and well-wishers, so I'm going to have to wait till the party to talk to him. I won't tell him about where Connor went, though, or about Amanda and Leo. Maybe with everything going on, he won't notice for a while.

As I head over to rejoin my parents, I spot a red envelope on the ground right where Angelina had been sitting. At first I think it must be a card for David that she dropped by mistake. But when I pick it up, I see Angelina's name written on the outside, not David's. The envelope has already been opened.

I slide the card out just enough to recognize the valentine I'd picked out for Bucky on my first trip to the store for him. Well, well. Isn't *that* interesting. I push the card back in, and drop the envelope in my bag. I'm sure Angelina will want this.

Even though we could all have squeezed into the SUV, Dad insisted on driving Uncle Roger's sports car again. So when it's time to leave for the party, I contort myself into the backseat and wait for Dad to join the line of cars leaving the parking lot. But one by one, people pass us.

"Um, Mom?" I ask. "Why isn't Dad pulling out?"

She turns around to face me. "He's stalling. We want to ask you something, but we're not sure how to bring it up."

I cringe. Here it comes. They're going to ask about David. I guess it was inevitable. They've never even seen me *talk* to a boy before. I take a deep breath to steady myself. I figure I'll just be honest and tell them how I feel.

"All right, here goes," Mom says. "I know —"

"We just held hands!" I blurt out. "It doesn't mean we're going to get married! I mean, who marries the person they date at thirteen? Wait, don't answer that!"

My parents share a puzzled look. Then my dad laughs. "Thank you for sharing, but that's not what we wanted to talk to you about."

I sink down into the seat and cover my face.

"Tara?" Mom says. "Do you want to say anything else about . . . what you just said? I mean, we'd be happy to talk to you about it."

I shake my head, still covering my face.

She reaches over and gently pulls my hands away. "It's okay, honey. David seems like a wonderful boy."

I have to force myself to leave my hands in my lap. "Can we just go back to talking about whatever you wanted to talk about?"

Mom takes a deep breath, and with one last glance at Dad says, "I know we made a deal that we wouldn't move again . . ."

I groan. "Are you serious, Mom? Angelina isn't looking for us anymore. She said your debt is repaid."

"I know," Mom says, fiddling with her seat belt strap, "but there's a house for sale down the street from Bethany's, and we made an offer on it this morning."

My jaw falls open.

"Unless you still don't want to move, of course. A deal's a deal. We can cancel our offer on the house."

I start bouncing up and down in the seat, coming dangerously close to banging my head on the roof. I'm so happy I probably wouldn't notice. "That would be totally bonza!" I shout.

"Is that a yes?" Dad asks.

"Yes! Yes! Yes!"

• • • • • • • • • • •

Later, after what was no doubt the best day of my entire life, I sit down to write the rest of my essay about what I've learned this summer. Even though I'm not going back to my old school (Tara = Still Jumping for Joy!!) I want to finish what I started.

First I reread what I'd written after my first week in Willow Falls. Then, before I come up for air, I've written another whole page.

I've learned that the universe doesn't care what our motives are, only our actions. So we should do things that will bring about good, even if there is an element of selfishness involved. Like the kids at my school might join the Key Club or Future Business Leaders of America, because it's a social thing and looks good on their record, not because they really want to volunteer at the nursing home. But the people at the nursing home still benefit from it, so it's better that the kids do it than not do it. And if they never did it, then they wouldn't find out that they actually liked it.

I have learned that almost anyone will help you if you ask for it.

I've learned that mothers can love their babies even before they're born and then will do all sorts of crazy things to try to keep them safe. Which leads to another thing I've learned — that everyone should be allowed to keep their secrets. But if they eat away at you with guilt, or make you move your family to a different town every year, you should *not* keep them.

I've learned that if you wait long enough, you might get a second chance at something you gave up on. And sometimes you'll be the one to give the second chance to someone else.

I've learned that sometimes you can meet your favorite movie star and he can turn out to be even greater than you thought, and that it's possible to be really happy for your new friend that he likes her and not even be jealous.

That said, I've also learned that it's possible to die from embarrassment when your dad, upon meeting aforementioned movie star at the premiere of his new movie, says, "Hey, you're the guy on my daughter's wall! She kisses your picture every night!"

I've learned that everyone can do their part to repair the world, and that the more you look for them, the easier it becomes to spot all the little pieces.

And most of all, I've learned that the sidelines may be safer, but life is played on the field.

Aussie Glossary

ace: great!
agro: aggressive
ankle biter: small child
arvo: afternoon
bingle: car accident
biscuit: cookie
blokes: male friends
bloody: very
bonza: excellent
brekkie: breakfast
cactus: broken
chewie: gum
chuck a sickie: take the day off work/school when you're not really sick
chuck a U-ee: make a u-turn
cobber: friend
don't fret your freckle: don't stress
dunny: bathroom
furphy: false rumor
g'day: hi!
give it a burl: try it

gobsmacked: astounded
good on ya: congratulations! well done!
I'll be stuffed: well, I'll be; an expression of pleased surprise
knocker: someone who criticizes
London to a brick: it's absolutely certain
make a quid: make a living
mate's rate: a special discount given to someone who's a friend
mates: friends
not my bowl of rice: I'm not interested in that
nut out: figure out
oldies: parents
pinch: steal
port: suitcase
rellies: relatives
ripper: really great
she'll be apples: it'll be all right
spit the dummy: be very upset
yabber: talk a lot

Turn the page for a magical look at . . .

The Last Present by Wendy Mass!

"In every moment something sacred is at stake."
— Rabbi Abraham Joshua Heschel

Prologue

Ten Years Ago

When you've drawn breath for nearly a hundred years, not much surprises you. So when Angelina D'Angelo stepped into the Willow Falls birthing center that hot July day, she didn't expect anything out of the ordinary. She figured she'd be in and out in ten minutes, tops.

But the elevator was broken and she had to take the stairs two flights up. Then a new guard kept asking to see the badge she'd forgotten to affix to her green nurse's outfit. She'd been coming here at least once a week for decades and had gotten used to no one stopping her. A bit rattled, she took a good five minutes to sort through all the badges in her pocket before she found the right one.

She quickened her pace toward the nursery. The clock above the door showed three till noon. She still had time. A quick scan of the room led her to the baby, bundled tight in pink. GRACE ALYSA KELLY, the note card on her bassinet read. GIRL. TIME OF BIRTH: 11 A.M. WEIGHT: 6 POUNDS, 4 OUNCES. A little thing she was. And yet so much depended on her.

With an ease that came from having done this many times before, she scooped the baby into her arms. Bending close, she began to murmur the words that would keep the baby safe.

They poured from her mouth like honey, making the air thick and sweet. The duck-shaped birthmark on Angelina's cheek wiggled as she spoke, but the baby's eyes were too unfocused to be entertained by it.

Knock! Knock!

Angelina looked up in surprise, the words tangling on her tongue. A boy no more than three years old stood at the nursery window, jumping up and down and rapping on the glass wall. She glanced at the clock. 11:59. She bent her head again to continue. Now where was she?

"Grace!" the boy shouted joyfully. "I'm your big brother!"

Angelina scowled. "Hush, Connor!" she scolded in as loud a voice as she dared. "You'll wake all the babies!"

The boy continued waving and stomping, not questioning why she would know his name. Where were his parents? She turned her back on him and resumed her benediction. But wait, had she said this part already? Her heart fluttered with an unfamiliar feeling. Fear.

Thirty seconds left.

Knock! Knock!

She didn't turn to look. A drop of sweat slid down her forehead. Angelina couldn't remember the last time anything had made her sweat. Couldn't someone make that boy go away?

The door to the nursery pushed open and one of the young nurses whose name she never bothered to learn strolled in. "Time to bring that one to her mother for feeding."

Angelina didn't have to check the clock to know she had run out of time.

"Do you want me to bring her?" the young nurse asked.

"You look like you could use a rest."

Without a word, Angelina placed the baby in the woman's waiting arms. Then she straightened up, threw a withering look at the boy still banging on the window, and left the nursery. She would have to wait a full year to try again. She couldn't fail twice. Not with this baby. Grace was special.

And it was up to Angelina D'Angelo to keep everyone else in Willow Falls from knowing it.

What's on your wish list?
13 Gifts
WENDY MASS
SCHOLASTIC
The Last Present
A Willow Falls book from the author of 11 Birthdays
WENDY MASS
SCHOLASTIC
TWICE UPON A TIME
Beauty and the Beast
The Only One Who Didn't Run Away
WENDY MASS
Author of 11 Birthdays
SCHOLASTIC
Switched at Birthday
Natalie Standiford
SCHOLASTIC
Once Upon a Cruise
SCHOLASTIC
Playing Cupid
SCHOLASTIC
hot cocoa hearts
SCHOLASTIC
you're bacon me crazy
SCHOLASTIC
wish
SCHOLASTIC
scholastic.com/wish
SCHOLASTIC and associated logos are trademarks and/or registered trademarks of Scholastic Inc.
WISH2